Far Rainbow

The Second
Invasion from Mars

Far Rainbow

Translated from the Russian by Antonina W. Bouis

The Second Invasion from Mars

Translated from the Russian by Gary Kern

Introduction by Theodore Sturgeon

Arkady Strugatsky and Boris Strugatsky

COLLIER BOOKS
A Division of Macmillan Publishing Co., Inc.
New York

COLLIER MACMILLAN PUBLISHERS
London

Macmillan Publishing Co., Inc.
866 Third Avenue, New York, N.Y. 10022
Collier Macmillan Canada, Ltd.

Library of Congress Cataloging in Publication Data

Strugatskii, Arkadii Natanovich.
    Far rainbow/The second invasion from Mars.

    Translation of Dalekaia radug and of Vtoroe
nashestvie marsian.
    1. Science fiction, English—Translations from
Russian. 2. Science fiction, Russian—Translations
into English. I. Strugatskii, Boris Natanovich,
joint author. II. Strugatskii, Arkadii Natanovich.
Vtoroe nashestvie marsian. 1980. III. Title.
IV. Title: The second invasion from Mars.
PZ4.S919Far 1980 [PG3476.S78835] 891.73′44
80-298
ISBN 0-02-025610-8

First Collier Books Edition 1980

Far Rainbow/The Second Invasion from Mars
is also published in a hardcover edition by
Macmillan Publishing Co., Inc.

Printed in the United States of America

Introduction

It is a Strugatsky hallmark not merely to present wonders, but to have the characters take them for granted, in the expectation that readers will follow suit. In *Far Rainbow* there is considerable explanation, for example, of "zero physics" and the theory of instantaneous matter transmission over stellar distances and associated phenomena. It is not an explanation one is expected to understand fully, any more than Hannibal could be expected to understand a tunnel diode, for the advance in technology is of that magnitude. The special Strugatsky trick is to convince you absolutely that the people in the story understand it; for the authors have grasped the secret of storytelling: good fiction is never primarily about ideas, but only about people and their interaction with ideas and with one another. Pivotal as the technology and its effects on the planet Rainbow may be, it will be the people in these pages who will involve you. You will care about them very much indeed as it comes to you that this is a tragedy in the purest form of ancient Greek drama: a story of the inevitable. You will be made to care by witnessing not only their peril, but their love and laughter, and the meticulous etching of their varied personalities.

Those who have enjoyed the sequential novel *Noon: 22nd Century* will have the pleasure of meeting an old friend here, the astronaut Gorbovsky. If you have wondered what ever became of him, you can now know. This may not please you, but you will never forget it. In a moment of ascending tension, he walks through a terribly threatened crowd, trying to guess their reaction to the doomsday news he is about to give them: "I believe in you, he thought stubbornly. I believe in you no matter what. I believe in you, you frightened, wary, disillusioned fanatics. People."

In this moment, he speaks for the Strugatskys. It has been said that every writer has one thing to say, and he says it over and over again in everything he writes. If this is true, then the foregoing is what the Strugatskys say in every one of their amazingly different and distinctive works.

The Second Invasion from Mars is a fable.

A fable is a story exemplifying a moral, a statement that, on reflection, one finds to be larger than the narrative itself.

All living literature is fable. Living literature is, like all living things, literature that grows as the reader grows. An eight-year-old will be enchanted by the image of Gulliver tied down on the sands by threadlike ropes manned by all those tiny little people and by his subsequent adventures with them. At twenty or so, the reader might learn that the story is an incisive lampoon of English and Irish politics of the day, complete with devastating caricatures of contemporary dignitaries. Ultimately, he might find a deeper level of human meaning, in which caring and compassion are shown to be the true sources of Swift's derision.

So you may read this fable for itself, and enjoy this conglomeration of village idiots: the bumbling retiree whose diary carries the narration, with his pompousness, his capacity for instant rationalization of cowardice, his slavish yet stubborn pursuit of his pension, his stamps, his cognac, and his self-respect; his wayward daughter and his acidulous housekeeper; the drunken honey-dumper who keeps driving his noisesome cess-truck into the architecture; the bird-brained constable who arrests him daily and jails him to sleep it off; and the damndest Martians you have ever encountered.

Stitched through this comic opera is wit of a high order. "Our policemen," writes the narrator in his diary, "should be intellectuals, models for the youth, heroes to be emulated, people you can safely entrust with weapons and authority, but also with educational work. But Charon considers such a police force 'a company of eggheads.' He says no state would want my kind of police force because it would start arresting and reeducating the very people the state finds most useful, beginning with the Prime Minister and the Chief of Police."

And this: "In such a small town as ours, everyone knows the teacher. The parents of your pupils imagine for some reason that you are a wonder-worker and are able by your personal example to keep the children from following in their parents' footsteps."

You noticed that name Charon. The dundering diarist's name is Apollo—Phoebus Apollo. There is a Polyphemus (who has only one leg), an Achilles, a Zephyrus. Apollo's amorous daughter (wife of Charon) is Artemis. The town madam is Persephone. Everyone has names like that, and there's no end to the delving that can be done to reach the many levels of puckishness involved.

This town could be any town, the people (under the clown suits) any people anywhere.

And when you're done laughing, the moral of this fable is utterly terrifying.

—THEODORE STURGEON
Los Angeles, 1979

Far Rainbow

Chapter 1

TANYA'S hand, warm and slightly chapped, lay over his eyes, and he wasn't interested in anything else. He was aware of the bitter salty smell of the dust, the prairie birds chirping in their sleep, and the dry grass that prickled and tickled the back of his neck. The ground was hard, and it was uncomfortable lying like this, and his neck itched unbearably, but he didn't move, listening to Tanya's quiet, even breathing. He was smiling and glad that it was dark, because his smile, he was sure, was indecently stupid and smug.

Then just at the wrong time, the phone signal went off at the laboratory on the hill. Let it. It wouldn't be the first time. Tonight all calls were just at the wrong time.

"Rob, dear," Tanya whispered, "don't you hear it?"

"I don't hear a thing," Robert muttered.

He blinked so that his lashes would tickle Tanya's hand. Everything was far, far away and absolutely unnecessary. Patrick, forever groggy from lack of sleep, was far away. Malyaev, the Ice Sphinx, was far away. That whole world of constant hurry and pressure, constant superintellectual arguments, constant dissatisfaction and anxiety, that whole nonsensory world where they despise the obvious, where they welcome only the unclear, where people have forgotten that they are men and women—all that was far, far away. ... Only the plains at night, hundreds of miles of plains, existed, nothing but empty land that had swallowed the broiling day and was warm and filled with dark, stimulating fragrances.

The phone shrilled again.

"Again," said Tanya.

"Let it. I'm not here. I'm dead. I was eaten by the earthmovers. I'm fine right here. I love you. I don't want to go anywhere. Why should I? Would you go?"

"I don't know."

"That's because you don't love me enough. A person who loves enough never has to go anywhere."

"Theorist."

"I'm no theorist. I'm a practicalist. And as a practicalist I ask you, why should I suddenly go off somewhere? One must know how to love. And you don't know how. You only talk about love. You don't love love. You love to talk about it. Am I talking too much?"

"Yes. Terribly."

He removed her hand from his eyes and put it to his lips. Now he could see the sky, swathed in clouds, and the red warning light at the twenty-yard level on the tower supports.

The phone rang and rang, and Robert pictured Patrick, pushing on the button, and getting angrier and angrier, his kind, fat lips pouting.

"I'm going to unplug you," Robert said in a muffled voice. "Tanya, would you like me to shut him up forever? I might as well do everything forever. Our love will be forever, and he'll shut up forever."

He could see her face in the darkness—luminous, with huge shining eyes. She pulled her hand away and said, "Let me talk to him. I'll tell him that I'm a hallucination. People are always having hallucinations at night."

"He never has hallucinations. He's that kind of guy, Tanya. He never fools himself."

"Do you want me to tell you what he's like? I love to guess people's personalities on the basis of a videophone call. He's a stubborn, mean, and tactless man. And nothing in the universe could force him to sit with a woman in the plains at night. That's him—in a nutshell. And the only thing he knows about night is that it's dark."

"No," said Robert. "You're right about the woman. But let's be fair. He's really kind and gentle. A pussycat."

"I don't believe it," Tanya said. "Just listen." They listened. "Is that a pussycat? That's an obvious *tenacem propositi virum*, 'a man steadfast in his intentions,' as Horace put it."

"Really? I'll tell him."

"Go ahead. Go and tell him."

"Now?"

"Immediately."

Robert got up, and she stayed seated, hugging her knees.

"But kiss me first," she added.

In the elevator, he pressed his forehead against the cool wall and remained that way for a while, eyes shut, laughing, and running his tongue over his lips. There wasn't a single thought in his head, only a triumphant voice that exulted: "She loves! Me. She loves me! So there! She loves me!" Then he discovered that the elevator had stopped a long time ago, and he tried to open the door. He couldn't find it right away, and somehow the laboratory turned out to be filled with excess furniture: he found himself knocking over chairs, banging into tables, and bumping into cabinets until he finally realized that he had forgotten to turn on the lights. Roaring with laughter, he felt for the switch, picked up an overturned armchair, and sat down at the videophone.

When Patrick appeared on the screen, Robert greeted him in a friendly manner.

"Good evening, my little piglet! Why aren't you asleep, sweetie pie?"

Patrick was looking at him in bewilderment, his inflamed eyelids blinking rapidly.

"What are you staring at, puppy boy? You rang and rang, dragging me away from highly important things, and now your're silent!"

Patrick finally opened his mouth:

"Are you . . . ? You're. . . ." He pounded his head with his fist, and a questioning look appeared on his face.

"And how!" Robert exclaimed. "The solitude! Loneliness! The forebodings! And then, the hallucinations! I almost forgot about them!"

"Are you kidding?" Patrick asked seriously.

"No! You don't kid on duty. But don't pay any attention to me and get on with it."

Patrick blinked with uncertainty.

"I don't understand," he admitted.

"How could you!" Robert said gloatingly. "Emotions, Patrick, that's what we're talking about! You know? . . . How can I put it so you'll understand? . . . Well, how about not completely algorithmical excitation in the supercomplex logical complexes. Got it?"

"Uh-huh." Patrick scratched his chin and gathered his thoughts. "You asked why I'm calling you, Rob? Here's the problem. There's a leak somewhere again. Maybe it's not a leak, and maybe it is. Just in case, check the ulmotrons. The Wave is kind of strange today. . . ."

Robert looked out the open window in puzzlement. He had completely forgotten all about the eruption. It turned out that he was sitting there because of the eruptions. Not because Tanya was there, but because somewhere out there was the Wave.

"Why aren't you talking?" Patrick asked patiently.

"I'm looking to see how the Wave is doing," Robert replied angrily.

Patrick's eyes bugged.

"You can see the Wave?"

"Me? Where did you get that idea?"

"You just said you were looking at it."

"Yes, I am!"

"Well?"

"That's it. What do you want from me?"

Patrick's eyes grew wide again.

"I misunderstood," he said. "What were we talking about? Oh yes! So definitely check the ulmotrons."

"Do you know what you're saying? How can I check the ulmotrons?"

"Somehow," Patrick said. "At least the connections.... We're completely lost. I'll explain it to you.... Today the Institute transported matter toward Earth—but you know all that." Patrick waved his outspread fingers in front of his face. "We were expecting a powerful Wave, but we're registering some tiny dribble. Do you see the picture? A thin, tiny dribble.... Dribble...." He moved closer to the video-phone, so that the screen only showed a huge, bleary eye. The eye blinked furiously. "Understand?" The speaker blared. "Our equipment registers a quasi-zero field. The Young Counter shows a minimum.... Almost negligible. ... The fields of the ulmotrons overlap in such a way that the resonating surface falls into the focus hyperplane, can you imagine? A quasi-zero field is made up of twelve components, and the receiver channels it into six precise components.... So the focus is hexacomponential...."

Robert thought of Tanya, patiently waiting outside. Patrick kept babbling, moving closer and further away, his voice alternately blaring and hardly audible, and Robert, as usual, very quickly lost his train of thought. He nodded, picturesquely furrowed his brow, and raised and lowered his eyebrows, but he didn't understand a thing, and thought with unbearable shame that Tanya was sitting down there, chin tucked into her knees, and waiting while he finished his important conversation, which was unintelligible to the unenlightened, with the leading zero-physicists of the planet, while he told the leading zero-physicists his own, completely original point of view on the problem that was causing them to disturb him so late at night, and while the leading zero-physicists, amazed and shaking their heads in awe, entered his point of view into their notebooks. . . .

Patrick stopped talking and looked at him strangely. Robert knew that expression well, it pursued him throughout his life. Various people—both men and women—had looked at him that way. First they looked at him indifferently or kindly, then expectantly, then curiously, but sooner or later the moment came when they looked at him like that. And each time he didn't know what to do, what to say, and how to behave. And how to go on living.

He took a chance.

"I guess you're right," he announced with concern. "However, all this has to be thought through carefully."

Patrick lowered his eyes.

"Think about it," he said, smiling uncomfortably. "And please, don't forget to check the ulmotrons."

The screen went black and the sound went off. Robert sat, hunched over, holding onto his cold rough elbows. Someone once said that a fool who realizes that he's a fool is no longer a fool. Perhaps once upon a time that was true. But a stupid utterance is always stupid, and I don't know any other way. I'm a very interesting person: everything that I say is old, everything I think is trite, and everything that I've managed to accomplish has been done two centuries ago. I'm not only a blockhead, but I'm a rare blockhead, a museum piece, like a village chief's staff of power. He remembered how old man Nicheporenko looked meditatively into Robert's loyal eyes and said: "My dear Sklyarov, you look like an ancient god. And like any god, please forgive me, you are totally incompatible with science. . . ."

Something cracked. Robert sighed and stared in surprise at a chunk of the arm of the chair, held tight in his white fist.

"Yes," he said aloud. "That I can do. Patrick can't. Nicheporenko can't either. Only I can."

He put the broken piece on the table, got up and went over to the window. It was dark and hot outside. Maybe I should leave before they fire me? But what will I do without them? And without that amazing feeling in the morning that maybe today that invisible and impenetrable sheath in my brain will burst, the one that keeps me from being like them, and then I'll be able to understand them readily, and I'll suddenly see something completely new in the mush of logic and mathematical symbols, and Patrick will pat me on the back and say joyously: "That's rea-ea-lly terrific! How did you do it?" And Malyaev will manage to squeeze out, despite himself: "Not bad, not bad . . . that wasn't just lying on the surface. . . ." And I'll begin to respect myself.

"Freak," he muttered.

He had to check the ulmotron, and Tanya could sit and watch how it's done. Good thing that she didn't see my face when the screen went out.

"Tanya, love," he called out the window.

"Yes?"

"Tanya, did you know that last year Roger used me as the model for *World Youth*?"

Tanya, after a brief silence, said softly:

"Wait, I'll come up there."

Robert knew that there was nothing wrong with the ulmotrons, he sensed it. But he decided to check them out anyway, everything that could be checked in the lab end: first of all, to relax after the conversation with Patrick, and second, because he knew how to work with his hands and loved it. It always relaxed him and for a short time gave him a happy sense of self-worth and usefulness, without which it's absolutely impossible to live in our times.

Tanya—a sweet and sensitive person—sat out of the way quietly at first, and then, just as silently, began helping him. Patrick called again at three, and Robert told him that there was no leak. Patrick was discouraged. He wheezed for a while on the screen, computing something on a scrap of paper, then rolled the paper into a tube and as usual posed a rhetorical question: "And what are we supposed to think about that, Rob?"

Robert stole a look at Tanya, who had just come out of the shower and quietly sat out of range of the videophone, and answered carefully to the effect that he didn't see anything special about it. "It's the usual, ordinary dribble," he said. "There was one like it after yesterday's zero-transport. And last week, too." Then he thought and added that the power of the dribble corresponds roughly to a hundred grams of the transported mass. Patrick said nothing, and Robert thought that he was wavering. "It's all in the mass," Robert said. He looked at the Young Counter and added confidently, "Yes, a hundred—hundred fifty grams. How much did you send today?" "Twenty kilograms," Patrick replied. "Ah, twenty kilos. . . . Then that doesn't work." And then Robert had a flash of insight. "What formula are you using to calculate power?" he asked. "The Drambe," Patrick replied matter-of-factly. That's just what Robert had thought: Drambe's formula evaluated power with precision only to an order of magnitude, and Robert had worked out his own a long time ago, carefully worked out and developed and written down and even framed with colored ink, a universal formula for determining the power of degenerated matter. And now, it seemed, the time had come for a demonstration of all his formula's good points.

Robert was about to take up pencil and paper, but Patrick suddenly disappeared from the screen. Robert waited, biting his lip. Someone asked, "Are you hanging up?" Patrick didn't answer. Carl Hoffman came up to the screen, nodded vaguely and pleasantly to Robert and called out: "Patrick, will you be using the phone?" Patrick's voice muttered off-screen: "I don't understand a thing. I'll have to deal with this very carefully." "I said, are you going to be using the phone?" Hoffman repeated. "No, no, I'm not . . ." Patrick replied grumpily. Then Hoffman, smiling guiltily, said, "I'm sorry, Rob, we're getting ready to go to sleep around here. I'll hang up, all right?"

Gritting his teeth so hard that his ears clicked, Robert slowly and methodically placed a sheet of paper before him, wrote his wonderful formula several times, shrugged and said in a hearty tone, "That's what I thought. Everything's clear. Now let's have some coffee."

He was absolutely disgusted with himself and sat in front of the breakfront with the coffee things until he felt that he could control his face once more. Tanya said, "You make the coffee, all right?"

"Why me?"

"You make it, I'll watch."

"What is it?"

"I love to watch you work. You work in an absolutely perfect way. You don't make any excess moves."

"Like a robot," he said, but he felt good.

"No. Not like a robot. You work perfectly. And perfection always brings joy."

"*World Youth*," he muttered. He was blushing with pleasure.

He put out the cups and rolled the table over to the window. They sat down and he poured the coffee. Tanya sat with her side to him, her legs crossed. She was marvelously beautiful, and he was struck again with a puppylike awe and confusion.

"Tanya," he said, "this can't be real. You must be a hallucination."

She smiled.

"You can laugh as much as you like. I know without your telling me that I look really pathetic now. But I can't do anything with myself. I want to nuzzle up to you and wag my tail. And I want you to pat me on the back and say 'Silly, you big silly!' "

"Silly, you big silly!" Tanya said.

"What about my back?"

"That's later. And nuzzling is later too."

"All right, later. And now? Would you like me to make a collar for myself? Or a muzzle?"

"No muzzle," Tanya said. "What would I want with you in a muzzle?"

"What do you want with me without one?"

"I like you without a muzzle."

"An auditory hallucination," Robert said. "What could you possibly like about me?"

"You have good-looking legs."

His legs were his weak point. They were powerful, but too heavy. The World Youth's legs were sculpted from Carl Hoffman's legs.

"I thought so," Robert said. He gulped the last of his coffee. "Then I'll tell you why I love you. I'm an egoist. Maybe the last egoist left in the universe. I love you because you are the only person who can put me in a good mood."

"That's my specialty," Tanya said.

"A marvelous specialty. The only bad thing is that the old and the young get in a good mood because of you. Particularly the young. Total strangers. With normal legs."

"Thank you, Robbie."

"The last time we were in the children's colony I noticed one kid. His name is Valya . . . or Varya . . . blond kid, freckles, green eyes."

"His name is Varya," Tanya said.

"Don't be picky. I'm accusing you. That Varya looked at you, dared to look at you with his green eyes in a way that made my hands itch."

"The jealousy of a blatant egoist."

"Of course it's jealousy."

"And now picture his jealousy."

"What?"

"And imagine how he sees you. A six-foot-tall World Youth. Athlete, handsome, zero-physicist, carrying his teacher on his shoulder, and the teacher is melting with love. . . ."

Robert laughed happily.

"Tanya, how could that be? We were alone that time!"

"You were alone. We educators are never alone."

"Yes," Robert thought aloud. "I remember those days, I do. Pretty teacher and fifteen-year-old jerks. . . . I was so bad that I threw flowers in her window. Does that happen frequently?"

"Very," Tanya said thoughtfully. "Particularly with the girls. They develop faster. And you know what our male teachers are like. Starship crewmen, heroes . . . that's a dead end in our work for now."

"Dead end," thought Robert. And, of course, she's happy to have it. They're all pleased with dead ends. It gives them a perfect excuse for breaking through walls. And they spend their lives breaking through one wall after another.

"Tanya," he said. "What's a fool?"

"An insult," she replied.

"What else?"

"A sick man who cannot be helped by any medicines."

"That's not a fool," Robert countered. "That's a malingerer."

"It's not my definition. It's a Japanese saying. 'There's no medicine that can cure a fool.' "

"Aha," Robert said. "That means a man in love is also a fool. 'A man in love is sick and incurable.' You've comforted me."

"Are you in love?"

"I'm incurable."

The clouds parted and exposed the starry sky. Morning was coming.

"Look, there's the sun," Tanya said.

"Where?" Robert asked unenthusiastically.

Tanya turned off the light, sat on his lap and, pressing her cheek against his, pointed it out.

"See the four bright stars? That's the Maiden's Scythe. To the left of the very top one there's a faint star. That's where we were born, girls. I was born earlier, you were born later.

That's our sun. Little Olya, of course, was born here, on Rainbow, but her mother and father were born there. And next year during summer vacation we'll all fly over there."

"Oh, Tatyana Alexandrovna!" Robert squealed. "Will we really fly there? Oh! Oooh!" He kissed her cheek. "Oh, we'll all go! On a D-Sigma starship? And we'll all go? Oh, can I take my dolly? Oh-oh, Varya is kissing you!" And he kissed her again.

She hugged his neck.

"My girls don't play with dolls."

Still holding her in his arms, Robert stood up, carefully went around the table and only then, in the greenish light of the electrical equipment, saw a tall human form in the chair by the work table. He shuddered and stopped.

"I think you can turn on the lights now," the man said, and Robert realized who it was.

"And then there were three," said Tanya. "Let me down, Rob."

She balanced herself and then bent over, looking for her right shoe.

"You know, Camill," Robert began in irritation.

"I know," Camill said.

"Amazing," Tanya said, putting on her shoe. "I'll never believe that our population density is one person per million square kilometers. Would you like some coffee?"

"No, thanks," Camill said.

Robert turned on the light. Camill, as usual, was sitting in a most uncomfortable position that jarred the eye. As usual, he was wearing a white plastic helmet that covered his forehead and ears, and as usual, his face expressed condescending boredom, and there was neither curiosity nor embarrassment in his round, unblinking eyes. Robert, squinting in the light, said, "At least tell me you just got here."

"I did. And I didn't look at you or listen to what you were saying."

"Thank you, Camill," Tanya said merrily. She was combing her hair. "You're very tactful."

"Only lazy bums are tactless."

Robert got mad.

"By the way, Camill, why are you here? And what's this new manner of appearing like a ghost?"

"I'll answer in order," Camill said calmly. That was his manner, too, to answer things in order. "I came here because an eruption is beginning. You know perfectly well"—and he even shut his eyes to express boredom—"that I come here every time an eruption begins in front of your post. Besides—" he opened his eyes and stared silently at the equipment, "besides, I like you, Robbie."

Robert looked over at Tanya. Tanya was listening carefully, her hand in the air, still holding the comb.

"As for my manner," Camill went on in a monotone, "it's strange. Every man's manner is strange. Only one's own seems natural."

"Camill," Tanya said unexpectedly. "How much is six hundred eighty-five times three million eight hundred fifty-three?"

To his great surprise, Robert saw something like a smile spread across Camill's face. It was a creepy sight. A Young Counter might have smiled that way.

"A lot," Camill said. "Somewhere around three billion."

"Strange," Tanya sighed.

"What's strange?" Robert asked stupidly.

"Minimal accuracy," Tanya explained. "Camill, tell me, why won't you have a cup of coffee?"

"Thank you, but I don't like coffee."

"Then, goodbye. It's a four-hour flight to Children's Colony, Robbie. Will you walk me downstairs?"

Robert nodded and looked with dismay at Camill. Camill was looking at the Young Counter. Like it was a mirror.

As usual on Rainbow, the sun rose in a perfectly clear sky—a tiny, white sun, surrounded by a triple halo. The night wind had died down, and the atmosphere had become even stuffier. The yellow-brown plain with bald spots of salt flats seemed dead. Shimmering foggy mounds rose over the marshes—the vapors from airborne salts.

Robert shut the window and turned on the air conditioning; then slowly, enjoying the cool air, he repaired the arm of the chair. Camill was walking softly and noiselessly around the lab, throwing glances out the window that faced north. Apparently, he wasn't hot in the least, but Robert was hot just looking at him, his heavy white jacket, his long white trousers, his shiny round white helmet. Zero-physicists frequently wore those helmets during experiments in order to protect themselves from radiation.

A whole day of duty lay ahead, twelve hours of the broiling sun above the roof, until the eruptions dissolved and all the repercussions of the preceding day's experiment passed. Robert threw off his jacket and pants, stripping down to his shorts. The air conditioning was on maximum, and there was nothing else he could do.

It would have been nice to splash the floor with liquid air. There was some liquid air, but not too much, and he needed it for the generator. I'll have to suffer, thought Robert docilely. He sat down in front of the equipment again. At least it was cool in the armchair and the upholstery didn't stick to his skin.

In the final analysis, they say, the important thing is to find your place. My place is here. And I do my small tasks no worse than anyone else. And in the final analysis, it's not my fault that I'm not capable of doing more. And the point isn't even whether I've found my place or not. It's just that I can't leave here, even if I wanted to. I'm simply chained to these people, who irritate me so, and to this major undertaking, of which I understand so little.

He remembered how amazed he had been at the prospect back in school: the instantaneous transportation of matter through vast distances in space. This undertaking had been proposed in contradiction to everything that was known about absolute space, the space-time continuum, kappa-space. . . . In those days they had called it "breakthrough of the Riemannian manifold." Then "hyperexudation," then "Sigma-exudation," then "zero-helixing." And then finally, "zero-transportation," or zero-T. "Zero-T setup." "Zero-T problematics." "Zero-T tester." "Zero-physicist." "Where do you work?" "I'm a zero-physicist." An awed and amazed look. "Listen, would you please explain zero-physics to me? I just can't understand it." "Neither can I." Hmmm . . .

Actually, there was enough to tell. About that amazing metamorphosis of the elementary conservation laws, when the zero-transference of a small platinum cube on the equator of Rainbow elicits on the planet's poles—and for some reason only at the poles!—gigantic gushers of ores, fiery geysers that can blind a man, and the terrible black Wave, mortally dangerous to any living thing.

And about the violent, terrifying combat going on among the zero-physicists themselves, about the unmendable break among these marvelous men, who, you would think, would be working shoulder to shoulder, but had split into two camps (even though very few knew about it): while Etienne Lamondois stubbornly led zero-physics down the path of zero-transportation, the school of young scientists considered that the Wave was the most important problem in zero-physics, the new genie of science, trying to break out of the bottle.

And about the fact that for reasons that were unclear they still couldn't transport living matter, and the miserable dogs, eternal martyrs, arrived at the finish point as blobs of organic matter. . . . And about the zero-test subjects, the "roaring dozen" headed by the astounding Gaba, those healthy, super-trained guys who'd spent the last three years hanging around Rainbow in constant readiness to get into the starting chamber instead of the dogs. . . .

"We'll be parting soon, Robbie," Camill suddenly said.

Robert had dozed off. Camill was standing at the northern window with his back to him. Robert straightened up and ran his hand over his face. He realized he was sweating.

"Why?" he asked.

"Science. It's so hopeless, Robbie."

"I've know that a long time," Robert grumbled.

"Science is a labyrinth as far as you're concerned. Dead ends, dark alleys, sudden turns. You don't see anything but walls. And you don't know anything about the final goal. You've announced that our aim is to reach the end of infinity, that is, you've basically announced that there is no goal. The measure of your success is not the path to the finish line, but the path from the start. It's your good fortune that you can't realize abstractions. Aim, infinity, eternity—they're only words for you. Abstract philosophical categories. They don't mean anything in your everyday life. But if you had a glimpse of that labyrinth from above. . . ."

Camill stopped. Robert waited and then asked, "Have you seen it?"

Camill didn't answer, and Robert decided not to press it. He sighed, rested his chin on his fist, and shut his eyes. A man talks and acts, he thought. And all that is the external manifestation of some processes in the depths of his nature. Most people have a shallow nature, and therefore any movement in it is immediately visible on the surface, as a rule, in the form of empty gabble and meaningless arm waving. But in people like Camill these processes must be very powerful in order to rise to the surface. He'd love to take just a tiny peek inside him. Robert pictured a gaping abyss, with shapeless phosphorescent shadows whirling about in the bottom.

Nobody liked him. Everyone knew him—there wasn't a single person on Rainbow who didn't know Camill—but no one liked him. I would go mad with that kind of loneliness, thought Robert, but Camill doesn't even seem to notice. He's always alone. I don't know where he lives. He appears suddenly and disappears just as suddenly. His white helmet is sighted in the Capital, then at open sea, and there are those who maintain that he's often been seen simultaneously in both places. That's local folklore, of course, but in general, everything that was said about Camill sounded like a bizarre joke. He had strangely formal manners. No one ever saw him work, but once in a while he showed up at the Council and said things no one could understand. Sometimes they did understand him, and then no one could argue with him. Lamondois once said that with Camill he always felt like the stupid grandson of a smart grandfather. In general, he made them feel that all the physicists on the planet from Etienne Lamondois down to Robert Sklyarov were on the same level. . . .

Robert felt that he was on the verge of boiling in his own sweat. He got up and headed for the shower. He stayed under the icy stream until his skin was covered with goosebumps and he lost the desire to get into the refrigerator and go to sleep.

When he got back to the lab, Camill was talking to Patrick. Patrick was furrowing his brow, flapping his lips in confusion, and looking at Camill with entreaty. Camill was speaking patiently and with great boredom:

"Try to take all three factors into account. All three at the same time. You don't need any theories here, just some imagination. The zero-factor in subspace and in both time coordinates. Can you do that?"

Patrick shook his head slowly. He was a pitiful sight. Camill waited a minute, then shrugged and hung up. Robert, drying himself with a rough towel, said determinedly, "Why were you like that, Camill? That's mean. That's insulting."

Camill shrugged again. It looked like his head, squashed down by the helmet, had dived down into his chest and then bobbed up.

"Insulting?" he said. "And why not?"

There was no answer to that. Robert felt instinctively that

there was no point in arguing morality with Camill. Camill simply wouldn't understand what he was talking about.

He hung up the towel and started making breakfast. They ate in silence. Camill settled for a piece of bread with jam and a glass of milk. Camill never ate much. Then he said:

"Robbie, do you know if the Arrow has taken off?"

"Day before yesterday," Robert said.

"Day before yesterday . . . that's bad."

"What do you need with the Arrow, Camill?"

Camill said matter-of-factly: "I don't need the Arrow."

Chapter 2

GORBOVSKY asked them to stop on the outskirts of the Capital. He got out of the car and said, "I really feel like a walk."

"Let's go," said Mark Falkenstein and he too got out.

The straight shiny highway was empty, the plain around them was yellow and green, and ahead, through the juicy Earthlike vegetation, they could see the multicolored walls of the city buildings.

"It's too hot," Percy Dixon argued. "It's a load for the heart."

Gorbovsky picked a flower from the roadside and brought it to his face.

"I like the heat," he said. "Come with us, Percy. You're getting flabby."

Percy slammed the door shut.

"As you like. To tell the truth, I've gotten quite tired of you two over the last twenty years. I'm an old man, and I'd like a rest from your paradoxes. And do me a favor, don't come up to me on the beach."

"Percy," Gorbovsky said, "why don't you go to the Children's Colony? I don't know exactly where it is, but there are children there, naive laughter, simple mores. . . . 'Mister!' they'll call out. 'Let's play mammoth!' "

"Just watch your beard," Mark added, grinning. "They'll pull on it."

Percy mumbled something to himself and drove off. Mark and Gorbovsky walked over to a path and slowly went alongside the highway.

"The Beard is getting old," Mark said. "He's tired of us."

"Don't be silly, Mark," Gorbovsky said. He took a player from his pocket. "He's not tired of us. He's just tired. And then, he's disillusioned too. It's no joke—the man spent twenty years on us: he really wanted to see what influence space would have on us. And for some reason, there's no influence. . . . I want Africa. Where's my Africa? Why are all my recordings always mixed up?"

He followed Mark down the path, the flower in his teeth, tuning his player and stumbling. He found Africa and the yellow and green plain resounded with drums. Mark looked back over his shoulder.

"Will you spit out that garbage," he said.

"Why do you call it garbage? It's a flower."

The drums were restless.

"Could you at least lower that?" Mark said.

Gorbovsky lowered the volume.

"More, please."

Gorbovsky pretended to lower the volume.

"Like that?" he asked.

"I don't understand why I haven't broken that thing yet," Mark said into space.

Gorbovsky quickly turned the sound very low and put the player in his breast pocket.

They were walking past cheery, multicolored houses, surrounded by lilacs, with identical mesh cones of the solar receivers on their roofs. An orange cat stalked across their path. "Kitty-kitty-kitty," Gorbovsky called happily. The cat dashed into the tall grass and stared out with wild eyes. Bees buzzed in the heated air. A throaty snore came from somewhere.

"What a hick town!" Mark said. "The Capital! They sleep till nine. . . ."

"Why are you like that, Mark? I, for one, find this place rather sweet. The bees . . . that little pussycat. What else do you need? Would you like me to turn up the sound?"

"No," Mark said. "I don't like these lazy hamlets. Lazy people live in lazy hamlets."

"I know your type," Gorbovsky said. "You want struggle, no one agreeing with anyone else, ideas striking sparks, and a fist fight wouldn't be bad, either, but that would make it too perfect. . . . Wait, wait! That looks like stinging nettle. . . . Pretty, but very painful."

He crouched in front of a thick bush with large, black-striped leaves. Mark said impatiently, "What are you sitting around for, Leonid Andreyevich! Haven't you ever seen a stinging nettle?"

"Never in my life. But I've read about it. And you know, Mark, I think I'll take you off the ship's roster. . . . You've changed, you're spoiled rotten. You've lost the ability to take pleasure in life's simple things."

"I don't know what life's simple things are," Mark said, "but all these flowers and nettles, all these paths and roads —all that simply rots the brain, Leonid Andreyevich. There's still so much wrong with the world, it's much too early to lose yourself in all this bucolic stuff."

"There are things wrong," Gorbovsky agreed. "But there always were and there always will be. What kind of life is it without something wrong? But in general, things are very good. Listen, someone's singing . . . despite all the things wrong. . . ."

A gigantic atomic truck came barreling down the highway toward them. Several half-naked, huge men sat on the boxes in the truck. One of them, lost in his pleasure, was banging away at a banjo, and they were all singing along:

> I need a wife,
> Pretty, sweet, or even harried,
> As long as she's a girl,
> And not already married . . .

The atomic truck sped past, and the wave of hot air that followed flattened the grass for a second. Gorbovsky said, "You should have liked that, Mark. It's nine and people are up and working. Did you like the song?"

"That's not it, either," Mark said stubbornly.

The path swerved away from the road, going around a huge cement pool with dark water. They walked through the patch of waist-high grass. It was cooler—overhead the black acacia leaves hung down.

"Mark," Gorbovsky said in a whisper, "here comes a girl!"

Mark stopped dead in his tracks. A tall, plump brunette came out of the grass, wearing white shorts and a short white jacket with all the buttons pulled off. She was dragging a heavy cable with obvious effort.

"Hello!" Gorbovsky and Mark said in unison.

The girl started. Fear crossed her face.

Gorbovsky and Mark exchanged a look.

"Hello, young lady!" Mark barked.

The brunette let go of the cable and looked downcast.

"Hello," she whispered.

"I have the feeling, Mark," said Gorbovsky, "that we've interrupted something."

"Do you need some help?" Mark offered gallantly.

The girl looked up at him, without raising her head.

"Snakes," she suddenly said.

"Where?" Gorbovsky yelled in terror and lifted one foot.

"Snakes in general," the girl explained. She looked Gorbovsky over. "Did you see the sunrise today?" she inquired stealthily.

"We saw four sunrises today," Mark said casually.

The girl squinted and fixed her hair with a calculated gesture. Mark introduced himself.

"Falkenstein. Mark."

"D-starship officer," Gorbovsky added.

"Ah, a D-starship," the girl said strangely. She picked up the cable, winked at Mark, and disappeared in the grass. The cable rustled on the path. Gorbovsky looked at Mark. Mark was looking at where the girl had been.

"Go ahead, Mark, go," Gorbovsky said. "It's completely logical. The cable is heavy, the girl is weak and pretty, and you're a big strong starflyer."

Mark thoughtfully stepped on the cable. The cable started jerking, and a voice from the grass said:

"Get him, Simon, get him!"

Mark quickly moved his foot. They went on.

"A strange girl," Gorbovsky said. "But, pretty! By the way, Mark, why didn't you marry?"

"Whom?" Mark asked.

"Come on, Mark. Don't be like that. Everybody knows. A very nice woman. Very thin and delicate. I always thought that you were too crude for her. But she didn't seem to think so...."

"I just didn't get married," Mark said unwillingly. "It didn't work out."

The path led them back out to the highway. Now there was a line of long white cisterns on the left, and up ahead the silver spire of the Council gleamed in the sun. It was still empty all around.

"She loved music too much," Mark said. "We couldn't take a choriol along on every flight! And I've had enough of your player, too. Percy can't stand music."

"Every flight," Gorbovsky picked up. "The whole point is, Mark, that we're too old. Twenty years ago we wouldn't have weighed which was more valuable—love or friendship. And now it's too late. Now we're stuck. But don't lose hope, Mark. Maybe we'll still meet some women who will mean more to us than all the rest."

"Not Percy," Mark said. "He doesn't have any other friends except us. And Percy in love...."

Gorbovsky pictured Percy in love.

"Percy would make a wonderful father," he offered tentatively.

Mark frowned.

"That wouldn't be honest. A child doesn't need a good father. It needs a good teacher. And a man needs a good friend. And a woman, someone to love. And why don't we change the subject."

The square in front of the Council was empty except for the big clumsy airbus at the driveway.

"I'd like to see Matvei," said Gorbovsky. "Come with me, Mark."

"Who's Matvei?"

"I'll introduce you. Matvei Vyazanitsyn. Matvei Sergeyevich. He's the director here. An old friend, a starflyer. An original lander. You should remember him, Mark. I guess not, that was before."

"Well," said Mark. "Let's go. A courtesy call. But turn off your player. It's not appropriate for the Council."

The director was very happy to see them.

"Terrific," he bellowed, asking them to sit down. "This is terrific, I'm so glad you flew in! Good for you, Leonid! What a great guy! Falkenstein? Mark. Of course, of course . . . but, why aren't you bald? Leonid definitely told me that you were bald. . . . Ah, yes, that was Dixon he was talking about. Of course, Dixon is famous for his beard, but that doesn't mean a thing—I know lots of bald men with beards! But that's all nonsense! It's hot here, have you noticed? Leonid, you don't eat well, you look like a muscular dystrophy patient. Let's have lunch together . . . and for now, let me offer you some drinks. I have orange juice, tomato juice, and pomegranate . . . our own, homemade! Yes! Wine! We make our own wine, right here on Rainbow, can you imagine, Leonid? Well? Strange, I like it a lot. . . . Mark, how about you? I would never have guessed that you don't drink wine.

Ah, you don't drink the local wines! Leonid, I have a thousand questions for you. I don't know where to start, and in another minute or so I won't be a human being anymore. I'll be a crazed administrator. Have you ever seen a crazed administrator? You'll see one now.... I'll be judge, I'll scold, I'll distribute wealth! I'll rule, having divided and conquered! Now I can understand what a lousy life all those kings and emperors and dictators led. Listen, friends, just please don't leave. I'll burn away at work, and you just sit and commiserate. Nobody commiserates with me around here.... You are comfortable here, aren't you? I'll open the window, let the breeze in.... Leonid, you can't imagine. ... Mark, you can move back into the shade.... So Leonid, do you realize what's going on here? Rainbow has gone berserk, and it's been this way for over a year."

He heaved himself into a groaning armchair in front of a dispatcher's control board—a huge, shaggy man, tanned almost black, with whiskers that looked like a cat's—tore open his shirt almost down to his navel, and looked over his shoulder delightedly at the two starflyers who were diligently sipping their iced drinks. His mustache twitched, and he was about to open his mouth, when a thin pretty girl with hurt in her eyes appeared on one of the six screens.

"Comrade Director," she said very seriously, "my name is Harrington, you may not remember me. I once spoke with you about the ray barrier on Alabaster Mountain. The physicists refuse to remove the barrier."

"What do you mean refuse?"

"I spoke with Rodriguez—he's the zeroist in charge, I believe? He announced that you don't have the right to interfere in their work...."

"They're putting you on, Ellen!" Matvei said. "Rodriguez is in charge just like I'm a dandelion. He's a servomachinist and knows less about zero-physics than you do. I'll get on it right away."

"Please, we really appreciate it."

The director, shaking his head, clicked the dial.

"Alabaster!" he barked. "Let me talk to Pagava!"

"Yes, Matvei?"

"Shota? Hello, pal. Why aren't you removing the barrier?"

"I have. Who says I haven't?"

"Oh, good. Tell Rodriguez to stop bugging people, or he'll have to come see me! Tell him that I remember him well! How's your Wave doing?"

"You see—" Shota stopped. "The Wave is interesting. It's too long to go into now, I'll tell you later."

"Well, good luck!" Matvei, leaning over his forearm, turned to the flyers. "By the way, Leonid." He shouted. "By the way. What do they say about the Wave?"

"Who?" Gorbovsky asked calmly, sipping on his straw. "You mean on board the Tariel?"

"What do you think about the Wave?"

Gorbovsky thought.

"I don't think anything," he said. "Maybe Mark does." He looked at the navigator quizzically.

Mark was sitting formally upright, holding the glass in his hand.

"If I'm not mistaken," he said, "the Wave is a certain process related to zero-transportation. I know very little about it. Zero-transportation interests me, of course, as it does any spaceflyer"—he bowed slightly to the director—"but they don't assign much significance to zero-problematics on Earth. I think that Earth physicists find it too localized an issue and in the applied sciences at that."

The director harrumphed.

"How do you like that, Leonid?" he said. "A localized problem! Yes, our Rainbow is obviously too far away from you, and everything that happens here seems minuscule. My dear Mark, it's this very localized problem that fills my life entirely, and I'm not even a zeroist! I'm exhausted, friends! The day before yesterday I personally refereed Lamondois and Aristotle, and now as I look at my hands"—and he held out his powerful tanned hands—"honest, I just can't believe that they're not covered with bites and scratches. And there were two mobs under the windows, and one was shouting, 'The Wave! The Wave!' and the other cried, 'Zero-T! Zero-T!' And do you think that was a scientific difference of opinion? No! It was an archaic domestic squabble over electric power! Do you remember that funny, but I must confess not very understandable, book about the man who was whipped because he never put out the light in the bathroom? *The Golden Goat* or *The Golden Ass* or something. Well, so Aristotle and his band were trying to whip Lamondois and his crowd for taking over the entire energy reserve. . . . Honest Rainbow! Just last year Aristotle and Lamondois were walking around arm-in-arm. Zeroists were friends, comrades and brothers, and it never occurred to anyone that Forster's infatuation with the Wave would break the planet in two! What a world I live in! There's a shortage of everything: a shortage of energy, a shortage of apparatus; there's a battle over every mealymouthed lab assistant! Lamondois' people steal energy, Aristotle's lurk to catch and proselytize to outsiders—those poor tourists who come here to relax or to write something positive about Rainbow! The Council—the Council, mind you!—has turned into a debating room! I've asked them to send me a copy of *Robert's Rules.* . . . Lately all I've been reading is historical novels. Honest Rainbow! Soon I'll have to set up a police force and jury trials! I'm getting to use completely crazy terminology. Yesterday I called Lamondois the defendant and Aristotle the plaintiff! I can say words like jurisprudence and police presidium without a stutter!"

One of the screens lit up. Two round-faced girls of ten or so showed up. One was wearing a pink dress, the other blue.

"Well, you talk!" said the pink one in a loud whisper.

"Why me, when we decided that you would? . . ."

"We decided it would be you!"

"Creep! . . . Hello, Matvei Semyonovich! . . ."

"Sergeyevich! . . ."

"Matvei Sergeyevich, hello!"

"Hello, girls," the director said. His face made it clear that he had forgotten something and that they had reminded him of it. "Hello, chickens. Hello, baby mice!"

Pink and blue began gabbling.

"Matvei Sergeyevich, we'd like to invite you to Children's Colony for our summer festival."

"Today at twelve o'clock!"

"At eleven!"

"No, twelve!"

"I'll be there!" the director shouted happily. "I'll definitely be there! And I'll be there at eleven and at twelve!"

Gorbovsky finished his drink, poured himself another one, and then stretched out in the chair, his legs way out in the middle of the room, and put the glass on his stomach. He felt good and comfortable.

"I'll go there, too," he announced. "I have absolutely nothing to do. I'll give a speech there. I've never given a speech in my life, and I'm doing to try."

"Children's Colony!" The director flopped over his arm again. "The Colony is the only place where order prevails around here! Children are marvelous people! They understand the word No. . . . And you can't say that about our zeroists, oh no! Last year they gobbled up two million megawatt hours! And this year it's already fifteen and they've put in a request for sixty. The whole problem is that they refuse to acknowledge the word No."

"Neither did we," Mark noted.

"My dear Mark! We all lived in a good time. It was a period of crisis in physics. We didn't need more than they gave us. And what for? What did we have? D-processes, electronic structures. . . . Only a few men were working on joined space, and then only on paper. . . . And now? Now we're in a period of madness in discrete physics. All these zero-problems! Some skinny kid, wet behind the ears, a lab assistant, needs thousands of megawatts for every experiment, special equipment which cannot be made on Rainbow, and which will, naturally, fall apart after the experiment. . . . You brought us a hundred ulmotrons—thanks! But we need six hundred! And energy . . . energy! Where am I supposed to get it? You didn't bring us any energy! And moreover, you need energy yourselves! . . . Kaneko and I turned to the Machine: give us the optimal strategy! The poor thing can't help. . . .'"

The door flew open, and a man of medium height, very well dressed and graceful, rushed in. Grass stuck out of his smooth, black hair, and his immobile face contained a controlled madness.

"Speak of the devil . . ." the director said, extending his hand to him.

"I'm requesting a discharge," the man said in a crisp metallic voice. "I don't feel that I'm capable of working with people any longer, and therefore I want to be retired. . . . Forgive me," he said and bowed shortly to the starflyers, "the name is Kaneko—I'm the energy planner for Rainbow. The former energy planner."

Gorbovsky hurriedly scraped his foot along the slippery floor trying to get up and bow at the same time. He raised his juice glass over his head and looked like a drunken toga-garbed guest at a party given by Lucullus.

"Honest Rainbow!" the director said worriedly. "What happened now?"

"A half hour ago Simon Galkin and Alexandra Postysheva secretly plugged into the zone's power station and took all the energy for the next two days," he said, with a shudder. "The Machine was counting on honest people. I am unaware of a subprogram that takes into account the existence of Galkin and Postysheva. Their behavior is inexcusable, but, unfortunately, not new for us. I might have been able to handle them myself, but I'm not a specialist in the martial arts. And not an acrobat, either. And I'm not working in a kindergarten either. I can't worry about people trying to trick me . . . and setting traps for me. . . . They camouflaged their patch with some thick bushes behind the ravine, and stretched a wire across the path. They knew that I would be running to stop the huge drain. . . ." He stopped talking and began pulling twigs out of his hair.

"Where's Postysheva?" the director said, blood rising to his face. Gorbovsky sat up straight and tucked in his feet in fright. Mark's face held lively interest.

"Postysheva will be here in a second," Kaneko replied. "I'm also certain that she instigated this outrage. I called her in here in your name."

Matvei picked up the microphone of the PA system and said, "Attention, Rainbow! This is the director. I know about the energy drain incident. I am working on it."

He stood, sidled over to Kaneko, put his hand on his shoulder and muttered guiltily, "What can you do, pal? . . . I told you, Rainbow's gone mad. Be patient, friend! I'm being patient, too. I'll let Postysheva have it good. She won't be happy to see me, I promise you that."

"I understand," Kaneko said. "Please forgive me—I was incensed. With your permission I will go to the spaceport. Today's most unpleasant task awaits me—handing out the ulmotrons. You know a ship landed today with a load of ulmotrons? . . ."

"Yes," the director said with feeling. "I know. Here," he said, pointing his square jaw at the starflyers, "I'd like you to meet my friends. The commander of the Tariel, Leonid Andreyevich Gorbovsky and his first officer Mark Falkenstein."

"Pleased to meet you," Kaneko said, bowing his twiggy head. Mark and Gorbovsky also bowed.

"I'll try to keep the damage to your ship down to a minimum," said Kaneko without a smile; then he turned, and headed for the door. Gorbovsky followed him anxiously with his eyes.

The door opened just as Kaneko reached it, and he politely stepped aside. The brunette they had seen earlier, in the white jacket with the missing buttons, came in. Gorbovsky noted that her shorts were burned on the side and her hands were sooty. Next to her Kaneko, graceful and well-kempt, seemed like a visitor from the distant future.

"Forgive me, please," the brunette said in a velvety voice. "May I come in. Did you call for me, Matvei Sergeyevich?"

Kaneko, turning his head away, walked around her and disappeared out the door. Matvei returned to his chair and leaned hard into the armrests. His face had turned blue again.

"Do you really think, Postysheva," he began barely audibly, "that I don't know whose ideas these are?"

A rosy-cheeked youth wearing a beret set at a rakish angle appeared on the screen.

"Forgive me, Matvei Sergeyevich," he said, smiling merrily. "I wanted to remind you that two cases of ulmotrons are for us."

"They'll be handed out according to the sign-up list, Carl," Marvei barked.

"According to the sign-up list, we're first," the young man said.

"In that case, you'll be first," Matvei said, not taking his eyes off Postysheva and looking angry and unapproachable.

"Forgive me once again, Matvei Sergeyevich, but we're very concerned by the behavior of Forster's people. I saw them send out their truck to the spaceport."

"Don't worry, Carl," Matvei said. He couldn't control himself and smiled. "Just look at that, Leonid! He's here to tattle! Who? Hoffman! And on whom? On his own teacher, Forster! Go on, go on, Carl! No one will get them out of turn!"

"Thank you, Matvei Sergeyevich," said Hoffman. "Malyaev and I are counting on you."

"Malyaev and him!" said the director, rolling his eyes to the ceiling.

The screen went black, and lit up a half second later. An elderly, crotchety-looking man wearing sunglasses with some kind of attachment on the frames mumbled grumpily:

"Matvei, I want to clear something up about the ulmotrons ____"

"They'll be handed out in order, in turn," Matvei said.

The brunette sighed languorously, looked sharply at Mark, and then sat down on the edge of a chair with a docile expression.

"We're supposed to get them out of turn," said the man wearing glasses.

"Then you'll get them out of turn," said Matvei. "There's a list of people who don't have to be on the list, and you're eighth on it. . . ."

The brunette, bending over gracefully, was examining the hole in her shorts, and then, spitting on her finger, cleaned the soot from her elbow.

"Just a minute, Postysheva," Matvei said and bent toward the mike. "Attention Rainbow! This is the director. The ulmotrons that arrived on the starship Tariel will be distributed according to the lists ratified by the Council and there will be no exceptions." And turning back, "So, Postysheva . . . I called you in to tell you that I'm tired of you. I was easy on you. Yes, I was patient. I put up with everything. You can't accuse me of cruelty. But Honest Rainbow! There are limits to everything. In other words, tell Galkin that I have taken you off the project and am sending you back to Earth on the very next ship."

Postysheva's huge, marvelous eyes immediately filled with tears. Mark shook his head bitterly, Gorbovsky looked downcast. The director, jaw jutting, looked at Postysheva.

"And it's too late to cry now, Alexandra," he said. "You should have cried before. With us."

A pretty woman in a pleated skirt and blue blouse came into the office. She had very short hair and her reddish bangs kept falling into her eyes.

"Hello!" she said smiling. "Matvei, am I disturbing you? Oh!" she said, seeing Postysheva. "What's this? We're crying?" She hugged Postysheva and pulled her head to her breast. "Matvei, did you do that? You should be ashamed! You must have been cruel! Sometimes you're unbearable!"

The director's mustache twitched.

"Good morning, Gina," he said. "Let go of Postysheva; she's being punished. She profoundly insulted Kaneko and she stole energy——"

"What nonsense!" Gina exclaimed. "Relax, child! What words: 'stole,' 'insulted,' 'energy.' From whom did she steal energy? Not from the Children's Colony! What does it matter which of the physicists uses up the energy—Alexandra Postysheva or that horrible Lamondois!"

The director rose majestically.

"Leonid, Mark," he said. "This is Gina Pickbridge, senior biologist of Rainbow. Gina, this is Leonid Gorbovsky and Mark Falkenstein, starflyers."

The starflyers stood up.

"Hello," Gina said. "No, I don't want to meet you.... How can two healthy handsome men be so callous? How can you sit there and look at a crying girl?"

"We're not callous!" Mark protested. Gorbovsky looked over at him in amazement. "We are just ready to interfere——"

"Then do! Interfere!" Gina said.

"Really now, comrades," the director bellowed. "I don't like this at all! Postysheva, you are excused. Go on... what's the matter, Gina? Let go of Postysheva and state your business ... there now, you see, she's bawled all over your sweater. Postysheva, I told you to leave!"

Postysheva got up and, face in her hands, left. Mark looked questioningly at Gina.

"Well, of course," Gina said.

Mark tugged at his jacket, gave Matvei a severe look,

bowed to Gina and left. Matvei weakly waved his hand in the air.

"I give up," he said. "There's no discipline at all. Do you realize what you're doing, Gina?"

"I do," she said, approaching the table. "All your physics and all your energy isn't worth one of Alexandra's tears."

"Tell that to Lamondois. Or Pagava. Or Forster. Or, for example, Kaneko. And as for the tears, everyone has his own weapon. And no more about it, by your leave. I'm listening."

"All right, enough is enough," Gina said. "I know that you're as stubborn as you are kind. That is to say, infinitely stubborn. Matvei, I need people. No, no," she raised a small hand. "This is very risky and interesting. All I have to do is beckon and half the physicists will run away from their mean supervisors."

"If you beckon," Matvei said, "the supervisors will come running as well."

"Thank you, but what I had in mind was hunting squid. I need twenty people to chase the squid from Pushkin Bay."

Matvei sighed.

"What are the squid doing wrong?" he said. "I don't have the personnel."

"Then ten people. The squid are systematically ravaging the fish preserves. What are your testers doing now?"

Matvei brightened.

"That's right!" he said. "Gaba! Where's Gaba now? Aha, I remember. . . . Everything's in order, Gina, you'll have your ten men."

"Good. I knew that you were kind. I'll go have breakfast, and let them find me. Good-bye, dear Leonid. If you'd like to take part, we'd be happy to have you."

"Phew!" Matvei said when the door shut. "A wonderful woman, but I'd rather work with Lamondois . . . how about your Mark?"

Gorbovsky grinned and poured some more juice. He stretched out blissfully in the chair and with a quiet "Do you mind?" turned on the player. The director leaned back in his chair.

"Yes!" he said meditatively. "Leonid, do you remember the Blind Spot, and Stanislav Pishta screaming into the atmosphere? . . . By the way . . . you know. . . ."

"Matvei Sergeyevich," the voice from the monitor said. "A message from the Arrow."

"Read it," Matvei said, sitting up.

" 'I'm going out into deritrinitation. Next communication in forty hours. Everything's fine. Anton.' The connection was bad, Matvei Sergeyevich. There's a magnetic storm. . . ."

"Thanks," Matvei said. He turned anxiously to Gorbovsky, "By the way, Leonid, what do you know about Camill?"

"That he never removes his helmet," Gorbovsky said. "I once asked him about it directly when we were out swimming. And he gave me a direct answer."

"And what do you think about him?"

Gorbovsky thought.

"I think it's his business."

Gorbovsky didn't want to talk about it. He listened to the drums for a while, and then said, "You understand, Matvei, somehow it turns out that people think I'm Camill's close friend or something. And everyone asks me this and that about him. And I don't like the subject. But if you have any concrete, specific questions, ask."

"I do," Matvei said. "Is Camill crazy?"

"No, not at all! He's just a typical genius."

"You understand, I keep thinking: why is he always predicting and predicting? He has this mania for prediction."

"And what does he predict?"

"Well, trifles," Matvei said. "The end of the world. The trouble is that there is absolutely no one who can understand him. . . . Well, let's forget it. What were we talking about?"

The screen lit up once more. It was Kaneko. His tie was askew.

"Matvei Sergeyevich," he said, panting. "Please verify the list. You must have a copy."

"Oh, I'm so tired of all this!" Matvei said. "Leonid, you must forgive me. I'll have to go out."

"Of course, go on," Gorbovsky said. "I'll take a walk over to the spaceport. See how my Tariel is doing."

"Come to my place for lunch at two," Matvei said, as he left.

Gorbovsky drained the glass, got up, and happily turned up the drums to maximum level. . . .

Chapter 3

BY ten the heat was unbearable. The acrid vapors of the airborne salt seeped from the burning plains through the cracks of the shut windows. Mirages danced over the plain. Robert set up two powerful fans by his chair and flopped down, fanning himself with an old magazine. He consoled himself with the thought that it would be a lot worse by three, and then, before you knew it, it would be evening. Camill was still by the north window. They were no longer talking.

The monitor spewed out an endless blue tape, covered with jagged lines; the Young Counter slowly, so slowly the eye couldn't see it happen, filled up with a deep purple light; the ulmotrons squeaked, reflections of nuclear flame dancing behind their small glass windows. The Wave was developing. Somewhere beyond the northern horizon, above the endless, vast expanse of burnt-out land, gigantic gushers of hot, poisonous dust poured into the stratosphere. . . .

The videophone went off, and Robert immediately assumed a more businesslike position. He thought that it was Patrick or—which would have been terrible in this heat—

Malyaev. But it was Tanya, fresh and happy, and you could see that there was no 110-degree heat there, no smelly vapors from the dead plain, that the air was sweet and cool, and that the wind from the nearby sea brought the fragrance of flowers that were revealed at ebb tide.

"How are you doing without me, Robbie?" she asked.

"Bad," he complained. "It stinks. It's hot. You're not here. I'm terribly sleepy, and I can't fall asleep."

"Poor baby . . . I had a good nap in the helicopter. I'll be having a tough day today too. It's the summer festival—a general mass of confusion, guests, and speeches. The kids are running around half-crazy. Are you alone?"

"No. There's Camill by the window, and he doesn't hear or see you. Tanya, I'm expecting you today. But where?"

"Is your shift over? Then let's fly south!"

"All right. Remember the cafe in Fishville? We'll eat minogi and drink young wine . . . icy cold!" Robert groaned and shut his eyes. "Now all I'll do is wait for evening. Oh, how I'll be waiting!"

"Me too—" She looked around. "Kisses, Robbie," she said. "Wait for my call."

"I sure will," he had time to say.

Camill was still looking out the window, hands clasped behind his back. His fingers were in constant motion. Camill had unusually long, pale, flexible fingers with short nails. They wove and unwove in strange patterns, and Robert caught himself trying to do the same thing with his fingers.

"It's begun," Camill said suddenly. "I suggest you take a look."

"What's begun?" Robert asked. He didn't feel like getting up.

"The plain is moving," Camill said.

Robert reluctantly got up and walked over to him. At first he didn't notice anything. Then he thought he saw a mirage. He was looking so hard that he leaned forward and smacked his forehead against the windowpane. The plain was moving. It was rapidly changing color—a horrible reddish mush was creeping over yellow space. Below, under the watchtower, you could see the red and yellow dots rustling and rumbling among the dried-out stalks.

"Mama mia!" Robert gasped. "The red graineater. What are you standing around for?" He raced to the videophone. "Shepherds!" he shouted. "Man on duty!"

"Speaking . . ."

"This is Plains Post! The graineater is coming from the north! The whole plain is covered with graineater!"

"What? Repeat, please . . . who's speaking?"

"This is Plains Post, Observer Sklyarov! The red graineater is coming from the north! Worse than the year before last! Understand? The whole plain is boiling over with it!!"

"I read you . . . loud and clear. . . . Thanks, Sklyarov. . . . What a mess! All our people are in the south! What a mess . . . well, all right. . . ."

"Wait!" Robert shouted. "Listen, call Alabaster or Greenfield Station, they're full of zeroists, they'll help out!"

"Got it! Thanks, Sklyarov. When the graineater stops moving, please let us know immediately. . . ."

Robert jumped over to the window again. The graineater was pouring in, there was no grass to be seen.

"This is awful," Robert said. "This is really a mess."

"Don't exaggerate, Robert," Camill said. "This isn't so bad. This is merely interesting."

"Yeah, it'll eat up all our fields," Robert said bitterly, "and we'll be stuck without grain, without livestock. . . ."

"No, we won't, Robbie. It won't have time."

"I hope so. That's my only hope. Just look at it go. The whole plain is red."

"It's a cataclysm," Camill said.

Twilight descended unexpectedly. A huge shadow fell across the plain. Robert looked around and ran to the west window. A broad trembling cloud was blocking the sun. And, once more, Robert couldn't immediately determine what was happening. At first he was just surprised, because there were never clouds on Rainbow in the daytime. But then he saw that it was birds. Thousands upon thousands of birds were flying from the north, and even through the shut windows he could hear the rustle of their wings and their sharp, piercing cries. Robert backed up to the table.

"Where are the birds coming from?" he muttered.

"Everything is running for its life," Camill said. "Everything. If I were you, Robbie, I'd be running too. The Wave is coming."

"What Wave?" Robert bent over and looked at the monitoring equipment. "There is no Wave, Camill. . . ."

"No?" said Camill calmly. "All the better. Let's stay and watch."

"I had no intention of running. I'm just surprised by all this. I guess I should report this to Greenfield. The main question is where are all these birds coming from? It's all desert up there."

"There are lots of birds there," Camill said calmly. "There are huge blue lakes, rushes. . . ."

Robert looked at him suspiciously. He had been working on Rainbow for ten years, and he had always been sure that to the north of the Hot Parallel there was nothing, no water, no grass, no life. I should take the flyer and go up there with Tanya, he thought. Lakes, rushes. . . .

The phone rang again, and Robert turned to the screen. It was Malyaev himself.

"Sklyarov," he said in his usual hostile tone, and Robert, as usual, felt guilty of something, of everything, including the graineater and the birds. "Sklyarov, listen to this order. Immediately evacuate your post. Take both ulmotrons with you."

"Fyodor Anatoliyevich," Robert said. "The graineater is coming, the birds are flying, and I was just about to call you——"

"Stick to the point. I repeat. Take both ulmotrons, get in

the helicopter, and head straight for Greenfield. Did you understand me?"

"Yes."

"It is now—" Malyaev looked down. "It is now ten forty-five. At eleven hundred you must be airborne. Keep in mind that I'm releasing the charybdises, so keep at a higher altitude just in case. If you don't have time to dismount the ulmotrons, abandon them."

"What's happened?"

"The Wave is coming," Malyaev said and looked Robert in the eyes for the first time. "It's across the Hot Parallel. Hurry."

Robert stood for a second, gathering his thoughts. Then he looked at the monitors again. According to them, the eruption was diminishing.

"Well, that's not my business," Robert said aloud. "Camill, would you help me?"

"I can't help anyone now," Camill replied. "But, that's not my business. What do you need—help dragging out the ulmotrons?"

"Yes. But first they have to be dismounted."

"Do you want some good advice?" Camill asked. "Good advice number seven thousand eight hundred thirty-two."

Robert had turned off the electricity and, burning his fingers, was unscrewing the plug and socket units.

"Let's hear your advice," he said.

"Drop those ulmotrons, get in the helicopter, and fly off to your Tanya."

"Good advice," Robert said, quickly cutting the plugs. "A pleasant idea. Help me pull it out. . . ."

The ulmotron hung by the center, a fat smooth cylinder about four feet long. They got it out of its nest and carried it into the elevator. The wind began howling and the tower began vibrating.

"Enough," said Camill. "Let's go down together."

"I have to get the other one."

"Robbie, you won't be using this one. Listen to my advice."

Robert looked at his watch.

"There's time. Go downstairs and roll it out onto the ground."

Camill shut the door. Robert went back to the setup. Red twilight suffused the windows. There were no more birds but the sky was swathed in murkiness, through which the small disk of the sun barely glimmered. The tower was shuddering and weaving in the wind.

"I hope to make it," Robert thought aloud.

He dragged out the second ulmotron, hoisted it on his shoulder, and headed for the elevator. Behind his back, the glass shattered in the windows with a resounding crash, and clouds of stinging sand mixed with overheated wind tore into the lab. Something hit him hard on the legs. Robert fell to his knees fast, leaning the ulmotron against the wall, and urgently pressed the elevator button. The motor whined and immediately fell silent.

"Cam-ill," Robert called, pressing his face against the grating.

No one answered. The wind howled and whistled in the broken windows, the tower swayed, and Robert could barely stand on his feet. He pressed the button again. The elevator wasn't working. Then, fighting the wind, he made his way to the window and looked out. The plain was covered with crazily swirling dust. Something shiny showed for a second at the foot of the tower, and Robert felt a chill when he recognized it as the torn and damaged wing of the pterocar. Robert shut his eyes and licked his dry lips. His mouth was filled with sharp bitterness. A good trap, he thought. A good place for Patrick. . . .

"Camill!" he shouted at the top of his lungs.

But he could barely hear his own voice. Through the window . . . he couldn't go through the window, the wind would blow him off. Should he bother at all? The pterocar was destroyed. . . . So this was it. No, he had to get down.

What's Camill doing down there? In his place, I would have fixed the elevator by now. . . . The elevator!

Stepping over the ruins, he returned to the gate and grabbed it. Well, "World Youth," he thought, let's see your stuff. The door was made well. If the supports of the tower had been made this well, the elevator would still be operating. Robert leaned his back against the door and pushed his feet against the wall. Well . . . heave! He saw spots before his eyes. Something cracked, either the door or his back. Again. The door gave. It'll fly out, he thought, and I'll fall down the shaft. Twenty yards head first, and then the ulmotron will fall on top of me. He changed position, back against the wall, feet into the door. Crash! The lower half of the door flew off, and Robert fell on his back, striking his head. He lay motionless for a few seconds. He was all wet. Then he looked into the hole. Far below he could see the top of the cabin. It was very scary to climb down there, but just then the tower began listing, and Robert was sent sliding down. He didn't resist, because the tower kept listing and listing and there was no end to it.

He descended, grabbing onto the struts and girders to slow his slide, and the heavy, stinging wind pressed him into the warm metal. He had time to notice that there was a lot less dust and that the wall was lit by sunlight once more. The tower kept listing. He was in such a rush to find out what had happened to the pterocar and where Camill had gotten to, that he jumped from the shaft some four yards to the ground. He hit the ground hard with his feet and then his hands. And the first thing he saw was Camill's fingers clawing the dry earth.

Camill was lying under the fallen pterocar, his glassy round eyes open wide, and his thin long fingers clutching the earth, as though he had been trying to drag himself out from under the broken copter, or perhaps because he had been in terrible pain before death. Dust covered his white jacket; there was dust on his cheeks and open eyes.

"Camill!" Robert called out.

The wind was shaking and mauling a piece of the broken wing above his head. The wind was carrying streams of yellow dust. The wind was whistling and screaming in the girders of the listing tower. The tiny sun blazed viciously in the murky sky. It seemed shaggy.

Robert got up on his feet and, falling against the pterocar, tried to move it. He managed to lift the heavy vehicle for a second, but only for a second. He looked at Camill again. Now his entire face was covered with dust, and his white jacket was rust-colored, and only the ridiculous helmet was free of dust, the plastic shining merrily in the sun.

Robert's legs started to wobble, and he sat down next to the dead man. He wanted to cry. Farewell, Camill. Honest, I loved you. No one loved you, but I did. Of course, I didn't always listen to you, just like the others, but honest, the only reason I didn't listen was that I had no hopes of ever understanding you. You were head and shoulders above the rest, and even more above me. And now I can't even shove this pile of garbage off your crushed chest. The rules of friendship call for me to stay by your side. But Tanya is waiting for me, maybe even Malyaev is waiting for me, and then, I desperately want to live. And there's no feeling or logic that are of any help here. I know that I can't get away, yet I'm still going. I'll run, I'll slog, maybe I'll crawl, but I'll leave and move until my last breath. . . . I'm a fool, I should have taken your good advice number seven thousand, but as usual I didn't understand you, though what was there to understand?

He felt so worn out that it was a major effort to get up and go. And when he turned for a last look at Camill he saw the Wave.

Far, far away over the north horizon, beyond the reddish haze of settling dust, a blinding stripe, as bright as the sun, sparkled in the bleached sky.

It's over, Robert thought weakly. I won't get far. It'll be here in half an hour and go on, and there'll only be a smooth black desert here. The tower will remain of course, and nothing will happen to the ulmotrons, and the pterocar will remain, and the torn wing will droop in the hot windless air. And maybe Camill's helmet will remain. There won't be anything left of me. And, as if in farewell, he looked at himself—he pounded his chest, felt his biceps. Too bad, he thought. And then he saw the flyer.

The flyer was behind the tower—a small two-seater, looking like a colorful turtle, speedy, economical, extraordinarily simple and easy to drive. It was Camill's flyer. Of course, Camell's flyer.

Robert took several uncertain steps toward it, and then ran like hell, going around the tower. He didn't take his eyes off it—afraid that it would disappear—tripped on something and fell splat on the prickly grass, scraping his chest and stomach. Jumping up, he looked back. The heavy cylinder of the ulmotron was still rolling softly from the collision. Robert looked north. A black wall was rising on the horizon. Raising a cloud of dust, Robert ran to the flyer, jumped onto the seat and, finding the controls, gave full throttle from a dead start.

The plains zone extended all the way to Greenfield, and Robert drove through it at an average speed of 300 mph. The flyer raced over the plain like a flea—in huge jumps. The blinding stripe was soon hidden behind the horizon once again. Everything seemed normal in the prairie—the dry, prickly grass, the trembling haze over the salt flats, and the infrequent patches of dwarf shrubs. The sun blazed mercilessly. And for some reason there was no trace of the graineater, or the birds, or the hurricane. Probably the hurricane had swept away the birds and lost itself in the fruitless, eternally empty expanses of Northern Rainbow, apparently destined by nature itself to be the site of the crazy experiments of the zero-physicists. Once, when Robert was still a tyro, when the Capital was still called a station and Greenfield didn't exist at all, the Wave passed through these parts, brought on by the grandiose experiments of the late Lu Fun-chan, and everything all around was turned black, but just seven years later the sturdy grasping grass had pushed the bare lands back far north to the areas of eruption.

Everything will return, thought Robert. Everything will be like it used to be, but Camill will be no more. And if someone ever suddenly appears in a chair behind my back, I'll know for sure that it's only a ghost. And now I'll go see Malyaev and tell him right to his face: "I abandoned your ulmotrons. . . ." And he'll hiss at me: "How could you, Sklyarov?" and I'll say, "I don't give a damn about your ulmotrons; Camill died because of your ulmotrons." And he'll say, "That's really too bad, but you should have brought the ulmotrons." And then I'll lose my temper and tell him everything: "You're an icicle," I'll say. "A snowman with an electric motor. How dare you think about ulmotrons when Camill is dead. . . . You're a callous bastard!"

A hundred fifty miles from Greenfield he saw the charybdises—gigantic telemechanical tanks, with huge open jaws of the energy gulpers. They were moving in a chain from horizon to horizon, at the proper half-mile distance from one another, rumbling and roaring with thousand-horsepower motors. They left broad strips of upturned soil, plowed down to the basalt core of the continent. The tank tracks blazed in the sun. And far to the right in the murky sky hovered a barely visible dot—that was the scout helicopter, controlling the movement of these metallic monsters. The charybdises were attacking the Wave.

The energy gulpers didn't seem to be on yet, but just in case, Robert gained altitude sharply and began his descent only when he suddenly saw Greenfield through the haze—several white houses and the square remote control tower, surrounded by lush vegetation. On the northern edge, crushing a palm grove, a stationary charybdis glowered darkly, and its bottomless energy gulper pointed directly at Robert; there were two other charybdises on either side of the settlement. Two helicopters flew up over the tower and headed south. On the square, amid the green lawns, the feathery wings of the pterocars sparkled in the sun. People scurried about near the pterocars.

Robert pulled up to the entrance of the tower and jumped onto the steps. Someone jumped back and a woman's voice called out: "Who's that?" Robert grabbed the handle of the glass door and stopped, completely taken aback by his reflection—almost naked, covered with baked-on dust, eyes angry, a broad black scratch across his chest and stomach. . . . All right, he thought, then pulled on the door. "It's Robert!" they shouted. He slowly went upstairs and ran into Patrick. Patrick stared at him, mouth agape. "Patrick," Robert said. "Patrick, friend, Camill is dead. . . ." Patrick blinked and then quickly brought his hand to his mouth. Robert went on. The door to the dispatcher's was open. Malyaev was in there along with Shota Petrovich Pagava, head of the northern zeroists, and Carl Hoffman, and some other people, biologists, he thought. Robert stopped in the doorway, holding onto the jamb. People were running up the stairs behind him and someone shouted: "How does he know?"

"Camill . . ." Robert rasped and began coughing.

They all stared at him.

"What's the matter?" Malyaev demanded sharply. "What's the matter with you, Sklyarov, why are you in that condition?"

Robert approached the table and leaned his dirty fists on some papers, said right to his face:

"Camill is dead. He was crushed."

It became very quiet. Malyaev's eyes narrowed.

"Crushed? How? Where?"

"He was crushed by the pterocar," Robert said. "Because of your precious ulmotrons. He could have easily saved himself, but he was helping me drag your precious ulmotrons, and he was crushed. And I left your ulmotrons there. You can pick them up after the Wave passes. Understand? I left them. They're lying around out there right now."

They gave him a glass of water. He took the glass and

drank greedily. Malyaev was silent. His pale face had turned completely white. Hoffman played with some circuits without looking up. Pagava got up and stood with lowered head.

"This is very sad," Malyaev finally said. "He was a great man." He wiped his forehead. "A very great man." He looked at Robert again. "You're very tired, Sklyarov. . . ."

"I'm not tired."

"Get cleaned up and get a rest."

"And that's it?" Robert asked bitterly.

Malyaev's face took on its habitual expression—indifferent and hard.

"I'll detain you one more minute. Did you see the Wave?"

"Yes. I saw the Wave too."

"What type of Wave?"

Something clicked in Robert's brain and everything was back to usual. There was the powerful and wise supervisor Malyaev and his eternal lab assistant and observer Robert Sklyarov, aka "World Youth." . . .

"I think the third type," he said docilely. "A Lu-wave."

Pagava looked up.

"Goo-ood!" he said in an unexpectedly hearty voice. And then his face fell again, and he leaned on the table and sat down. "Ay, Camill, Camill!" he muttered. "Poor guy!" He grabbed his large, protruding ears and shook his head over the papers.

One of the biologists, giving Robert nervous side glances, tapped Malyaev on the shoulder.

"Forgive me," he said guiltily. "Why is that good, that it's a Lu-wave?"

Malyaev finally stopped drilling his cruel eyes through Robert.

"That means," he said, "that only the northern grain fields will perish. But we're not yet sure that it is a Lu-wave. The observer might have been mistaken."

"But how can that be?" the biologist wailed. "We had agreed . . . you have those . . . 'charybdises' . . Can't you stop it? What kind of physicists are you?"

Hoffman said, "We might be able to stop the Wave's iner-
tia at the line of discrete fallover."

"What do you mean 'might be able'?" an unfamiliar
woman exclaimed, standing next to the biologist. "Do you
understand that this is an outrage? Where are your guaran-
tees? All your fine talk? Do you realize that you're leaving
the planet without grain or meat?"

"I do not accept these complaints," Malyaev said coldly.
"I commiserate deeply, but your complaints should be directed to Etienne Lamondois. We don't set up zero-experi-
ments. We merely study the Wave. . . ."

Robert turned and slowly headed for the door. And they
don't care about Camill, he thought. The Wave, the crops,
meat . . . why did they dislike him so? Because he was
smarter than all of them put together? Or don't they love
anyone at all? There were some people in the doorway, familiar faces, upset, sad, worried. Someone took his elbow.
He looked down and met the small sad eyes of Patrick.

"Let's go, Rob, I'll help you wash up."

"Patrick," Robert said, putting his hand on his shoulder.
"Patrick. Get away from here. Leave them if you want to
remain human."

Patrick's face grimaced with a martyred look.

"Don't, Rob," he muttered. "Don't. It'll pass."

"It'll pass," Robert repeated. "It'll all pass. The Wave. Life.
And everything will be forgotten. Does it matter when it will
be forgotten—now or later?"

Behind him, the biologists were arguing openly. Malyaev
was demanding: "The situation report!" Shota was shouting: "Don't stop the measurements even for a second! Use
all the automation! The hell with it, you'll leave it there!"

"Let's go, Rob," Patrick asked.

And just then, drowning out the talk and shouting, the
familiar montonous voice bellowed in the dispatcher's
speaker:

"Attention!"

Robert wheeled around. His knees were weak. On the

huge screen he saw Camill's ugly helmet and round unblinking eyes.

"I don't have much time," Camill said. It was Camill, real
and alive—his head was shaking, his thin lips were moving,
and the tip of his long thin nose bobbed in rhythm. "I can't
get in touch with the director. Immediately call back the
Arrow. Immediately evacuate the entire north side. Immediately!" He turned his head and looked off to the side, and
they could see his dust-smeared cheek. "There's a Wave of a
new type directly behind the Lu-wave. You must—"

An explosion, a cracking sound, and the screen went
dead. A deathly silence hung over the dispatcher's room,
and suddenly Robert saw Malyaev's horrible eyes squinting
at him.

Chapter 4

THERE was only one spaceport on Rainbow, and there was only one starship at the spaceport—sigma-D-starship Tariel Two. It was visible from afar—the pale blue dome some seventy yards high rose like a cloud over the flat dark green roofs of the service stations. Leonid Andreyevich Gorbovsky made two unsure circles over it. It was difficult to land right next to the starship: a solid circle of various vehicles surrounded the ship. From his vantage point he could see the clumsy robot-service workers, attaching themselves to the six tank nipples; the bustling safety cybers, feeling along every inch of surface; and the gray mother robot, which directed a dozen little squirmy analyzers. It was a familiar sight, one that gladdened his proprietary eye.

However, there was a complete disregard of all regulations by the loading dock. The silent spaceport cybers had been pushed aside, and a great number of transport vehicles of all types huddled there. There were the usual trucks, the recreational vehicles called Diligences, passenger vehicles like the Testudo and Leopard, and even a Mole, a clumsy earth-boring vehicle used in mining. They were all performing

complicated maneuvers around the dock, crowding one another. To one side, in the terrible sun, sat several helicopters
and some empty crates, which, Gorbovsky realized, had
once held ulmotrons. Some people sat miserably on the
crates.

Still searching for a spot to land, Gorbovsky began his
third circle and discovered that his flyer was being followed
by a heavy pterocar, the driver of which was hanging out the
open door and signaling him. Gorbovsky landed among the
helicopters and crates, and the pterocar thudded down next
to him.

"I'm after you," the driver said, jumping out of the cab.

"I don't recommend it," Gorbovsky said softly. "I don't
care about any lines. I'm captain of this ship."

The driver's face came alive with excitement.

"Fantastic!" he whispered, carefully looking around.
"We'll show these zeroists. . . . What's the captain's name?"

"Gorbovsky," said Gorbovsky, bowing slightly.

"And the first officer?"

"Falkenstein."

"Marvelous," the pterocar driver said in a businesslike
tone. "So, you're Gorbovsky, and I'm Falkenstein. Let's go."

He took Gorbovsky by the arm. Gorbovsky held back.

"Listen, Gorbovsky, we're not risking a thing. I know these
ships very well. I came here on a landing craft myself. We'll
make our way to the hold, each take an ulmotron, and hide
in the sleeping quarters. When all this is over"—he gestured
casually at the vehicles—"we'll get out calmly."

"What if the real first officer comes?"

"The real first officer will have a long hard time proving
that he's the real one," the impostor said.

Gorbovsky giggled and said, "Let's go."

The self-appointed first officer smoothed his hair, took a
deep breath, and resolutely moved forward. They squeezed
in between the vehicles. The impostor talked incessantly—
and suddenly developed a deep bass voice.

"I feel," he proclaimed loudly, "that cleaning out the diffusers will only hold us up. I propose that we merely change half the sets, and concentrate on examining the lining. . . . Comrade, move up your car a bit. It's in the way. . . . So, Valentin Petrovich, when we get out into derintrinitation— Back up your truck a bit, there, fellows. I can't understand, why are you all crowding around here? There's a line, there's a list, the law, you know—send your representatives. . . . Valentin Petrovich, I don't know about you, but I find the locals quite uncivilized. We didn't see anything like this even on Pandora among the Takhorgs. . . ."

"You're absolutely right, Mark," Gorbovsky said, having a wonderful time.

"What? Oh, yes . . . terrible mores."

A girl in a silk scarf looked out of her truck and asked, "First officer and captain, I presume?"

"Yes!" the impostor said challengingly. "And as first officer, I would suggest that you read the instructions on the procedure for unloading one more time."

"You think that's necessary?"

"Definitely. You've brought your truck inside the twenty-yard zone against all regulations. . . ."

"You know, friends," a merry young voice called out, "this first officer has a lot less imagination than the first two."

"What do you mean by that?" the impostor demanded. He had something of a fake Nero in his face.

"You see," the girl wearing the scarf said, "there on those crates, you see two first officers and one captain. And the empty crates held ulmotrons that were taken away by the engineer—a modest young woman. She's now being chased by a representative of the Council."

"How do you like this, Valentin Petrovich?" the fraudulent first officer yelled. "False advertising, eh?"

"I have the feeling," Gorbovsky said quietly, "that I'm not going to get on my own ship."

"A correct interpretation," the girl said. "And not a new one."

The self-proclaimed first officer tried a headlong dash, but the truck on the right moved left, the yellow and black Diligence on the left moved right, and the angry, earth-chomping Mole blocked his path to the door.

"Valentin Petrovich!" he cried. "I cannot guarantee the ship's preparedness for takeoff in these circumstances!"

"Old stuff!" the driver of the Diligence said.

The loud merry voice went on:

"Some first officer! What a bore! Now remember the second one—he was amusing at least! He pulled up his T-shirt to show scars from meteorites!"

"No, the first one was better," the Mole driver said.

The fraudulent first officer, lowering his head in abject defeat, picked clumps of dirt from the Mole's shiny teeth.

"Well, and what do you have to say for yourself?" the Diligence driver said to Gorbovsky. "Why are you silent? You have to say something . . . something convincing."

They all waited curiously.

"Actually, I could have gone in through the passenger hatch," Gorbovsky said thoughtfully.

The fraudulent first officer looked up at him hopefully.

"No, you couldn't have," the driver shook his head. "It's locked from inside."

During the ensuing pause, they heard Kaneko's voice: "I can't give you ten sets, please understand, Comrade Prozorovsky!"

"You must understand, Comrade Kaneko! We ordered ten. How can I go back with six?"

Someone interrupted: "Take them, Prozorovsky. . . . Take the six for now. We'll have four free next week, and I'll send them over."

"Promise?"

The girl in the scarf said, "I really feel sorry for Prozorovsky. They have sixteen circuits working on ulmotrons."

"Poor people," the Diligence driver sighed.

"And we have five," the fraudulent first officer said. "Five circuits and only one ulmotron. Why couldn't they have brought two hundred?"

"We could have brought three or four hundred," Gorbovsky said. "But everyone needs ulmotrons nowadays. They've set up six new U-conveyors on Earth."

"U-conveyors!" the girl laughed. "That's easy to say! Do you have any idea of the technology involved in an ulmotron!"

"Just very generally."

"Sixty kilograms of ultramicroelements . . . put together by hand, with half-micron tolerances. . . . What self-respecting person would do that kind of work? Would you?"

"They're calling for volunteers," Gorbovsky said.

"Hah!" the Mole driver said. "Be Kind to Physicists Week!"

"Well, Valentin Petrovich," the fraudulent first officer said, "looks like they won't let us in. . . ."

"My name is Leonid Andreyevich," Gorbovsky said.

"And mine's Hans," the man admitted. "Let's go sit on the crates. Maybe something will happen."

The girl in the scarf waved to them. They made their way out of the car maze and sat down on the crates with the other men who had unsuccessfully posed as officers of the starship. They were greeted with sympathetic and mocking silence.

Gorbovsky felt the crate. The plastic was rough and hard. The sun was hot. There was absolutely nothing here for him to do, but, as usual, he really wanted to meet these people, learn who they were and how they'd come to be here and how things were in general. He pushed several crates together, asked, "Mind if I lie down?", lay down, stretching out to his full length, and clamped a micro air-conditioner near his head. Then he turned on his player.

"My name is Gorbovsky," he presented himself. "Leonid. I was the captain of this ship."

"I also was the captain of this ship," a heavyset, dark-faced man sitting to his right announced glumly. "My name is Alpa."

"And I'm Vanin," said a thin young man, naked to the waist and wearing a boater. "I was and am the first officer. At least <u>until I get my ulmotron.</u>"

"Hans," the pseudo-Falkenstein introduced himself and sat in the grass close to the micro air-conditioner.

The third fraudulent first officer apparently hadn't heard them. He sat with his back to them and was writing something on a pad on his knees.

A long sleek Leopard pulled out from the mass of cars. A door opened, empty boxes that had once held ulmotrons were tossed out, and the car raced off into the plains.

"Prozorovsky," Vanin said enviously.

"Yes," Alpa said bitterly. "Prozorovsky doesn't have to lie. He's Lamondois' right arm." He sighed deeply. "I never lied. I can't stand lying. And now I feel bad."

Vanin made a profound pronouncement: "If a man begins lying without any desire to, that means that something has gone haywire. Serious repercussions."

Alpa said, as though continuing an interrupted conversation, "Jokes aside, but take Lamondois. He's racing headlong to reach zero-T. Zero-T, as is to be expected, will present us with a mass of offshoots. But Lamondois is forced to chop most of them off; he simply must ignore them. Because he has no opportunity to follow every offshoot to its logical development. And moreover, he is forced to consciously disregard truly amazing and astounding phenomena. That's what happened with the Wave. An unexpected, amazing, and, as I see it, dangerous phenomenon. But pursuing his goal, Lamondois was willing even to create a breach in his own camp. He fell out with Aristotle, he refuses to protect the wavists. He's going deeper and deeper and his problems are becoming narrower and narrower. The Wave is far behind him. It's merely an irritation for him, he doesn't even want to hear about it. And it, by the way, is burning all our crops. . . ."

The loudspeaker above the spaceport rumbled into action:

"Attention, Rainbow! This is the director. Chief Gaba of the testers' brigade and the brigade come to see me immediately."

"Lucky men," said Hans. "They don't need any ulmotrons."

"They have their own problems," Vanin said. "I watched them train once—not for me, I'd rather be a pseudo—first officer. . . . And then you sit around for two years without doing what you're trained for and hear people say, 'Well, just wait a little longer. Maybe tomorrow. . . .' "

"I'm glad that you bring up things that are left behind," Gorbovsky said. "The blank spots of science. I'm interested in that, too. I think we have some problems back there . . . for instance, the Massachusetts Machine." Alpa nodded. Gorbovsky turned to him. "You must remember it. It's not brought up very often nowadays. The computer heyday is over."

"I don't recall hearing about the Massachusetts Machine," Vanin said. "Well?"

"You know that old fear: that machines will be smarter than man and take over. . . . A hundred fifty years ago in Massachusetts they started up the most advanced computer ever created. With phenomenal speed and almost infinite memory, and so on . . . and that computer worked for exactly four minutes. They unplugged it, cemented up all the entrances and exits, diverted all the power sources away from it, laid mines around it, and put up barbed wire. Good old-fashioned barbed wire—you can believe this or not."

"What was the problem?" Vanin asked.

"It began controlling itself," Gorbovsky said.

"I don't understand."

"Neither do I, but it was all they could do to turn it off when they did."

"Does anyone understand?"

"I talked to one of its creators. He took me by the shoulder and looked me in the eyes and said: 'Leonid, it was terrifying.'"

"That's terrific!" Hans said.

"Ah, baloney," Vanin said. "That doesn't interest me."

"It does me," Gorbovsky said. "They could turn it on again, you know. Of course, that's forbidden by the Council, but the ban could be lifted."

Alpa grumbled: "Every age has its sorcerers and ghosts...."

"By the way, speaking of sorcerers," Gorbovsky went on. "I immediately thought of the case of the Devil's Dozen."

Hans's eyes lit up.

"The Case of the Devil's Dozen, of course!" Vanin said. "Thirteen fanatics ... where are they now?"

"Wait a minute," Alpa said. "Are they the scientists who tried to graft themselves with computers? They were killed!"

"So they say," said Gorbovsky. "But that's not the point. The precedent was set."

"Well," Vanin said, "they call them fanatics and sorcerers, but I think there's something attractive about them. Lose all the weaknesses, passions, emotional upheavals.... Sheer reason plus the unlimited possibilities of perfecting the organism. A researcher who doesn't need equipment, who is his own equipment and his own transport. And no lines for ulmotrons ... I can picture that perfectly. A human flyer, a human-reactor, a human lab ... untouchable, immortal...."

"Forgive me, but that's not a human being," Alpa grumbled. "That's the Massachusetts Machine."

"But how did they die if they were immortal?" Hans asked.

"They destroyed themselves," Gorbovsky said. "I guess it's not so great being a human lab."

A man scarlet-faced from exertion, carrying an ulmotron cylinder on his shoulder, appeared from the cars. Vanin jumped down from the crate and ran to help him. Gorbovsky thoughtfully observed them load the ulmotron into the heli-copter. The scarlet-faced man was complaining:

"It's not bad enough that they give you one instead of three. Or that you lose half your day. You also have to prove that you have the right to get it! They don't believe you! Can you imagine—they don't believe you! They don't!"

When Vanin returned, Alpa said, "All this is rather fantas-tic. If you're interested in the rear guard, you'd be better off paying attention to the Wave. Every week there's another zero-transport. And every zero-T brings on the Wave. A larger or smaller eruption. And they deal with the Wave in an amateurish way. We may end up with another Massachu-setts Machine, but without an off switch. Camill—you know Camill?—sees it like a phenomenon of planetary scope, but his arguments are hard to follow. It's very hard working with him."

Alpa sighed and put away his pipe. "Problems, prob-lems," he said. "Contradictions, synthesis, the rear, the front. . . . Have you noticed who's sitting here? You, you . . . him . . . me—losers. Science's rejects. Science is over there—getting ulmotrons." He wanted to say something else, but the loudspeaker came back on.

"Attention, Rainbow! This is the director. Leonid Andrey-evich Gorbovsky, Captain of starship Tariel Two. Comrade Kaneko, Energy Planner for the planet. Please come to my office immediately."

The drivers stuck their heads out the car windows. Indes-cribable satisfaction was written all over their faces. They all stared at the fraudulent starflyers. Vanin, tucking his head into his shoulders, spread his hands in dismay. Hans called out merrily: "That's not for me. I'm the first officer!" Alpa groaned and covered his face with his hands. Gorbovsky quickly got up.

"It's time for me to go," he said. "And I really don't feel like it. I haven't had time to let you know what I think, so here's my point of view, in brief. Don't grieve, don't wring your hands in anguish. Life is beautiful. And it is precisely because there's no end to contradictions and new twists. And as for turmoil and trouble—well, I've always liked the writer Kuprin. He has a character, a man who has ruined his life with vodka, leading a wretched existence. I remember word for word what he says." Gorbovsky cleared his throat. " 'If I should fall under a train, and the wheels slice through my body, and my guts mingle with the sand and get twisted up in the wheels, and if in that last instant someone were to ask me, "And *now* is life beautiful?" I would answer in an ecstasy of gratitude, "Oh, how beautiful life is!" ' " Gorbovsky smiled shyly and flipped on the player in his pocket. "That was written three centuries ago, when mankind was still crawling on all fours. So let's not complain. . . . I'll leave you the air-conditioner—it's awfully hot here."

Chapter 5

MATVEI was not alone. A small dark-haired man sat on his desk, leaning back on his arms and dangling his feet; he had black eyes and he was as lively as a high school senior. This was Etienne Lamondois, the head of contemporary zero-physics, "the fast physicist," as his colleagues had dubbed him.

"May I?" Gorbovsky asked from the doorway of Matvei's office.

"Ah, here he is," Matvei said. "Do you know each other?"

Lamondois jumped down from the desk and, stepping close to Gorbovsky, warmly shook his hand.

"Happy to meet you, Captain," he said, smiling pleasantly. "We were just talking about you."

Gorbovsky backed away and sat down. "And we were talking about you," he said.

Etienne bowed in a lively manner and went back behind the director's desk.

"And so, I continue," he said. "The charybdises are ready to do mortal battle. I have to give Malyaev the credit—he created absolutely marvelous machines. It's curious that the northern Wave is of a completely new type. Those boys have already named it. P-Wave: how do you like that? After big-nosed Shota. Dammit, I must admit that I'm tearing my hair out. How could I not have noticed this marvelous phenomenon before? I'll have to apologize to Aristotle. He was right. He and Camill. I bow to Camill. I bowed to him before, but now I think I understand what he had in mind. By the way, do you know that Camill died?"

Matvei's head jerked up.

"Again?"

"Ah, you know already! A strange story. He died and was resurrected. I've heard of things like that. There's nothing new under the sun. The same thing happened to Christ. By the way, can you believe that Sklyarov could have abandoned him to the Wave? I don't. So, the northern Wave has reached the belt of control stations. The first, the Lu-Wave has been broken up, the second, the P-Wave, is pushing up on the charybdises at the rate of twenty kilometers an hour. So the northern fields, probably, will be destroyed. The biologists were sent out in helicopters. . . ."

"I know," the director said. "They complained."

"What can you do! They were behaving in an understandable but nevertheless undignified manner. The Wave's movement has been stopped at the ocean. We're observing a phenomenon there that Lu would have given up half a lifetime to see: the deformation of a ring Wave. This deformation satisfies kappa-equation, and if the Wave is a kappa-field, then everything that poor Malyaev has been struggling with becomes clear: D-permeability, and the gusher's telegenics, and secondary ghosts! . . . Dammit, in these three hours we've learned more about the Wave than we have in ten years. Matvei, bear in mind that as soon as this is all over we'll need a U-register, maybe two of them. Consider this a requisition. Ordinary computers won't help. Only Lu-algorithms, only Lu-logic!"

"All right, all right," Matvei said. "What's happening in the south?"

"In the south we have the ocean. You don't have to worry about the south. The Wave has reached Pushkin Bay, burned the Southern Archipelago, and stopped. I have the impression that it won't go any further, and I'm really sorry, because the observers ran away from there so fast that they abandoned all the machinery, and we know almost nothing about the Southern Wave." He snapped his fingers to underscore his regret. "I understand that you're interested in something else entirely. But what can you do, Matvei! Let's look at things realistically. Rainbow is a physicists' planet, a laboratory. The energy stations are gone and you can't get them back. When this experiment is over, we'll build them anew, together. We'll need lots of energy! And as for the fishing industry, damn it . . . the zeroists are prepared to sacrifice squid chowder! Don't be mad at us, Matvei."

"I'm not mad," the director said with a deep sigh. "But there is something very childish about you, Etienne. Like a child, you play and break things that adults cherish." He sighed again. "Please try to save at least the southern crops. I wouldn't want us to lose our autonomy."

Lamondois looked at his watch, nodded, and left without a word. The director looked at Gorbovsky.

"How do you like it, Leonid?" he asked, laughing sadly. "Yes, my friend. Poor Postysheva, she's an angel compared to these vandals. When I think that in addition to all my other wounds I now have to worry about restoring all the utilities and sanitation systems, my skin crawls." He tugged at his mustache. "But on the other hand, Lamondois is right. Rainbow is a physicists' planet. But what will Kaneko say, what will Gina say? . . ." He shook his head and shuddered. "Yes! Kaneko! Where's Kaneko?"

"Matvei," Gorbovsky said. "Why have you called me in?"

The director, turning his back to him, was fiddling with the keys of the selector.

"Are you comfortable?" he asked.

"Yes," Gorbovsky said. He was already lying down.

"Would you like something to drink?"

"Yes."

"Get it in the fridge. Are you hungry?"

"Not yet. But I will be."

"We'll talk then. And meanwhile, don't bother my work."

Gorbovsky got juice from the refrigerator and a glass, mixed himself a cocktail, and lay back in the chair. The chair was soft and cool, the drink icy and delicious. He lay contentedly, sucking on the straw with eyes half shut, and listened to the director talk with Kaneko. Kaneko said that he couldn't get away—they wouldn't let him go. The director asked who wasn't letting him go. I'll send Gaba over there, the director said. Kaneko replied that it was noisy enough as it was. Then Matvei told him about the Wave and reminded him in an apologetic tone that on top of everything else, Kaneko was the chief of ISS on Rainbow. Kaneko said angrily that he didn't remember that at all, and Gorbovsky felt sorry for him.

The directors of the Individual Safety Service always elicited pity from him. Eventually, every mastered, and sometimes not completely mastered, planet is swamped, with outsiders—tourists, retired people (with their entire families), artists looking for new impressions, losers seeking solitude or hard work, various dilettantes, hunters, and so on —not on any lists, unknown to anyone on the planet, connected to no one and often carefully avoiding any contact. The head of ISS had to get to know each of the outsiders personally, instruct them, and keep an eye on them, making sure that each outsider reported in by a signal on a registering machine. On vicious planets like Yowlah or Pandora, where a novice could fall into all kinds of danger at every step, the ISS commandos saved many lives. But on Rainbow, with its flat, solid surface, mild climate, friendly fauna, and gentle, always calm sea, the ISS had apparently turned into an empty formality, as was inevitable. And polite, proper Kaneko, feeling the ambiguity of his position, did not spend his time instructing writers who had come to work in peace or keeping an eye on the meanderings of lovers and newlyweds, but on his planning or some other real work.

"How many outsiders are on Rainbow now?" Matvei asked.

"About sixty. Maybe a few more."

"Kaneko, friend, all the outsiders have to be found immediately and sent to the Capital."

"I don't quite understand the point of that," Kaneko said politely. "The threatened areas are almost never visited by outsiders. It's naked plain there, it smells bad, it's very hot...."

"Please, let's not argue, Kaneko," Matvei said. "The Wave is the Wave. At a time like this it's better to have all uninterested parties close at hand. Gaba will show up here any minute with his bums, and I'll send him to you. Organize things."

Gorbovsky, setting his straw aside, took a gulp straight from the glass. Camill is dead, he thought. And having died, was resurrected. Things like that have happened to me, too. Of course, that Wave has created considerable panic. And during a panic there's always someone who dies and then you're very surprised when you run into him at a cafe a million miles away from where he died. His mug is scratched up, his voice hoarse and hearty, he's listening to jokes and putting away his sixth serving of marinated shrimp and Szechuan cabbage.

"Matvei," he called out. "Where's Camill now?"

"Ah, so you don't know yet," the director said. He went over to the small table and poured himself a cocktail of grenadine and pineapple syrup. "Malyaev called me from Greenfield. Camill had somehow ended up in a frontier post, hung around, and was swept over by the Wave. Some complicated story. That Sklyarov—the observer—rushed in on Camill's flyer, had a fit and announced that Camill was squashed, and ten minutes later Camill was on the screen at Greenfield, prophesying as usual, and then disappeared once again. Now how can he be taken seriously after such business?"

"Yes. Camill is an original. Who's Sklyarov?"

"One of Malyaev's observers, I just told you. A diligent, nice guy, not too bright. . . . It's impossible that he could have abandoned Camill. . . . Malyaev always gets these crazy ideas. . . ."

"Don't pick on Malyaev, he's just being logical," Gorbovsky said. "But enough of that. Let's talk about the Wave instead."

"All right," the director said distractedly.

"Is it very dangerous?"

"What?"

"The Wave. Is it dangerous?"

Matvei breathed hard.

"In general, the Wave is mortally dangerous," he said. "The trouble is that the physicists never know how it will behave ahead of time. For example, it can dissipate at any moment." He paused. "Or not dissipate."

"And there's no place to hide from it?"

"I haven't heard of anyone trying. They say that it's quite a horrible sight."

"You mean you've never seen it?"

Matvei's mustache bristled.

"You might have noticed," he said, "that I don't have too much time to travel around the planet. I'm always waiting for someone, placating someone, or else someone's waiting for me. . . . I assure you that if I had any spare time. . . ."

Gorbovsky asked gingerly, "Matvei, you probably wanted me to help look for the outsiders, right?"

The director looked at him angrily. "Are you hungry?"

"N-no."

Matvei walked around the office.

"I'll tell you what's upsetting me. First of all, Camill had predicted that this experiment would end badly. They didn't pay any attention. Neither did I, consequently. And now Lamondois admits that Camill was right."

The door flew open and a young, huge black man, teeth flashing, rushed in. He was wearing white shorts, white jacket, and white shoes with no socks.

"I've arrived!" he announced, waving his huge hands. "What do you wish, oh my director? Do you want me to destroy a city or build a palace? Guessing your wishes, I tried to capture the most beautiful of women for you, by the name of Gina Pickbridge, but her charms were stronger, and she remained in Fishville, from where she sends not particularly flattering regards."

"I had absolutely nothing to do with this," the director said. "Let her send her greetings to Lamondois."

"Yes, let her!" the black man exclaimed.

"Gaba," the director said, "do you know about the Wave?"

"Is this a Wave?" he demanded disdainfully. "Now when I get into the start chamber and Lamondois pushes the button, then you'll have a real Wave! But this—this is nothing, a ripple, just piffle! But I attend and am eager to obey."

"Is the brigade with you?" the director asked patiently. Gaba silently motioned out the window. "Go with them to the spaceport; you'll be at Kaneko's disposal."

"My head and my eyes are his," said Gaba. Just then the powerful voices outside the window struck up a song to an old spiritual played on a banjo:

> On merry Rainbow
> Rainbow, Rainbow . . .

Gaba reached the window in one giant stride and hollered, "Quiet!"

The song died down. A clear, pure voice woefully sang:

> Dig my grave both long and narrow,
> Make my coffin neat and stro-o-ong . . .

"I'm off," Gaba said with some embarrassment and hopped over the window ledge. There was howling below.

"Bums," grumbled the director, grinning. He closed the

window. "They're bored, the poor infants. I don't know what I'd do without them."

He stood at the window, and Gorbovsky, squinting, stared at his back. His back was very broad, but somehow so hunched and pathetic-looking that Gorbovsky started worrying. Matvei, a starflyer and landing pilot, simply couldn't have a back like that.

"Matvei," Gorbovsky said. "You really need me?"

"Yes," the director said. "Very much." He kept looking out the window.

"Ennui, foreboding, cares," Matvei declaimed.

Gorbovsky squirmed to get more comfortable, turned on his player softly and said in a low voice, "All right, friend. I'll sit here with you just like this."

"Uh-huh. You just sit awhile, please."

A guitar sang sadly and languidly, the sky blazed outside, and it was cool and dark in the office.

"Wait. We'll wait," the director said loudly and then returned to his chair. They both were silent.

"Oh!" Gorbovsky said suddenly. "I'm so impolite! I forgot completely! How's Jenny?"

"Fine, thanks."

"She hasn't returned?"

"No. She hasn't. I think she doesn't even want to think about it now."

"Still Alex?"

"Of course. It's amazing how important that turned out to be for her."

"Remember how she promised and swore: as soon as he's born—"

"I remember. I remember more than you can imagine. She suffered terribly with him at first. Complained. 'No,' she said, 'I don't have any maternal feeling. I'm a monster. Wood.' And then something happened. I didn't even notice it. Of course, he's a marvelous little piglet. Very friendly and sweet. I was walking in the park with him one evening. Suddenly he says: 'Papa, what's that sitting down there?' I didn't understand at first. Then . . . you see, there was a breeze, the street lamp was swaying, and its shadow on the wall. . . . 'Sitting down.' A very precise image, no?"

"Yes," Gorbovsky said. "He'll be a writer. But it would be a good idea to send him to boarding school."

Matvei just waved the idea away.

"Can't even talk about it," he said. "She wouldn't give him up. And you know, at first I argued, but then I thought: why? Why take away a person's reason for living? He's her reason for living. I don't understand that, but I believe it, because I see it. Maybe it's because I'm so much older. And Alex came too late into my life. I sometimes think how lonely I would be if I didn't know that I could see him every day. Jenny says that I love him not as a father, but as a grandfather. It's possible. You understand what I'm talking about?"

"I do. But it's not anything I know. I've never been lonely, Matvei."

"Yes," Matvei said. "As long as I've known you, there have always been people hovering around you, people who need you desperately. You have a wonderful personality, and everyone loves you."

"That's not true," Gorbovsky said. "It's me who loves everybody. I've lived almost a hundred years and imagine this, Matvei, I haven't met a single unpleasant person."

"You're a rich man," Matvei pronounced.

"By the way," Gorbovsky remembered. "A new book was published in Moscow. *Nothing's More Bitter Than Your Joy.* By Sergei Volkovsky. A new bombshell by the emotionalists. Genkin reacted with a vitriolic article, which was quite witty, but not convincing. He maintained that literature has to be pleasant to dissect. The emotionalists laughed sarcastically. Probably the fight is still going on. I'll never understand it. Why can't they tolerate one another?"

"That's easy," Matvei said. "Everyone feels that he's making history."

"But he is!" Gorbovsky countered. "Everyone really does

make history. After all, those of us in science and industry are always under their influence in one way or another."

"I don't care to argue about it," Matvei said. "I don't have time to think about this. I'm not under their influence."

"Well, let's not argue," Gorbovsky said. "Let's drink some juice. If you like, I'll even have some local wine. If it really will help you."

"Only one thing will help me now. That's Lamondois coming in here crestfallen and telling me that the Wave has dissipated."

They drank juice for a time, looking at each other over the rims of their glasses.

"Nobody's called you in a while," Gorbovsky said. "It's kind of strange."

"The Wave," Matvei said. "They're all busy. Differences are forgotten. They're all running away."

The door at the back of the office opened, and Etienne Lamondois appeared. His face was thoughtful and he moved with an extraordinarily slow and measured tread. The director and Gorbovsky watched him walk in silence, and Gorbovsky felt an unpleasant, nauseous sensation. He had no idea what had happened or was happening, but he already knew that he wouldn't be lying around comfortably anymore. He turned off his player.

Lamondois stopped at the desk.

"I think this will make you unhappy," he said slowly and evenly. "The charybdises didn't withstand the Wave." Matvei's head sank into his shoulders. "The front was broken in both the north and the south. The Wave is spreading with an acceleration of ten meters per second per second. Communications with the control stations are broken. I just had time to order the evacuation of valuable equipment and archives." He turned to Gorbovsky. "Captain, we're counting on you. Be so kind as to tell me what your freight capacity is?"

Gorbovsky, without replying, looked at Matvei. The director's eyes were shut. He aimlessly stroked the desk's surface with his huge hands.

"Freight capacity?" Gorbovsky repeated and stood up. He went over to the director's control board, bent over toward the microphone and said: "Attention, Rainbow! First Officer Falkenstein and Engineer Dixon immediately report to the starship."

Then he came back to Matvei and put his hand on his shoulder. "It's nothing terrible, friend," he said. "We'll fit. Give the order to evacuate Children's Colony. I'll take care of the nursery." He looked over at Lamondois. "My freight capacity is small, Etienne," he added.

Etienne Lamondois' eyes were black and calm—the eyes of a man who knows he's always right.

Chapter 6

ROBERT saw it all happen.

He was crouching on the flat roof of a remote control tower carefully disconnecting the receiving antennas. There were forty-eight of them—thin, heavy aerial rods mounted on a gliding parabolic frame, and each one had to be twisted out carefully and packed with all caution and care in a special casing. He was in a great hurry and kept looking over his shoulder to the north.

A tall blank wall stood over the northern horizon. Along its crest, where it pressed up against the tropopause, was a border of blinding light, and higher up, pale violet explosions faded in the empty sky. The Wave was moving toward them, inexorably, but very slowly. He couldn't believe that it was being held back by a chain of clumsy machines that looked tiny from the roof of the tower. It was strangely still and hot, and the sun seemed strangely bright, the way it is on Earth just before a storm, when a hush descends and the sun still shines but half the sky is covered with heavy blue-black clouds. There was something particularly vicious, un-usual, almost otherworldly in that silence, because usually the Wave's advance was preceded by high-intensity hurricanes and countless lightning bolts.

And now it was completely still. Robert could hear hurried voices from the square below, where they were loading the expensive equipment, the observers' journals, and the data from the automatic machines. It was all heaped up in a heavy helicopter. He could hear Pagava heatedly berating someone for taking down the analyzers too soon, and Malyaev slowly discussing a profoundly theoretical question with Patrick about the probable distribution of explosions in the energy barrier over the Wave. Greenfield's entire population was gathered in the tower under Robert's feet and in the square. The rebellious biologists and two groups of tourists who had spent the night in the settlement had been sent beyond the crop fields. The biologists had been packed off in a pterocar with the lab assistants, who had been ordered by Pagava to set up a new observation point beyond the fields, and a special airbus from the Capital had come for the tourists. Both the biologists and the tourists had been very unhappy, and now that they had left, only the happy remained in Greenfield.

Robert was working almost mechanically and, as usual when working with his hands, thought about a variety of things. His shoulder hurt a lot. Strange—he hadn't hit his shoulder. His stomach ached, but that was from stumbling over the ulmotron. He'd like to see what that ulmotron looked like now. And the pterocar. And . . . what will this place be like in three hours? Too bad about the flowers. . . . The children had worked all summer, coming up with the most fantastic combinations of flowers. That's when he met Tanya. "Tan-ya." He called out softly. How are you doing over there? He estimated the distance between the Wave and Children's Colony. No danger, he thought with satisfaction. They probably don't even know about the Wave, or the biologists' revolt, or that I was almost killed, that Camill. . . .

He stood, wiped his face with the back of his hand, and

looked south at the green fields of grain. He tried to picture the huge herds of cattle being driven into the interior of the continent; thought about how much work it would take to reestablish Greenfield after the Wave passed, how unpleasant it would be to go back to synthetic food after two years of abundance, back to artificial steaks, pears that taste of toothpaste, "city soups" made with chlorella, quasibiotic lamb chops and other miracles of synthesis, damn them all. . . . He thought about anything he could, but it didn't help.

He couldn't forget Pagava's amazed eyes, Malyaev's icy voice, or Patrick's exaggerated friendliness. The horrible part was that there was nothing he could do. To put it kindly, it all must seem very strange to others. But why be kind? It simply seemed quite obvious. A terrified observer looking disheveled comes in someone else's flyer and announces the death of his comrade. And the comrade, it turns out, was alive. The comrade, it turns out, died later, while the terrified observer was escaping in his flyer. But he had been squashed to death, Robert repeated for the umpteenth time. Maybe he had hallucinated the whole thing? Maybe he had been terrified into seeing things? No one had ever heard of such a thing. But neither had he heard of what had happened—if it *had* happened. Well, let them, he thought desperately. Let them not believe me. Tanya will believe me. Oh, let her believe me! The rest don't care, they forgot about Camill right away. They'll only think of him when they see me. They'll look at me with their theoretical eyes, analyzing, and juxtaposing, and weighing. And constructing the least contradictory hypotheses, but they'll never learn the truth. . . . And neither will I.

He unscrewed the last antenna, put it in the case, and put all the cases in a flat cardboard box; then a resounding boom came from the north, like a balloon bursting in a huge empty auditorium. Robert turned to see a long white torch rise against the asp-black background of the Wave. A charybdis was burning. The voices below shut up, and the helicopter motor whined and stopped. They were all probably listening and looking north. Robert was still figuring out what had happened when there was a rumble and a tremor and a reserve charybdis came rolling out from below the tower, mowing down the few remaining palm trees, opening the jaws of its gulper as it headed north. Its roar was deafening, and it rolled on to plug the gap, enveloped in a cloud of red dust.

It was a common sight: one of the charybdises hadn't released its excess energy into the basalt in time, and Robert bent over his cardboard box again, but something exploded at the foot of the black wall, and a fan of multicolored flames shot up, and then there was another column of white smoke, billowing and thickening before his eyes and stretching up to the sky. Another boom reached him. People below were shouting, and Robert saw several other torches to the east. The charybdises were exploding one after the other, and a minute later the thousand-mile-wide wall of the Wave, looking like a blackboard covered with chalk scrawls, rocked and crept forward, throwing out black blobs into the plains before its path. Robert swallowed with difficulty, grabbed the box, and ran down the stairs.

People were scurrying about in the corridors. Zina, frightened, ran past, clutching a bunch of tape boxes to her chest. Beak-nosed Hassan Ali-zadeh and Carl Hoffman were carrying a bulky sarcophagus containing the lab chemostaser with supernatural speed—they seemed windborne. Someone was calling: "Come here! I can't do this alone! Hassan! . . ." The sound of broken glass rang out in the vestibule. Pagava, trampling lamps and papers, was hopping up and down in the dispatcher's room and shouting into the screen: "Why can't you hear me? The charybdises are burning! I say, the charybdises are burning! The Wave is coming! I can't hear anything, understand? Etienne, if you understood, nod!"

Robert, grimacing with pain, hoisted the box on his shoulder and headed down to the vestibule. Someone behind him, breathing hard, was lumbering down the stairs. The vestibule was littered with pieces of wrapping paper and the parts of some apparatus. The door, made of shatterproof glass, was broken in half. Robert squeezed out sideways onto the porch and stopped. He watched the crammed, jammed pterocars rising up into the sky one after another. He saw Malyaev, silent, his face made of stone, shoving the young female lab assistants into the last pterocar. He saw Hassan and Carl, mouths open with exertion, trying to push their sarcophagus into the hatch of a helicopter and a man inside trying to help, and he saw the sarcophagus hit the man on his fingers time and time again. He saw Patrick, completely calm, sleepy Patrick, leaning against the rear light of the helicopter, looking intent and meditative. And turning his head, he saw the coal-black wall of the Wave, hiding the sky with a velvet curtain, almost over his head.

"Stop loading!" Pagava shouted by his ear. "Come to your senses! Immediately drop that coffin!"

The chemostaser fell on the concrete with a thud.

"Throw everything out!" Pagava shouted, running down from the porch. "Everyone into the helicopter, immediately! Can't you see? Who am I talking to? Sklyarov! Patrick, are you asleep?"

Robert didn't move. Neither did Patrick. Just then Malyaev, pushing hard, slammed the door to the pterocar and waved his arms. The pterocar's wings spread out, it hopped clumsily and, listing heavily, disappeared beyond the rooftops. Crates were flying out of the helicopter. Someone howled: "I won't give it up, Shota; not that!" "Yes, you will," Pagava roared. "And how!" Malyaev ran up to him, shouting and pointing at the sky. Robert looked up. A small guide helicopter, bristling with antennas like a hedgehog, dashed over the square with a screeching, overheated engine and, rapidly growing smaller, raced off to the south. Pagava raised his fists over his head:

"Where are you going?" he yelled. "Back! Back, you son of a dog! Stop panicking! Stop him!"

All this time Robert stood on the porch, balancing the cardboard box on his aching shoulder. He had the feeling that he was watching a movie. Here was a helicopter-unloading scene. Actually they were just dumping everything out of it. The helicopter was overloaded—you could see that from the way the chassis sagged. People were pushing and shoving around the helicopter. At first they shoved and screamed, but now they did it in silence. Hassan was sucking his knuckles; he must have skinned them. Patrick seemed to be asleep. A good time for it, and a terrific place. . . . Carl Hoffman, a pedantic man (what they call "a thoughtful and cautious scientist") was catching the crates as they tumbled out of the helicopter and stacking them neatly, probably as a form of self-expression. Pagava was jumping impatiently alongside the helicopter, constantly looking back at the Wave or at the control tower. He obviously didn't want to leave, and he was sorry that he was in charge. Malyaev stood to one side and also looked at the Wave—fixedly and with cold hostility. . . . And in the shade of the cottage where Patrick lived was his flyer. He wondered who had brought it over there and why? No one was paying any attention to the flyer and no one needed it; there were about ten people left, maybe more. The helicopter was a good one, a Griffin, powerful—but with a load like that it would only go at half normal speed. . . . Robert set the box down on the steps.

"We won't make it," Malyaev said. There was such sadness and bitterness in his voice that it surprised Robert. But he knew that they would all make it. He went up to Malyaev.

"There's another reserve charybdis," Robert said. "Would fifteen minutes be enough for you?"

Malyaev looked at him uncomprehendingly.

"There are two reserve charybdises," he replied and suddenly understood.

"All right," Robert said. "Don't forget Patrick. He's on the other side of the helicopter."

He turned and ran. They called after him, but he didn't look back. He ran as fast as he could, leaping over abandoned equipment, over flower beds with ornamental plants, over neatly trimmed hedges with aromatic white flowers. He was running to the western edge, and on his right a huge black velvet wall towered over the rooftops, pressing up against the zenith, and on his left the blinding white sun blazed. He rounded the last house and came up against the boundless charybdis stern. He saw the clumps of vegetation stuck in its caterpillar tracks, the petals of a torn flower, a broken palm tree trunk stuck between the idlers, and without looking up he climbed up the narrow ramp, burning his hands on the sun-baked rungs. Still without looking up, he slid down on his back into the manual-control cab, got in the seat, and pushed back the steel shield in front of his face, and his hands took over automatically and mechanically. His right hand reached out and turned on the ignition, the left one simultaneously turned on the coupling, switched the pilot to manual, and the right hand was already moving back, looking for the starter; and when the world around him began roaring, tumbling, and shaking, the left hand, quite unnecessarily, turned on the air conditioning. Then— consciously—he found the lever that controlled the gulper, pulled it toward himself as far as it would go, and then, and only then, he had the nerve to look out the windshield and see what was going on.

The Wave was directly in front of him. Probably no man since Lu had ever been that close to the Wave. It was solid black, without the slightest break or chink, and the plain, drenched in sunlight, showed clear against it. You could see every blade of grass, every bush. Robert could even see prairie dogs, frozen in little yellow columns at the entrances to their tunnels. . . .

A dry, ringing howl grew over his head—the gulper

started up. The charybdis swayed smoothly as it traveled. The buildings of the settlement jumped in the dust in his rearview mirror. He couldn't see the helicopter. Another hundred yards, no, fifty, and that would be enough. He glanced over to the left, and he thought that the Wave was bending a little. But it was very hard to judge. "Maybe I won't make it," he suddenly thought. He couldn't take his eyes off the white columns of smoke rising from beyond the horizon. The smoke dissipated quickly and was barely visible now. He wondered what there was that could burn in a charybdis. . . .

Enough, he thought, and put on the brakes. Or he wouldn't be able to escape either. He looked in the rearview mirror again. They were taking such a long time, he thought. The plain was darkening slowly in a large triangle in front of the charybdis, the gulper at the apex. The prairie dogs began jumping about nervously, and one, about twenty feet away, keeled over, its legs twitching.

"Run away, you little jerks," Robert said. "You can, you know. . . ."

And then he saw the other charybdis. It was a quarter mile to the east, greedily thrusting out the gulper, and the grass was darkening in front of it, too, squirming in the unbearable cold.

Robert was overjoyed. Good for him, he thought. Hero! That's brave! Could it really be Malyaev? And why not? He was a human being after all, and human feelings were not alien to him. . . . Maybe it was Pagava himself? No! they would never permit that. They would tie him up and stick him under the seat, and then stand on him to make sure he didn't kick. . . . No, terrific! Good for you! He pushed out the starboard hatch, leaned out and shouted:

"Hey! Hold on, pally! You and I will hold out here together for a year!"

He glanced at the meters and forgot everything else. The condensers were dying out: the glowing needle under the dusty glass was pushed right up to the limit. He took a quick look at the rearview mirror and felt a little better. He could see a quickly diminishing dot in the white sky over the settlement's rooftops. Another ten minutes, he thought. Now it was clearly visible that the Wave's front had bent in front of the settlement. The Wave was going around the area in which the charybdises were functioning.

Robert sat for a while with clenched teeth. He was expending all his energy to chase away the image of a burnt corpse in the driver's seat. It would be nice to be able to turn off the imagination at will. . . . He jumped and began opening all the hatches he could think of. The heavy one over his head. The one on the left—open it wide! The one on the right was already open—open it wider! The door behind his back, leading to the machinery compartment . . . no, better leave that shut—the explosion must go off in there, in the condensers. . . . Seal it up, seal it—Just then the other charybdis exploded.

Robert heard a short, deafening roar, he was stunned by a blast of hot air, and looking out of the hatch, he saw that there was a huge yellow cloud of dust where his neighbor had been, covering the plain, and the sky, and the Wave, and that in the depths of that cloud something was glowing with a bright, shuddering light. . . . Something rustled in the air and struck the charybdis's shields. Robert looked at the instrument panel and threw himself out the left hatch in one swift motion.

He fell face first in the dry grass and immediately jumped up, and, crouching, ran toward the settlement. He had never run like that in his life. His charybdis blew up after he reached the first house. He didn't even look back, he pulled in his neck, bent even lower, and ran even faster. Eternal glory to Thee, he repeated, glory to Thee. . . . Later he realized that he had been saying those words from the moment that he'd seen the terrible column of dust instead of the charybdis.

The square was empty, the lawns trampled; invaluable, unique instruments and boxes with unique, irreplaceable journals were scattered every which-way, and a light breeze lazily ruffled the unique diaries of unique observations. Panting, Robert crossed the square and ran up to the flyer. The engine was running, and Patrick was in the driver's seat with his usual sleepy air.

"There you are," Patrick said gently. Robert stared at him in disbelief. "I thought you had stayed back there. Get in quick, we have to get a move on. The Wave is coming at an unbelievable velocity!"

Robert fell into the seat next to him.

"Wait," he said, catching his breath. "Maybe the second driver is safe, too. Who was it? Malyaev, Hoffman?"

Patrick clumsily moved the shift, bringing the flyer into gear.

"The other driver was me," he said shyly.

"You?"

"Me," Patrick repeated and laughed nervously. He drove the flyer out on the road and finally raised it. "I felt that I was about to explode, so I got out and ran. That was some blast, huh? It pushed me all the way to the settlement."

The settlement turned slowly below them and slipped back. That Patrick, thought Robert in shock.

"Mine made a louder boom," Patrick said. "Didn't you think so, Robert, huh?"

"Where are you flying to?" Robert said.

"To Cold Springs," Patrick said. "That's where the new base will be."

Chapter 7

R OBERT looked over his shoulder. There was nothing to see now but the white sky and the green fields. I got away from it twice today, he thought. And there'll be a third time, too.

"What happens now?" he asked.

Patrick's fat lips formed a pout. "Nothing good. It has an enormous reserve of energy."

"Did you try to calculate it?"

"Yes."

"Well?"

Patrick just sighed.

Robert, knitting his brow, looked straight ahead. Then he turned on the radio and tuned in Children's Colony. He pressed the call button several times, but there was no response. I shouldn't worry, he thought. It's the summer holiday and all that. How strange that they don't know anything about it. It's better that they don't. Only I'll know.

He asked, "Where are we going?"

"You asked that already."

"Oh yeah . . . Patrick, my friend, do you really need to go to those springs so much?"

"Of course. Where else?"

Robert leaned back in his seat.

"Well," he said. "Too bad you stayed."

"What do you mean, too bad?"

"Can you go any faster?"

"I can. . . ."

"And even faster?"

Patrick said nothing. The engine throbbed, gasping air.

"We're always in a hurry," Patrick muttered. "Someone's always rushing us. Hurry, faster, faster . . . and a little faster, please? Yes, all right, we say. . . . There's no time to get our bearings. No time to think. No time to find out why and whether it's worth it. And then the Wave comes and we hurry some more."

"Give it some fuel," Robert said. He was thinking about something else entirely. "And bear right."

Patrick stopped complaining. Below them were green fields of ripening grain and a few scattered white buildings of the synoptic stations. They could see how the cattle had been driven south right through the fields. The cyber-shepherds looked like tiny, shiny stars from that height. None of this was of any use now.

"Have you heard anything about the Arrow?" Robert asked.

"No. The Arrow is far away. It won't get here in time. Drop that line of thought, Rob."

"Then what should I think about?"

"Nothing. Get comfortable and look around. I don't know about you, but I never noticed any of this before. I don't think I've ever seen that green wave in the grain made by the wind. . . . The Wave! Phooey! Do you know the first time I saw all of this? Know when? When I looked at the plains through the metal shields on the charybdis. I was looking at the blackness and suddenly I saw the plain and realized that it was doomed. And I felt so terribly sorry. And the prairie dogs looked at the Wave and didn't understand. . . . And do you know what else I discovered, Rob? We miscalculated somewhere."

Robert said nothing. Kind of late now, he thought. He should have at least looked out a window before.

They floated over white square buildings, cement walks and squares, striped energy antenna towers—it was one of the many energy stations in the northern belt.

"Land," Robert said.

"Where?"

"See that field? Where the pterocar is?"

Patrick looked overboard.

"You're right," he said. "But what for?"

"You'll take the pterocar, and give me the flyer."

"What have you got in mind?"

"You'll go on alone. I don't need to go to the springs. Land."

Patrick obediently landed. He was a terrible driver. Robert was looking at the field.

"Marvelous organization," he muttered. "We're knocking ourselves out, throwing everything out and abandoning things, and they have three pterocars for two guards."

The flyer landed clumsily between the pterocars. Robert bit his tongue.

"Ow," he said. "Well, come on, get out."

Patrick slowly and reluctantly got out.

"Rob," he said uncertainly, "maybe this is none of my business, but what do you have in mind?"

Robert slid over to his seat.

"Don't worry, nothing terrible. Can you manage the pterocar?"

Patrick stood with downcast eyes and a hangdog look.

"Rob," he said. "Be serious. There's a one-hundred-kilometer plasma barrier over the Wave. You won't be able to jump over that."

Robert looked at him in amazement.

"He died a long time ago," Patrick said. "You might have been mistaken the first time, but the Wave passed over there this time."

"What are you talking about? I have no intention of jumping over the Wave, damn it. I have something more important to do. Goodbye. Tell Malyaev I won't be back. Goodbye, Patrick."

"Goodbye," Patrick said.

"You still haven't told me if you can manage with the pterocar?"

"I can," Patrick said sadly. "I know the pterocar well. Ah, Rob. . . ."

Robert jerked the lever toward him, and when he looked back five minutes later, the energy station was hidden behind the horizon. It was a two-hour flight to the Colony. Robert checked the fuel gauge, listened to the motor, switched to the most economical ratio, and turned on the autopilot. Then he tried reaching Children's Colony again. The Colony was silent. Robert was going to turn the radio off, but decided to put it on autotune.

". . . ninth-grader Asmodey Barraux found a petrified organism that resembles a sea urchin on a field trip. The spot is rather far from the shore. . . ."

". . . director's meeting. There are strange rumors around here. They say the Wave has reached Greenfield. Should I return to base? I don't think this is the time to worry about ulmotrons." "No, be a friend, stick it out to the end. The day is wasted anyway."

". . . our people won't be enough. We don't have an Othello. To tell the truth, I think it's absurd to try to put on Shakespeare anyway. I don't think we're capable of a new interpretation, and to wait for. . . ."

"Vitya, do you read me? Vitya the most amazing news! Bullit has decoded the gene. Write this down. Six . . . eleven . . . I said eleven. . . ."

"Attention, Rainbow! Leaders of all search parties. Begin evacuating. Pay particular attention to getting all air transport of Medusa class and larger to the Capital."

". . . a small blue cottage right on the water. The air is so fresh, and the sun marvelous. I never did like the Capital and I never understood why they put it right on the equator. What? Of course, it's terribly muggy. . . ."

". . . Sawyer, Sawyer, this is Kaneko. Change direction immediately. The artists have been found. Go south. Find the third helicopter. The third helicopter has not returned."

"Attention, testers! Today at fourteen hundred hours there will be an unscheduled zero-transport of a human being to Earth. Please be at the Institute no later than thirteen hundred. . . ."

". . . I don't understand. I can't reach the director. All channels are in use. Do you know what's going on?"

"Adolf! Adolf! I beg you, respond! I beg you, return immediately! There's still a chance to get on the starship! . . ." The voice began fading out, but Robert held the tuner. "A horrible catastrophe! No one's announcing it for some reason, but I hear that Rainbow is doomed! Hurry back. I want to be with you now. . . ."

Robert released the dial.

". . . as usual. At Veselovsky's house. No, Sinitsa will be reading his new poetry. I find them interesting. I think you'll like them. No, it's no masterpiece, but. . . ."

". . . Why not, I understand completely. But judge for yourself. Tariel Two is a landing starship. . . . Have you estimated how many people it can carry? No, I'm staying here. So is Vera. It doesn't matter where it happens. . . ."

"Guides, guides! The rallying point is the Capital. Everyone to the Capital. Bring your Moles, we'll be digging shelters. Maybe we'll have time. . . ."

"You say the Tariel? I know it, of course. The pilot's Gorbovsky. Unfortunately, the freight capacity is small. Oh well . . . here's the list I recommend: from the discretists, Pagava;

the Wave specialists, Aristotle and maybe Malyaev; the barrierists, I would suggest Forster . . . what do you mean he's old? He's a great man! You're only forty, my friend, and you, I see, don't know the psychology of old men. . . . I've only got five or ten years to go and they won't let me live. . . ."

"Gaba! Gaba! Did you hear about the zero-transport? What? Busy? You're crazy . . . I'm flying over to the Institute. Why am I crazy? I know all that, yes . . . right now! What if it works? Well, goodbye . . . Look for my remains somewhere near Prozion. . . ."

"The physicists blew something up near the North Pole. We should go over and take a look, but there's a helicopter here and we're all invited to the Capital. . . . You too? Strange . . . well, see you there."

Robert turned off the radio. Tariel Two, a landing ship. . . . He took over the controls from autopilot and pushed the engine to its limit. The grain fields below had ended; he was in a zone of tropical rain forests. There was nothing visible in the tangle of bright green foliage, but Robert knew that below the ancient trees there were highways and that cars filled with refugees were racing west along them. Several bulky freight copters headed southwest low on the horizon. They disappeared from view and Robert was left alone. He took out the radiophone and dialed Patrick. Patrick didn't reply for a long time. Finally he heard his voice:

"Hello?"

"Patrick, it's me, Sklyarov. Patrick, what's new on the Wave?"

"Nothing, Rob. Pushkin Bay is flooded. Aozora burned down. Fishville is burning now. A few charybdises survived, they're being towed to the Capital. . . . Where are you?"

"That's not important," Robert replied. "How far from the Wave to Children's Colony?"

"Children's Colony? What do you care about the Colony? It's far from the Colony. Listen, Rob, if you survive, hurry to the Capital. We'll all be there in a half hour." He suddenly giggled. "They tried to get Malyaev into the starship. Too bad you weren't there. He broke Hassan's nose. And Pagava hid somewhere."

"They didn't try to put you on it?"

"Why are you being like that, Rob. . . ."

"All right, I'm sorry. So, the Wave is still far from the Colony?"

"I wouldn't say very far. An hour or an hour and a half. . . ."

"Thanks, Patrick. So long."

Robert tried to reach Tanya again, this time by radio-phone. He waited five minutes. Tanya didn't answer.

Children's Colony was empty. Silence hung over the glass dormitories, the gardens, the cheery cottages. There was none of the disordered panic that the zeroists had left behind at Greenfield. The sand paths were neatly swept, the school desks were in aligned rows in the garden, the beds were perfectly made. But a forgotten doll lay in the sand in front of Tanya's cottage. A big-eyed, fuzzy tame kalyam sat near the doll. It was sniffing it and looking up at Robert with friendly curiosity.

Robert went into Tanya's room. It was, as usual, clean, airy, and pleasant smelling. An open notebook lay on the desk, and a big fluffy towel was draped over the back of the chair. Robert touched it—it was still damp.

Robert stood in the doorway and then glanced casually at the notebook. He read his name twice before he realized it was for him. His name was printed in large block letters.

"ROBBIE! We're being evacuated hurriedly to the Capital. Look for me in the Capital. Find me. They haven't told us anything, but I think something terrible is coming. I need you, Robbie. Find me. Your T."

Robert tore the page out of the notebook, folded it into fourths, and put it in his pocket. He looked around Tanya's room one last time, opened the closet, touched her dresses, looked around again and left.

There was a good view of the sea from Tanya's cottage—calm, looking like solidified green oil. Dozens of paths led through the grass to the yellow beach, which was dotted with lounge chairs and blankets. Several boats lay keel up on the shore. And the horizon to the north blazed with bright sun reflections. Robert hurried to his flyer. He boarded and took another look at the sea. And he understood. That wasn't the sun, it was the crest of the Wave.

He sank tiredly into the seat. "It's the same thing in the south," he thought. "It's crowding us from the north and from the south. A mouse trap. A corridor between two deaths." The flyer was skimming the rain forests. "How much time is left?" he thought. "Two hours, maybe three? Two seats in the starship, ten?"

The forest under the flyer ended abruptly, and Robert saw a large passenger airbus, surrounded by a crowd of people, down in a large meadow. He braked and descended. Apparently the bus had had trouble, and all those people—strange how tiny they looked—were waiting for the pilot to fix it. He saw the pilot—a huge black man, burrowing in the engine. Then he realized that they were children, and then he saw Tanya. She was standing next to the pilot and holding parts for him.

The flyer was ten feet from the airbus, and they all turned to him. But Robert only saw Tanya, her marvelous exhausted face, her thin hands clutching the dirty metal to her chest, and her surprised, wide eyes.

"It's me," Robert said. "What happened, Tanya?"

Tanya stared at him in silence, and then he looked over at the black pilot and saw Gaba. Gaba smiled broadly and called out:

"Hey, Robert! Come here, help me! Tanya is a wonderful girl, but she's never worked on an airbus! Neither have I! And the engine keeps conking out!"

The children—seven-year-old boys and girls—looked at Robert with great interest. Robert went over to the airbus, and brushing his cheek gently against Tanya's hair in passing, looked into the engine. Gaba slapped his back. They were good friends. They found each other easily—Robert and the ten desperately bored zero-testers who had been sitting around without any work for two years, since the failed attempt with Fimka the dog.

When Robert saw the dismantled engine, it took his breath away. Gaba really didn't know anything about airbuses, that was obvious. There was nothing he could do—they were simply out of fuel, and Gaba had taken apart the engine for nothing. It happens, it happens even to the most experienced drivers: airbuses rarely run out of fuel. Robert stole a glance at Tanya. She was still clutching the dirty, oily pistons and waiting.

"Well?" Gaba asked heartily. "Were we on the right track with this thingamabob, whatever it's called?"

"Well," Robert said, "it's possible." He took the lever and tugged at it. "Does anyone know you're downed here?"

"I let them know," Gaba replied. "But they don't have enough cars. You know the story with embryos?"

"Well, well," Robert said meaninglessly, cleaning the lever and dropping it. He bent over so that they couldn't see his face.

"They needed more transportation. Kaneko began growing Medusas, but they turned out to be cyberkitchens. A slight mistake in equipment, no?" Gaba laughed. "How do you like that?"

"A laugh riot," Robert muttered through his teeth. He looked up and scanned the sky. He saw an empty, whitish sky and on the north, above the distant trees, the blinding bright crest of the Wave. He softly lowered the hood, muttering "So, we'll see!" and went around the airbus, where there was no one. He crouched down there, leaning his forehead against the shiny, polished chrome. On the other side of the bus Gaba started a children's counting song in his gentle, throbbing voice.

Opening his eyes, Robert saw his dancing shadow on the hot grass—the shadow of his raised hands and outspread fingers. Gaba was amusing the children. Robert got up and climbed into the bus. There was a boy in the driver's seat fiercely holding onto the steering wheel. He was making fantastic figures with the handles and levers, whistling and roaring as he played.

"Watch you don't tear it out," Robert said. The boy didn't pay any attention to him. Robert wanted to turn on the SOS light, but he saw that it was on. Then he looked at the sky again. The sky seemed a delicate blue seen through the spectrolite of the lantern, and it was completely empty. I have to decide, he thought. He looked at the boy. The boy was imitating the rushing wind.

"Come out, Rob," Gaba said. He was by the door. Robert went out.

"Shut the door," Gaba said. He could hear Tanya telling the kids something on the other side of the bus, and he could hear the boy beeping and whistling in the driver's seat.

"When will it be here?" Gaba asked.

"In a half hour."

"What happened to the engine?"

"No fuel."

Gaba's face turned ashen.

"Why?" he asked meaninglessly. Robert said nothing. "How about your flyer?"

"There wouldn't be enough for more than five minutes for a crate like this."

Gaba struck himself in the head with his fist and sat down in the grass.

"You're a mechanic," he said hoarsely. "Think of something."

Robert leaned against the bus.

"Remember the story of the wolf, the goat and the head of cabbage? . . . Here we have a dozen kids, a woman and the two of us. A woman whom I love more than anyone in the world. A woman whom I will save no matter what. So there. The flyer has two seats. . . ."

Gaba nodded.

"I understand. There's nothing to discuss. Let Tanya take the flyer and as many kids as will fit. . . ."

"No," Robert said.

"Why not? They'll be in the Capital in two hours."

"No," Robert repeated. "That won't save her. The Wave will be in the Capital in three hours. There's a starship there. Tanya must be on it. Don't argue with me!" he whispered fiercely. "There are only two possible variations here—either I go with Tanya, or you go with Tanya, but then you must swear by all that is holy that Tanya will be on that starship. Choose."

"You're mad," Gaba said. He got up slowly from the grass. "They're children. Come to your senses!"

"And the ones who stay behind, aren't they children too? Who's going to pick the three that go in the flyer to the Capital and then to Earth? You? Go choose them!"

Gaba's mouth opened and shut soundlessly. Robert looked north. He could see the Wave clearly. The glowing strip was rising higher and higher, dragging the black curtain after it.

"Well," Robert said. "Do you swear?"

Gaba shook his head slowly.

"Then goodbye," Robert said.

He took a step forward, but Gaba blocked his path.

"Children!" he said almost soundlessly.

Robert grabbed him by the lapels of his jacket and brought his face right up to his.

"Tanya!" he said.

They stared into each other's eyes silently for a few seconds.

"She'll hate you," Gaba said softly.

Robert let go and laughed.

"I'll be dead in three hours, too," he said. "I won't care then. Goodbye, Gaba."

They parted.

"She won't go with you," Gaba called.

Robert didn't answer. I know that, he thought. He came

around the airbus and ran to the flyer. He saw Tanya's face turned to him and laughing faces of the children surrounding Tanya, and he waved merrily to them, feeling pain in the muscles of his face, convulsively forming a casual smile. He ran up to the flyer, looked in, and then called out:

"Tanya, come help me!"

And Gaba appeared from behind the bus just then. He was on all fours.

"Who's just hanging around?" he yelled. "Who can catch Sher-Khan—the greatest tiger in the jungle?"

He roared and, kicking his legs, raced into the forest. For a few seconds, the children, mouths open, stared at him, then one whooped delightedly, another howled aggressively, and they all raced off after Gaba, who was peering out and roaring at them from the trees.

Tanya, looking around and smiling perplexedly, went over to Robert.

"Strange," she said. "You'd think there was no catastrophe coming."

Robert kept looking at Gaba. They were out of sight, but he could hear laughter and screams, crackling branches and Sher-Khan's terrible roars.

"What a strange smile you have, Robbie."

"Gaba is crazy," Robert said and was immediately sorry. He should have kept quiet. His voice wasn't obeying him.

"What's wrong, Rob?" Tanya asked.

He involuntarily looked up over her head. She also turned and looked up and pressed closer to him in fright.

"What's that?" she asked.

The Wave was nearing the sun.

"We have to hurry," Robert said. "Get in the flyer and lift up the seat."

She hopped into the cab easily, and he jumped in after her, wrapping his right arm around her shoulders so that she couldn't move, and took off without warning.

"Robbie!" Tanya whispered. "What are you doing?"

He didn't look at her. He was squeezing everything he could get out of the flyer. And with the corner of his eye he saw the field below, the solitary bus, and the tiny face looking up curiously from the driver's window.

Chapter 8

THE daytime heat had started abating when the last pterocars, overloaded and stuffed, landed, breaking their chassis, on the streets leading to the square in front of the Council Building. Now almost the entire population of Rainbow was in that spacious square.

From the north and south, rumbling columns of monstrous-looking earthboring Moles with the Scout insignia or the yellow lightning bolts of the Power and Energy crews slowly dragged into town. They camped in the middle of the square, and after intense consultation, during which only two men spoke—each for three minutes in a low voice—they began digging a deep shelter tunnel. The Moles clattered away, breaking up the asphalt, and then, one after the other, bending clumsily, burrowed underground. A large ring of excavated dirt formed around the hole, and the fetid sour smell of denaturized basalt hung in the air.

The zero-physicists filled the empty stories of the theater opposite the Council Building. They retreated all day, clinging with damaged charybdises to every observation point, to every remote control station, saving everything they had time to save, from equipment to scientific documentation, risking their lives every second, until Lamondois and the director forced them to come to the Capital. They were recognizable by their agitated, guilty and challenging looks, their unnaturally animated voices, their unfunny jokes with references to special circumstances, and their loud nervous laughter. Now, under the leadership of Pagava and Aristotle, they were sorting and microfilming the most valuable data for evacuation from the planet.

A large group of mechanics and meteorologists went out to the outskirts of town to set up conveyor shops to produce small rockets. They planned to load the most important documents on these rockets and launch them out of the planet's atmosphere into satellite orbit to be picked up later and brought back to Earth. Some of the outsiders joined the rocket makers—those who couldn't sit around with hands folded, and those who could be of actual help, and those who believed in the necessity of saving the important documents.

But on the square, jammed with Leopards, Medusas, trucks, Diligences, Moles, Griffons, there were still a lot of people. Biologists and planetologists who had lost their life's meaning in their last remaining hours, outsiders—artists and actors—stunned by the unexpected calamity, angry, lost, not knowing what to do, or where to go, or whom to complain to. Some very calm and self-possessed people chatted on various topics, gathering in clusters among the vehicles. And some other quiet people, silent and glum, sat in their cars or leaned against the walls of the building.

The planet was deserted. The entire population—every person had been called, moved, or hunted down from its most distant and remote corners and brought to the Capital. The Capital was on the Equator, and now the northern and southern expanses of the planet were empty. There were just a few people left, who announced that they didn't care, and somewhere over the rainforests they had lost an airbus with

children and their teacher and the heavy Griffon that had
been sent out to find them. For the last few hours, under the
building's silvery spire, the Council of Rainbow had been
meeting. From time to time the voice of the director or Kaneko over the loudspeaker called in the most unexpected
people, who ran to the building and disappeared behind the
door, and then ran out again, rushed into pterocars or flyers,
and left the city. Many of those who had nothing to do
watched with envious eyes. No one knew what they were
discussing at the Council meeting, but the loudspeakers had
already announced the most important things: the threat of
catastrophe was absolutely real; the Council had only one
landing starship with a small capacity at its disposal; Children's Colony was evacuated and the children were in the
city park in the care of their teachers and doctors; the starship liner Arrow was in constant communication with Rainbow and was on its way, but would not arrive for at least ten
hours. Three times an hour the square was given information
about the Wave's fronts. The loudspeaker thundered: "Attention, Rainbow! We are giving information on. . . ." And
then the square would fall silent, and everyone waited ea-
gerly, looking sadly at the tunnels from which came the
distant rumble of the Moles. The Wave was moving
strangely. Its acceleration increased sometimes—and then
the people looked glummer and lowered their eyes—and
decreased sometimes—and then the people brightened, and
uncertain smiles appeared on their faces. But the Wave was
moving on them, the crops were burning, the forests exploding, abandoned settlements blazing.

There were very little official news, perhaps no one had
the time to handle it, and as usual in such situations, the
main source of news became rumor.

The scouts and the builders were digging deeper into the
ground and the tired, grimy men who came up out of the
hole shouted, grinning merrily, that all they needed was two
or three hours, and they'd have a comfortable and deep shel-

ter for everyone. People looked upon them with some hope, and the hope was bolstered by the stubborn rumor that supposedly Etienne Lamondois, Pagava, and someone named Patrick had made calculations. According to their calculations, the northern and southern Waves meeting at the equator would "mutually energetically turn and deritrinitirate," absorbing vast amounts of energy. They said that after that there would be a snowfall six feet deep on Rainbow.

They also said that a half hour ago at the Institute of Discrete Space, whose sheer white walls could be seen by anyone standing on the square, they had finally succeeded in transporting a human being by zero-T to the solar system, and they even knew the man's name, the first zero-pilot in history, who was now supposedly safe on Pluto.

They also talked about the signals received from beyond the southern Wave. The signals were very strongly deformed by interference, but they decoded them, and apparently found out that several people who had voluntarily stayed on at an energy station in the Wave's path had survived and felt fine, which was proof that the P-Wave, as distinguished from the earlier known types, did not pose any threat to life. They even knew the names of the lucky ones, and there were even people who knew them personally. And for support they told the account of an eyewitness of how the famous Camill had jumped out of the Wave in a burning pterocar and flew past like a monstrous comet, shouting something and waving his hand.

A widespread rumor dealt with the supposed fact that an old starpilot, now working in the tunnel, had said something allegedly like this: "I've known the commander of the Arrow for a hundred years. And if he says that he won't be here in less than ten hours, it means that it won't take him more than three. And you don't have to believe the Council. They're a bunch of amateurs who have no idea what a modern starship is like and what it can do in experienced hands."

The world suddenly lost its simplicity and clarity. It was hard to separate truth from fiction. The most honest man, someone you'd known since childhood, could easily be lying to you just to keep up your spirits and comfort you and twenty minutes later you might see him despondent over the latest rumor, that is, that the Wave was not dangerous to your bodily health, but damages the mind, reducing you to a caveman mentality.

The people in the square saw a tall, large woman with a tearstained face lead a five-year-old boy in red shorts into the Council Building. Many recognized her—it was Jenny Vyazanitsyn, the wife of Rainbow's director. She left very quickly, accompanied by Kaneko, who led her politely but firmly by the elbow. She wasn't crying anymore, but her face was viciously determined and people moved to let her pass. The boy calmly chewed on a pretzel.

The ones who were busy had an easier time of it. Therefore a large group of painters, writers, and actors, having argued until they were hoarse, finally took a vote and moved to the outskirts to help the rocketters. They probably couldn't be of great help, but they were sure that there would be something they could do. Several went down into the tunnel, where they were now digging horizontally. And several experienced pilots got in pterocars and flew north and south, to join the Council's observers, who had been playing hide and seek with death for several hours.

The remaining ones saw a charred, dented and battered flyer land at the Council doorstep. Two people got out with difficulty, stood on shaky legs for a minute, and then went to the door, helping each other. Their faces were yellow and swollen, and it was with difficulty that they were recognized as young Carl Hoffman and zero-tester Timothy Sawyer, banjo player par excellence. Sawyer just shook his head and moaned, and Hoffman, after clearing his throat, mumbled their tale—they had tried to jump over the Wave, had got within twenty kilometers of it, but Tim's eyesight had gone and they'd had to return. It turned out that the Council had proposed transporting the populace to the other side of the Wave. Sawyer and Hoffman were scouts. And someone immediately said that two scouts had tried to dive under the Wave on the open sea on a research bathyscaphe, but hadn't returned yet, and no one knew what had happened to them.

By then there were about two hundred people on the square—less than half the adult population of Rainbow. The people tried to stay in groups. They talked quietly without taking their eyes from the Council windows. It grew quiet on the square: the Moles were deep down and you could barely hear their roar. The conversations were not jolly:

"My vacation is ruined again. For good, this time, I think."

"Shelter, underground. . . . The black wall is coming, and people are going underground. . . ."

"Too bad I don't feel like painting. Just look how beautiful the Council Building is. What depth of color. I'd love to paint it and give it a mood of tension and anticipation, but . . . I can't. It nauseates me."

"It's so strange. I don't believe we elected a secret council. All this hush-hush nonsense. Locked themselves up and decided the fate of the planet. . . . I don't really care what it is they're saying, but this simply is impolite, you know. . . ."

"I'm really worried about Ananyev. Look at him, he's been sitting that way for two hours, not talking to anyone, sharpening his knife . . . I'm going to go talk to him. Come along with me, all right?"

"Aozora burned down. My Aozora. I built it. Now it has to be built again. . . . And then they'll burn it again."

"I'm sorry for them. Here we are together, and honest, I'm not afraid of anything! But Matvei Sergeyevich can't even spend his last hours with his wife. It's so crazy. Why?"

"I'm sitting here and gabbing and that's because I feel that our only hope is the starship. And everything else is just a flash in the pan, nonsense, homespun theories. . . ."

"Why did I fly here? What was so bad about Earth? Rainbow, Rainbow, you've treated us badly. . . ."

And that moment the loudspeaker roared out:

"Attention, Rainbow! This is the Council. We are calling a general meeting of the populace! The meeting will begin in twenty minutes on the Council Square. I repeat. . . ."

Making his way through the crowd to the Council, Gorbovsky discovered that he was suddenly very popular. People let him pass, nodded at him and even pointed, said hello, asked, "Well, how are things, Leonid Andreyevich?" and whispered his name behind his back, naming the stars and planets he had dealt with, and the ships he had commanded.

Gorbovsky, long unaccustomed to such celebrity, bowed, saluted, smiled, and replied, "So far so good," and thought, "Just let someone try to tell me that the general masses aren't interested in starflying." At the same time he could almost physically sense the nervous tension that reigned on the square. It was something like those last moments before a final exam. He felt the tension himself. Smiling and smoking, he tried to assess the mood and collective thoughts of the crowd and tried to guess what they would say when he made his announcement. I believe in you, he thought stubbornly. I believe in you no matter what. I believe in you, you frightened, wary, disillusioned fanatics. People.

At the door he was overtaken and stopped by a man in a miner's outfit.

"Leonid Andreyevich," he said, smiling with concern. "Just a minute. Literally one minute."

"Of course," Gorbovsky said.

The man was rummaging through his pockets.

"When you get to Earth," he was saying, "please be so kind . . . Where could it have gone? . . . I don't think it would be too much trouble. . . . Aha, here it is. . . ." He pulled out an envelope folded over. "The address is printed on it. . . . Please don't refuse to mail it."

Gorbovsky nodded.

"I can write it out in script," he said gently and took the envelope.

"My handwriting is terrible. I can't read it myself, and I was in such a hurry now . . ." He stopped and then extended his hand. "Bon voyage. Thank you."

"How's your tunnel?" Gorbovsky asked.

"Fine," the man replied. "Don't worry about us."

Gorbovsky went into the Council Building and started up the stairs, trying to think of an opening remark to the Council. He couldn't come up with one. He got only as far as the second floor when he saw the Council members coming down toward him. Leading them, running his fingers along the bannister, came Lamondois with springy step, totally calm and even slightly distracted. He gave Gorbovsky a strange, unfocused smile and immediately looked away. Gorbovsky made way for him. The director was behind Lamondois, purple and fierce-looking. He muttered, "Are you ready?" and without waiting for a reply, walked on. The other members followed, men Gorbovsky did not know. They were discussing the question of an entrance to the tunnel loudly and animatedly, and the volume and the animation made it clear that their thoughts were elsewhere. And after the rest, slightly behind, came Stanislav Pishta, just as broad, darkly tanned, and bushy-haired as he had been twenty-five years before when he had commanded the Sunflower and he and Gorbovsky had stormed Blind Spot.

"Bah!" said Gorbovsky.

"Oh!" said Stanislav Pishta.

"What are you doing here?"

"Arguing with the physicists."

"Good for you," Gorbovsky said. "I will too. Meanwhile, tell me, who's in charge of Children's Colony?"

"I am," Pishta said.

Gorbovsky looked at him suspiciously.

"I am, really!" Pishta laughed. "Unlikely? But you'll see. On the square. When the battle begins. I assure you, it will be a completely unpedagogic sight."

They went down to the entrance slowly.

"Let them argue, that doesn't concern you," Gorbovsky said. "Where are the children?"

"In the park."

"Very good. Get over there and immediately—do you hear?—immediately start loading the children on the Tariel. Mark and Percy are waiting for you there. We've loaded the nursery already. Hurry up."

"You're great," Pishta said.

"What else?" Gorbovsky replied. "Now hurry."

Pishta slapped him on the back and ran down the stairs. Gorbovsky came outside after him. He saw hundreds of faces, all of them turned toward himself, and heard Matvei's voice thundering through the megaphone:

". . . and in fact we are now deciding the question of what is most valuable to humanity and to us, as part of humanity. The first speaker will be the head of the Children's Colony, Comrade Stanislav Pishta."

"He's gone," Gorbovsky said.

The director looked around.

"What do you mean, gone?" he whispered. "Where to?"

It was very quiet on the platform.

"Then let me," Lamondois said.

He took the megaphone. Gorbovsky saw his thin white fingers firmly cover Matvei's fat clenched fingers. The director turned over the megaphone only after a struggle.

"We all know what Rainbow is," Lamondois began. "Rainbow is a planet colonized by science and set up for physics experiments. All of humanity awaits the results of these tests. Everyone who comes to Rainbow and lives here knows where he's come to and where he's living." Lamondois spoke harshly and confidently; he looked handsome now—pale, erect, tense. "We are soldiers of science. We have given our lives to science. We gave it our love and the best of what we had. And what we've created no longer belongs just to us. It belongs to science and the twenty billion earthlings scattered across the Universe. Conversations on moral issues are always very difficult and unpleasant. And too often reason and logic cannot prevail over the purely emotional 'want' and 'don't want,' 'like' and 'don't like.' But there is an objective law that is the motive force of human society. It does not depend on our emotions. And it says: humanity must know. That is the most important thing for us: the battle between ignorance and knowledge. And if we want our actions to seem consistent with this law we must follow it, even if we must retreat from several ideas that are innate or inculcated in childhood." Lamondois stopped and unbuttoned his collar.

"The most valuable thing on Rainbow is our labor. We have studied discrete space for thirty years. We have gathered the best zero-physicists on Earth here. The ideas that sprang from our work are still in a stage of being mastered, for they are profound, full of potential, and as a rule, paradoxical. I would not be mistaken if I were to say that only here on Rainbow is there the experimental new material that will serve in the theoretical development of that concept. But even we specialists are incapable of saying now what gigantic, unlimited power over the world our new theory will give to man. Science will lose not thirty years, but a hundred, two hundred . . . three hundred years . . . that's the loss we face. . . ."

Lamondois stopped and red splotches appeared on his face. His shoulders drooped. A deathly silence hung over the city.

"I want to live very much," he suddenly said. "And the children . . . I have two, a boy and a girl, they're over there, in the park. . . . I don't know. You decide."

He lowered the megaphone and stood before the crowd, perspiring and looking older, pathetic even.

The crowd was silent. The zero-physicists standing in the front rows were silent, the miserable bearers of the new concept of space, the only ones in the whole Universe. The painters, writers, and actors were silent, knowing full well what thirty years of labor meant and knowing full well that no masterpiece was repeatable. On the mounds of upturned soil, the builders, who had worked for thirty years with the zeroists, were silent. The members of the Council were silent —men who were considered the wisest, most knowledgeable, and kindest, and who were to determine what was about to happen.

Gorbovsky saw hundreds of faces, young and old, men and women, and they all seemed the same to him, remarkably like Lamondois. He could picture clearly what they were thinking. They wanted to live so very much; the young because they had lived so little, the old because there was so little left. That was a thought that could be handled: apply some will power and the thought could be pushed back into the recesses of your mind. The ones who couldn't do it thought about nothing else, and all their energy was directed at hiding their mortal terror. And the rest . . . they were sorry about their work. They were sorry, so unbearably sorry for the children. Not even sorry—there were many people here who were indifferent to children, but it seemed somehow callous to think about anything else. And they had to decide. Oh, how hard that was—deciding! You had to decide and say out loud what you'd decided. And thereby take on the responsibility, extraordinary in its seriousness and weightiness, so that in the remaining three hours you could feel like a human being and not shrivel up from unbearable shame and not waste your last breath on berating yourself: "Fool! Bastard!" Mercy, thought Gorbovsky.

He went up to Lamondois and took the megaphone from him. Lamondois didn't even seem to notice.

"You see," Gorbovsky said in an inspired tone, "I'm afraid that there's been a misunderstanding. Comrade Lamondois is asking you to decide. But you see, there really isn't anything to decide. It's all been decided. The nursery babies and mothers with newborns are already on the ship." The crowd sighed audibly. "The rest of the children are being loaded now. I think they'll all fit. I don't think—I know. You must forgive me, but I decided on my own. I have the right to do that. I even have the right to decisively end any attempts to keep me from exercising that right. But I don't think it'll come to that. In general, Comrade Lamondois expressed some interesting ideas. I would enjoy debating with him, but I must go. Comrade parents, you have free access to the spaceport. But forgive me, you may not board the ship."

"That's it," someone in the crowd said. "And you're right. Miners, follow me!"

The crowd began moving and talking. Several pterocars took off.

"What are we basing things on?" Gorbovsky asked. "Our most valuable asset is our future. . . ."

"We don't have one," a bitter voice in the crowd said.

"On the contrary, we do! Our future is the children. What a new and fresh idea, no? And we must be fair. Life is a wonderful thing, and we know that already. But the children don't. Just think how much love awaits them! Not to mention zero-problems." There was applause in the crowd. "And now I'm off."

Gorbovsky shoved the megaphone into the hands of one of the Council members and walked over to Matvei. Matvei clapped him firmly on the back a few times. They looked at the thinning crowd, the animated faces, which suddenly became quite varied, and Gorbovsky muttered with a sigh:

"It's rather interesting. We keep perfecting ourselves, getting better, smarter, kinder and so on, and yet it's so nice when someone makes a decision for you. . . ."

Chapter 9

THE Tariel Two, a landing sigma-D-starship, was built to transport small groups of researchers with a minimal lab across vast distances. It was very good for unloading on planets with unpredictable atmospheres, had great speed reserves, was sturdy and dependable, and was made up of ninety-five percent energy capacitors. Naturally, the ship had living quarters—five tiny cabins, a tiny living area, a miniature galley, and a roomy bridge stuffed with control panels for all the equipment. There was a cargo compartment as well—a rather large space with bare walls and low ceilings, lacking air conditioning, and good (in an emergency situation) for setting up a traveling lab. Normally the Tariel Two took on ten people and their luggage.

They were loading the children through both hatches: the smaller ones through the freight one. People were crowded around the hatches, and there were many more than Gorbovsky had expected. It was immediately apparent that they weren't all parents and teachers. In the distance there were crates with undistributed ulmotrons and the apparatus for the Scouts on Lalanda. The adults were quiet, but it was very noisy near the ship—squeals, laughter, tiny voices raised in silly song—the noise that is so common in dormitories, playgrounds, and schoolyards. Gorbovsky didn't see any familiar faces, except Alexandra Postysheva off to one side. And she looked completely different—sad and depressed, dressed neatly and delicately. She was sitting on an empty crate, her hands on her knees, looking at the ship. She was waiting.

Gorbovsky got out of the pterocar and headed for the starship. When he passed Alexandra she smiled pathetically and said, "I'm waiting for Mark." "He'll be out shortly," Gorbovsky said gently and went on. But he was stopped, and realized that it wouldn't be so easy getting to the door.

A large bearded man in a panama hat barred his path.

"Comrade Gorbovsky," he said. "I beg of you, please take this."

He handed Gorbovsky a long, heavy tube.

"What's this?" Gorbovsky said.

"My last work. I'm Johann Sourd."

"Johann Sourd," Gorbovsky repeated. "I didn't know you were here."

"Take it. It weighs very little. It's the best thing I've ever done. I brought it here for an exhibition. It's *Wind*."

Gorbovsky's insides churned.

"Let's have it," he said and carefully put the rolled canvas away.

Sourd bowed.

"Thank you, Gorbovsky," he said, then disappeared into the crowd.

Someone grabbed Gorbovsky hard by the arm. He turned and saw a young woman. Her lips were trembling and her face was wet with tears.

"Are you the captain?" she wailed.

"Yes, yes, I'm the captain."

She grasped his hand and squeezed hard.

"My son is there . . . on the ship. . . ." Her lips trembled. "I'm afraid. . . ."

Gorbovsky made a surprised face.

"But why? He's perfectly safe."

"Do you promise?"

"He's perfectly safe there," Gorbovsky repeated. "This is a very fine ship."

"So many children," she sobbed. "So many children."

She let go of his hand and turned away. Gorbovsky stood around for a while indecisively and then went on, protecting Sourd's masterpiece with his arms and sides. But he was grabbed by the elbows from both sides.

"This weighs only six pounds," said a pale, angular man. "I've never, ever asked anyone for anything. . . ."

"I can see that," Gorbovsky agreed. It really was obvious.

"This is a summary of ten years of observations of the Wave. Six million photocopies."

"This is very important!" a second man stressed, holding Gorbovsky by the left elbow. He had thick lips, unshaven cheeks, and small, imploring eyes. "You understand, that's Malyaev. . . ." He pointed at the first man. "You must take this folder . . ."

"Be quiet, Patrick," Malyaev said. "Leonid Andreyevich, listen. . . . So that this never happens again . . . never . . ." He caught his breath. "So that no one ever gives us that shameful choice to make."

"Bring it along," Gorbovsky said. "My hands are full."

They let go of him and he took a step forward but struck his knee on a large, canvas-wrapped object that was being held with great difficulty by two young men wearing identical blue berets.

"Could you take it?" one panted.

"If you could . . ." the other said.

"We worked on it for two years. . . ."

"Please."

Gorbovsky shook his head and started walking around them carefully.

"Leonid Andreyevich," the first one said pathetically. "We beg you."

Gorbovsky shook his head again.

"Don't demean yourself," the second one said angrily. He let go of his end, and the wrapped object struck the ground with a resounding crack. "Well, what are you holding it for?"

He kicked the apparatus with unwonted ferocity, and limping badly, stalked off.

"Volodya!" the first one shouted anxiously. "Don't go crazy!"

Gorbovsky turned away.

"Sculptors naturally have no hope at all," a stealthy voice said near his ear. Gorbovsky merely shook his head. He couldn't talk. Behind his back, stepping on his heels, Malyaev breathed hoarsely.

Another group of people with rolls of canvas, packages and bags started off in unison and walked alongside.

"Perhaps it would be worthwhile to do it this way," one of them said nervously and hurriedly. "Perhaps everyone can bring his things over to the cargo hatch. . . . We know there isn't much chance . . . but what if there is room. After all, these are things, not people. . . . They can be shoved anywhere . . . somehow. . . ."

"Yes . . . all right," Gorbovsky said. "Please take care of it." He stopped and transferred the masterpiece to his other shoulder. "Tell everyone about it. Let them pile everything up by the cargo hatch. Ten feet from it and to the side . . . all right?"

There was movement in the crowd, and there were fewer people now. People with packages and bags started moving away, and Gorbovsky finally got out to the free space near the passenger hatch, where the children, lined up in pairs, were waiting their turn to get into the hands of Percy Dixon.

The younger children, in colored jackets, pants, and caps, were in a state of joyous excitement brought on by the prospect of a real starship flight. They were very busy with one another and the blue hugeness of the ship, and gave their parents, who were nearby, no more than an occasional look.

They didn't have time for parents. In the round opening of the hatch stood Percy Dixon, who had donned an ancient, long-forgotten parade dress uniform, heavy and tight, with hurriedly polished buttons, insignias and brightly colored braid and trim. The sweat was pouring down his hairy face, and from time to time he exhorted in a salty, marine voice: "Avast, me hearties! Take your places, raise anchor!" It was very jolly, and the overjoyed kids never took their wide eyes off him. There were also two teachers: the man held the lists in his hand and the woman merrily sang a song about a brave rhinoceros. The children, keeping their eyes on Dixon, sang along, each in his own manner.

Gorbovsky thought that if you were to stand with your back to the crowd, you might really think that dear old Uncle Percy had organized a jolly spin around Rainbow for the preschoolers. But just then Dixon picked up the next child and turned to pass him to someone inside, and a woman behind Gorbovsky cried hysterically, "It's my Tolik! Tolik!" and Gorbovsky turned and saw Malyaev's pale face and the strained faces of the mothers, smiling pathetically crooked smiles, and the tears in their eyes and the bitten lips, and the despair, and the hysterical woman who was led away struggling by a man in soil-smeared overalls. And someone turned away, and someone bent over and made his way from the spaceport, bumping into people, and someone else simply lay down on the concrete and held his head in his arms.

Gorbovsky saw Jenny Vyazanitsyn, plumper and prettier now, with huge dry eyes and a determined mouth. She was holding a calm fat boy in red pants by the hand. The boy was munching an apple and stared as hard as he could at the shining Percy Dixon.

"Hello, Leonid," she said.

"Hello, Jenny," Gorbovsky said.

Malyaev and Patrick walked away a bit.

"How thin you are," she said. "Still so thin. Even thinner and drier than before."

"And you've grown prettier."

"I'm not keeping you too much?"

"No, everything is going as it should. I only have to check the ship. I'm really afraid that we won't have room after all."

"It's very hard alone. Matvei is always busy, busy, busy. . . . Sometimes I think that he absolutely doesn't care."

"He does care very much," Gorbovsky said. "I talked to him. I know that he cares. But he can't do anything about it. All the children on Rainbow are his children. It can't be any other way for him."

She waved her free hand weakly.

"I don't know what to do with Alex," she said. "He's such a homebody. He's never even been to kindergarten."

"He'll get used to it. Children get used to things very quickly, Jenny. And don't you worry, He'll be fine."

"I don't even know who to talk to."

"All the teachers are good. You know that. They're all the same. Alex will be fine."

"You don't understand. He's not even on any lists."

"What's so terrible about that? Whether he's on a list or not, not a single child will remain on Rainbow. The lists are only to make sure we don't lose any here. Do you want me to go and tell them to put him on a list?"

"Yes," she said. "No . . . wait. May I go up aboard with him?"

Gorbovsky sadly shook his head.

"Jenny," he said gently. "Don't upset the children."

"I won't upset anyone. I only want to see what's it's like. . . . Who'll be with him. . . ."

"Children like him. Merry and kind."

"May I go up with him?"

"Don't, Jenny."

"I must. I must. He can't do it alone. How will he live without me? You don't understand anything. None of you does. I'll do whatever's necessary. Any kind of work. I can do anything. Don't be so heartless."

"Jenny, look around. Those are mothers."

"He's not like the rest. He's weak. Spoiled. He's used to constant attention. He won't be able to be without me. He won't! I know that better than anyone else! Are you going to take advantage of the fact that there's no one to complain to about you?"

"Would you really take away the place of a child who will have to remain here?"

"No one will remain," she said passionately. "I'm sure of it! They'll all fit! And I don't need any space! There must be machine rooms, some space. . . . I must be with him!"

"I can't do anything for you, Jenny. Forgive me."

"You can! You're the captain. You can do anything. You were always a kind man, Leonid."

"I'm kind now. You can't imagine how kind I am."

"I won't leave you," she said and stopped talking.

"Fine," Gorbovsky said. "But let's do this. I'll take Alex on board now, look the place over, and come back to you. All right?"

She looked intently into his eyes.

"You won't trick me. I know. I believe. You've never tricked anyone."

"I won't trick you. When the ship starts up you'll be next to me. Give me the boy."

Without taking her eyes from his face, she pushed Alex toward him as if in a dream.

"Go, go, Alex," she said. "Go with Uncle Leonid."

"Where?" he asked.

"To the ship," Gorbovsky said, taking his hand. "Where else. Right to this ship. To that man over there. Do you want to?"

"I want to go to that man," the boy announced. He didn't look back at his mother. They went up to the ramp, which the last children were ascending.

Gorbovsky said to the teacher, "Enter him on the list. Alexey Matveyevich Vyazanitsyn."

The teacher looked at the boy, then at Gorbovsky, and

nodded, writing down the name. Gorbovsky slowly went up the ramp, pulled Alexey Matveyevich by the hand over a tall coaming.

"That's called a tambur," he said.

The boy pulled on his hand, freed it, and walking right up to Percy Dixon, began examining him. Gorbovsky removed Sourd's painting from his shoulder and put it in the corner. What else? he thought. Oh yes! He went back to the hatch and, leaning out, took Malyaev's folder.

"Thank you," Malyaev said, smiling. "You didn't forget. Calm plasma. . . ."

Patrick was smiling too. Nodding, he backed toward the crowd. Jenny was standing right under the hatchway, and Gorbovsky waved to her. Then he turned to Dixon.

"Hot?" he asked.

"Terribly. I'd love a shower. But there are children in the shower room."

"Take them out."

"That's easy to say," Dixon sighed and grimaced as he tugged at his collar. "My beard gets stuck under the collar," he muttered. "It prickles. My whole body aches."

"Mister," said Alex. "Is your beard real?"

"You can try it," Percy said with a sigh and bent over.

The boy tugged at it.

"It's still not real," he announced.

Gorbovsky took him by the shoulder, but the boy pulled away.

"I don't want to go with you," he said. "I want to go with the captain."

"That's fine," Gorbovsky said. "Percy, take him to a teacher."

He went over to the door to the corridor.

"Just don't faint," Dixon said.

Gorbovsky rolled back the door. The ship had never seen such a sight. Squeals, laughter, whistling, whispers, shouts, banging, ringing, tiny footsteps, metal clanging on metal, infants mewling.... The incomparable smell of milk, honey, medicine, hot children's bodies, and soap, despite the air conditioning and the emergency fans. . . . Gorbovsky went down the corridor, carefully choosing places for his feet, gasping as he looked into open doors where children were jumping, dancing, singing lullabies to dolls, aiming rifles, tossing lassos, jammed in, sitting and crawling on pushed-back berths, tables, under tables, under berths—there were four dozen boys and girls from two to six. Harried teachers struggled to get from room to room. In the living area, from which most of the furniture had been thrown out, young mothers were feeding and diapering infants; the nursery was here too—five toddlers babbling in baby talk, crawling around on all fours in a fenced-off corner. Gorbovsky pictured all of that in a state of weightlessness, shut his eyes and went up to the bridge.

Gorbovsky didn't recognize it. It was empty. The control combine, which had taken up a third of the room, was gone. The control panel was gone, and the copilot's seat was gone. The console for the scanner screen was gone. The chair in front of the computer was gone. And the computer, half taken apart, gleamed with naked circuitry. The ship was no longer a starship. It had become a self-propelled interplanetary barge, with good speed, but good only for flights on inertial trajectories.

Gorbovsky shoved his hands into his pockets. Dixon was panting behind him.

"So," Gorbovsky said. "And where's Falkenstein?"

"Here." Falkenstein stuck his head out of the computer's bowels. He looked grim and determined.

"Good, Mark," Gorbovsky said. "And you're great too, Percy. Thanks."

"Pishta asked for you three times already," Mark said and disappeared once more inside the computer. "He's by the cargo hatch."

Gorbovsky crossed the bridge and went to the cargo hold.

He was horrified by what he saw. There, in a long and narrow room, dimly lit by two gas lights, stood schoolchildren closely jammed together. They stood silently, almost without moving, just shifting from leg to leg, and staring out the open hatch, where they could see the blue sky and the white roof of the faraway packing house. For a few seconds Gorbovsky stared at the children and bit his lip.

"Move the first graders into the corridor," he said. "Second and third grade, into the bridge . . . immediately."

"That's not all," Dixon said softly. "Ten people got lost somewhere on the way from the Colony . . . but it seems that they perished. A group of older kids refuses to board. And there's another group of children of outsiders, who just got here. . . . But you'll see for yourself."

"You do what I said," Gorbovsky suggested. "The first three grades into the corridor and bridge. And put a screen in here and show movies. Historical films. Let them see how things used to be. Act, Percy. And one more thing—make a human chain of the kids to Falkenstein. They can pass parts down the line; that'll keep them occupied a bit."

He squeezed his way to the hatch and ran down: At the foot of the ramp, surrounded by teachers, stood a large group of children of varying ages. To the left was a disorderly pile of Rainbow's most valuable cultural objects: bundles of documents, folders, machines, and mock-ups, burlap-covered sculptures, rolled-up canvases. To the right, some twenty feet away, stood a group of grim teenage boys and girls, and in front of them, Stanislav Pishta walked back and forth, looking very serious, his hands behind his back. Quietly, but distinctly, he was saying:

"Think of this as a test. Think less of yourselves and more about others. Aren't you ashamed of yourselves? Get a grip on yourselves, overcome this feeling!"

The teenagers said nothing. And the adults who crowded around the cargo hatch were silent too, oppressively so. Some of the kids looked around furtively, and it was obvious that they would have run away if they hadn't been surrounded by their mothers and fathers. Gorbovsky looked at the hatch. Even from there it was clear that the ship was stuffed to the gills. In the gatelike hatch the children stood in tight formation. They did not have the faces of children —they were too serious and too sad.

A huge, very handsome young man with longing, entreating eyes that clashed rudely with his physical appearance sidled up to Gorbovsky.

"A word with you, Captain," he said in a trembling voice. "Just a word. . . ."

"One minute," Gorbovsky said.

He went over to Pishta and embraced him.

"There will be room for everyone," Pishta was saying. "Don't let that worry you. . . ."

"Stanislav," Gorbovsky said, "have the rest loaded."

"There's no room," Pishta countered, not very logically. "We were waiting for you. It would be good if you could clear out the reserve D-chamber."

"The Tariel has no reserve D-chambers. But there will be space in a minute. Do it."

Gorbovsky was face to face with the teenagers.

"We don't want to go," one of them announced, a tall blond fellow with bright green eyes. "The teachers should go."

"Right!" said a small girl in jeans.

Behind them Percy Dixon shouted: "Throw them on the ground!"

Circuits fell to the ground from the hatch. The conveyor line had started up.

"Here's the thing, boys and girls," Gorbovsky said. "First of all, you can't vote yet, because you haven't finished school. Second, you have to have a conscience about this. Sure, you're young and want to perform heroic acts, but the point is, you're not needed here and you are needed on board ship. I'm afraid to think what will happen during an inertial flight. We have two seniors in every room with pre-schoolers, at least three agile girls in the nursery and to help the women with the newborns. In short, that's where your heroism is needed."

"Forgive me, Captain," the green-eyed youth said sarcastically, "but all these duties can be performed by the teachers."

"Forgive me, young man," Gorbovsky said, "but I assume you know the rights of a captain. As captain, I promise you that only two teachers will be on board. The important thing for you is to make an effort and picture how your teachers will go on living if they take your places on board. The games are over, boys and girls, you are now facing life the way it can be sometimes—luckily, rarely. And now you must excuse me, I'm busy. I can give you one last comforting thought. You will be the last to board. All of you."

He turned his back on them and bumped right into the young man with longing eyes.

"Oh, forgive me," he said. "I forgot all about you."

"You said that two teachers will be going," the young man said hoarsely. "Who?"

"Who are you?" Gorbovsky asked.

"I'm Robert Sklyarov. I'm a zero-physicist. But that's not the issue. I'll tell you everything in a minute. But first tell me, who's going?"

"Sklyarov . . . Sklyarov . . . I know the name. Where have I heard it?"

"Camill," said Sklyarov, forcing a smile.

"Ah," Gorbovsky said. "So you want to know who's coming with us?" He looked Sklyarov over. "All right, I'll tell you. Only you. The principal and the senior physician. They don't know it yet."

"No," said Sklyarov, grabbing Gorbovsky's hands. "One more . . . Turchina. Tatyana. She's a teacher. They adore her. She's a very experienced teacher. . . ."

Gorbovsky freed his hands.

"No," he said. "No, my dear Robert! Only children and mothers with their infants, understand? Only children and mothers with nursing infants!"

"She's one!" Sklyarov said. "She's a mother, too! She's going to have a baby...my baby! Ask her....She's a mother, too!"

Gorbovsky was shoved hard in the shoulder. He reeled and saw Sklyarov backing off in fright from a small thin woman, extraordinarily graceful and lovely, who was advancing on him with her beautiful face frozen like stone. Gorbovsky wiped his face with his hand and returned to the ramp.

Now only the senior kids and the teachers remained. The other adults—the parents and the ones who had brought their creations and those who apparently had been drawn to the ship by some vague hope, were slowly backing away and forming small groups. In the hatch, arms spread, Stanislav Pishta was shouting:

"Squeeze together children! Michael, call down to the bridge for them to squeeze together! A little more!"

Serious children's voices responded:

"They can't! We're all crowded now as it is!"

And Percy Dixon bellowed:

"What do you mean, you can't? And what about over here, behind the console? Don't be afraid, dearie, there's no electricity, go on, go on. ... And you ... and you, snubnose ... step lively! And you ... there ... there. ..."

And then Falkenstein's cold voice, like steel:

"Move over, kids. ... Let me through. ... Excuse me, little girl. ... Hey fellow, shove over. ..."

Pishta moved over, and Falkenstein appeared next to him, his jacket over his shoulder.

"I'm staying on Rainbow," he said. "You go without me, Leonid Andreyevich." His eyes searched the crowd, looking for someone.

Gorbovsky nodded.

"Is the doctor on board?" he asked.

"Yes," Mark replied. "The only adults are the doctor and Dixon."

Laughter cascaded from the hatch.

"Hey you," Dixon's strained voice called. "Come on, like this . . . hup, two . . . hup, two. . . ."

Dixon appeared in the hatch. He appeared over Pishta's head, and his upside-down face was sweaty and bright red.

"Hold me, Leonid," he whispered. "I'm falling."

The children were laughing. It really was very funny, a fat engineer, hanging like a fly on the ceiling, holding on to the pipes. He was heavy and hot, and when Pishta and Gorbovsky pulled him out and set him on his feet, he said, panting: "Old. I'm too old."

Blinking guiltily, he looked at Gorbovsky.

"I can't take it in there, Leonid. It's crowded, stuffy and hot. . . . This damn costume. . . . I'm staying here, and you and Mark go on. And to tell the truth, I'm tired of you two by now."

"Farewell, Percy," Gorbovsky said.

"Farewell, my friend," Dixon said, touched.

Gorbovsky laughed and patted his galloons.

"Well, Stanislav," he said, "You'll just have to manage without an engineer. I think you'll manage. Your tasks: enter an equatorial satellite orbit and wait for the Arrow. The rest will be done by the Arrow's commander."

Pishta was stunned into several seconds of silence.

"What's the matter with you, hah?" he said very softly, his eyes running over Gorbovsky's face. "What's the matter with you? You're a landing pilot! What's with these empty gestures?"

"Gestures?" Gorbovsky said. "I don't know how to make them. But you go on. You're responsible for everyone to the end." He turned to the teenagers. "March on board!" he shouted. "You go ahead, or you'll never get on," he said to Pishta.

Pishta looked at the depressed teenagers, slowly wending their way to the ramp, looked at the hatch with children's faces hanging out, clumsily pecked Gorbovsky on the cheek, nodded to Mark and Dixon, and getting on tiptoe, grabbed the pipes. Gorbovsky gave him a shove. The teenagers slowly filed in, pushing in one at a time, bravely yelling: "Well, move it! Who's crying back there? Heads up!" The last one in was the girl in jeans. She stopped for a second and looked hopefully at Gorbovsky, but he made a stone face.

"There's nowhere to go," she said quietly. "See? There's no room for me."

"You'll lose weight," Gorbovsky promised and, taking her by the shoulders, carefully pushed her inside. Then he asked Dixon, "Where are the movies?"

"It's taken care of. The movies will start at take-off. Children like surprises."

"Pishta!" Gorbovsky yelled. "Ready?"

"Ready!" Pishta replied.

"Start her up, Pishta! Calm plasma! Close the hatches! Boys and girls, I wish you calm plasma!"

The heavy hatch door silently began to glide shut. Gorbovsky, waving goodbye, stepped back from the coaming. Then he remembered.

"Ah! The letter," he shouted.

It wasn't in his front pocket or in the side one. The hatch was closing. The letter was in his inside breast pocket for some reason. Gorbovsky handed it to the girl in jeans and pulled back his hand. The hatch closed. Gorbovsky ran his hand over the light blue metal, without looking at anyone, then got down to the ground, and Dixon and Mark pulled away the ramp. There were just a few people around the ship, but there were dozens of flyers and pterocars circling in the sky.

Gorbovsky went around the pile of material valuables, tripped over a bust and went to the passenger hatch, where

Jenny Vyazanitsyn was supposed to be waiting for him. "If only Matvei would come," he thought glumly. He felt wrung out and used up, and was happy to see Matvei coming toward him. But he was alone.

"Where's Jenny?" Gorbovsky asked.

Matvei stopped and looked around.

"She was here," he said. "I talked to her by radiophone. What, are the hatches shut already?" He kept looking around.

"Yes, it's almost take-off," Gorbovsky said. He was looking around too. Maybe she's on a helicopter, he thought. But he knew that was impossible.

"Strange that Jenny's not here," Matvei said.

"Maybe she's on a helicopter," Gorbovsky said. He suddenly realized where she was. What a woman! he thought.

"I didn't get to see Alex," Matvei said.

A strange broad sound, like a convulsive shudder, sped over the spaceport. The huge blue ship silently tore away from the ground and slowly floated up. This is the first time I've seen my own ship take off, Gorbovsky thought. Matvei kept watching the ship and then, as if stung, turned to Gorbovsky and stared at him.

"What? . . . Wait a minute . . ." he muttered. "What's this? Why are you here? What about the ship?"

"Pishta's there," Gorbovsky said.

Matvei's eyes stopped.

"There it is," he whispered.

Gorbovsky turned. A shimmering solid strip glowed blindingly on the horizon.

Chapter 10

GORBOVSKY asked them to stop on the outskirts of the Capital. Dixon braked and looked at him expectantly.

"I'm going to walk," Gorbovsky said.

He got out. So did Mark and held out his hand to Alexandra Postysheva. The couple had sat in silence in the back seat all the way from the spaceport. They were holding hands tight, like children, and Alexandra, eyes shut, pressed her face against Mark's shoulder.

"Come with us, Percy," Gorbovsky said. "We'll pick flowers. It's cooled off. It will be very good for your heart."

Dixon shook his shaggy head.

"No, Leonid," he said. "Let's say goodbye instead. I'm driving."

The sun hung over the horizon. It was cool. The sun shone into what seemed to be a corridor with black walls: both Waves, the northern and southern, were high over the horizon.

"Right down the corridor," Dixon said. "Follow my eyes. Farewell, Leonid, farewell, Mark. And you, young lady, goodbye. Go on. . . . But first I will try for the last time to predict your behavior. This time it's particularly easy."

"Yes, it is," said Mark. "Farewell, Percy. Come on, honey."

Smiling gently, he looked at Gorbovsky, embraced Alexandra, and they went into the prairie. Gorbovsky and Dixon watched them go.

"A little late," Dixon said.

"Yes," Gorbovsky agreed. "But I still envy them."

"You enjoy envy. You do it with such gusto. I envy him, too. I'm jealous that someone will be thinking of him in his last moments, and no one will be thinking of me. . . . Or of you, Leonid."

"Do you want me to think of you?" Gorbovsky asked seriously.

"No, don't bother." Dixon squinted at the low sun. "Yes," he said. "This time, it looks like we won't get out of it. Farewell, Leonid."

He nodded and drove off, and Gorbovsky slowly strolled along the highway with the other people who were slowly walking back to town. He felt good and relaxed for the first time that crazy, tense, and terrible day. He didn't have to worry about anyone or anything, he didn't have to make decisions, everyone around him was independent, and he was totally independent, too. He had never been so independent in his life.

It was a beautiful evening, and if it hadn't been for the black walls to the right and left, slowly growing in the blue sky, it would have been perfect: quiet, transparent, cool enough, and shot through with the sun's slanting pink rays. There were fewer people on the highway; many had walked into the prairie, like Falkenstein and Alexandra, and many simply stayed on the shoulder.

In town the main street was decorated by the paintings that the artists were exhibiting for the last time—leaning up against tree trunks, buildings, on wires across the street, and

on lamp posts. People stood in front of paintings, remembering, quietly rejoicing, and a man was arguing loudly, and a
pretty thin woman cried bitterly, "What a shame . . . what a
shame!" Gorbovsky thought that he had seen her somewhere, but he couldn't remember where.

He heard unfamiliar music: in the open air cafe by the
Council Building a tiny, skinny man was playing a concert
choriol with incredible passion and spirit, and people at the
tables listened to him motionlessly as did people sitting on
the steps and the lawns around the cafe, and there was a
cardboard sign propped up against the instrument that said
in crooked letters: " 'Far Rainbow.' A song. Unfinished."

There were a lot of people around the tunnel, and they
were all busy. The huge, unfinished dome of the entrance
caisson shone in the sun. A line of zero-physicists moved
from the theater, each one carrying folders, boxes, packages.
Gorbovsky thought about the folder Malyaev had given him.
What had he done with it? Did he leave it in the bridge? Or
on the coaming? He shouldn't think about it . . . it wasn't
important. He should be totally carefree. Strange, could the
physicists be harboring hope? No tunnel could possibly save
us. But they could hope that the tunnel would save us. But
they could hope that the tunnel would save the fruits of their
labor. You can always hope for a miracle. It was funny that
the most skeptical and logical men on the planet were hoping for a miracle. . . .

In the alley leading to the Council courtyard sat a blind
man with a bandaged face, legs outstretched, dressed in a
worn pilot's suit. A shiny, chrome-plated banjo lay on his
lap. Head back, the blind man listened to the song "Far
Rainbow."

Fraudulent First Officer Hans came around a corner with
a huge bundle on his shoulder. Seeing Gorbovsky he smiled
and said, "Ah, Captain! How are your ulmotrons? Did you
get any? We're burying our archives. It's exhausting. What a
crazy day. . . ." He must have been the only man on Rainbow

who hadn't found out that Gorbovsky really was the captain of the Tariel.

Matvei called down from the Council window.

"The Tariel is in orbit," he shouted. "They just said goodbye. Everything is fine."

"Come on down," Gorbovsky said. "Let's go together."

Matvei shook his head.

"No, my friend," he said. "I have loads of work, and so little time. . . ." He stopped and then added in confusion, "I found Jenny, and do you know where?"

"I can guess," Gorbovsky said.

"Why did you do it?"

"Honest, I didn't," Gorbovsky said.

Matvei shook his head reproachfully and retreated into the room, and Gorbovsky went on.

He reached the beach, the beautiful yellow sand with multicolored umbrellas and lounge chairs, with cutters and sailboats at the dock. He lowered himself into a chair, stretched out with pleasure, folded his hands on his stomach, and looked west at the gorgeous setting sun. The black velvet curtains were coming from the left and right, and he tried not to look at them.

I would be taking off from Lalanda, he thought sleepily. The three of us would be in the bridge, and I would be telling them what a swell place Rainbow is, how I walked all around it in one day. Percy Dixon would be quiet, twirling his beard around his fingers, and Mark would be complaining that everything was old, dull and the same everywhere. And tomorrow at this time we would be out of deritrinitation. . . .

Head lowered, a beautiful girl walked by, the one who had interrupted his unpleasant conversation with Sklyarov at the spaceport. She was walking along the water's edge, and her face no longer seemed stony; she was just utterly exhausted. Fifty feet from him she stopped, stood for a while looking at the sea, and sat down on the sand, tucking her chin between her knees. Someone near Gorbovsky sighed deeply, and squinting sideways, Gorbovsky saw Sklyarov. Sklyarov was also looking at the girl.

"It's all meaningless," he said softly. "I lived a dull, useless life. And saved all the worst for the last day. . . ."

"Pal, what could be good on the last day?"

"You don't know. . . ."

"I know," Gorbovsky said. "I know everything."

"You can't know everything. . . . I can tell by the way you're talking to me."

"How?"

"Like I'm a regular person. But I'm a coward and a criminal."

"Come on, Robert. What kind of a coward and criminal are you?"

"I'm a coward and a criminal," Robert insisted stubbornly. "I'm probably worse than that because I was sure that what I did was right."

"There are no cowards and criminals," Gorbovsky said. "I'd sooner believe in a man who can be resurrected than in a man who is capable of a criminal act."

"Don't try to console me. I told you, you don't know everything."

Gorbovsky lazily turned to face him.

"Robert," he said. "Don't waste time. Go to her. Sit next to her. . . . I'm very comfortable here, but if you like, I'll help you. . . ."

"Everything turned out wrong," Robert said sadly. "I was sure that I would save her. I thought that I was prepared to do anything. But I wasn't. . . . I'll go," he said suddenly.

Gorbovsky watched him walk—first smoothly and confidently, then slower and slower, but he did reach her and sit down and she didn't move away.

Gorbovsky watched them for a while, trying to decide whether he envied them or not, and then fell asleep. He was awakened by something cold touching him. He opened one eye and saw Camill, his eternal silly helmet, his eternally ascetic and grim face and round unblinking eyes.

"I knew you were here, Leonid," Camill announced. "I was looking for you."

"Hello, Camill," Gorbovsky muttered. "It must be very boring, knowing everything."

Camill dragged over a chair and sat next to him, looking like a man with a broken back.

"There are more boring things," he said. "I'm tired of everything. It was an enormous mistake."

"How are things in the other world?" Gorbovsky asked.

"Dark," Camill said. He was silent. "I died and arose three times today. It was very painful each time."

"Three times," Gorbovsky said. "A record." He looked at Camill. "Camill, tell me the truth. I can't figure it out. Are you human? Don't be embarrassed. I won't have time to tell anyone."

Camill thought.

"I don't know," he said. "I'm the last of the 'Devil's Dozen.' The experiment failed, Leonid. Going from 'I want to but can't' to 'I can, but don't want to.' . . . It's so depressing, being able to and not wanting to. . . ."

Gorbovsky listened with eyes shut.

"Yes, I understand," he said. "Being able to and not wanting to—that's the machine in you. And being depressed, that's human."

"You don't understand a thing," Camill said. "You dream sometimes of the wisdom of the patriarchs who have no desires, no emotions, not even feelings. Disembodied reason. A Daltonic brain. The Great Logician. Logical methods demand absolute concentration. In order to get anywhere in science you have to think about one thing only day and night, read about one thing only, talk about one thing only. . . . But how can you get away from your own psyche? From the innate ability to feel? . . . After all, you have to love, and read about love, and you need green knolls, and music, and paintings, and frustration, and fear, and envy. . . . You try to limit yourselves and lose an enormous hunk of happiness. And you know very well that you're losing it. And then, to eradicate that knowledge and put an end to the painful duality, you castrate yourselves. You tear out the emotional half of humanity and leave only one reaction to the world surrounding you—doubt. 'Doubt everything!' " Camill stopped.

"And loneliness awaits you." He looked with great sadness at the evening sea, the cooling beach, the empty chaises that cast a strange triple shadow. "Loneliness," he repeated. "You always fled me, you people. I was always superfluous, a pushy and misunderstood eccentric. And now you'll leave again. And I'll be left alone. Tonight I'll be resurrected again for the fourth time, alone on a dead planet, covered with ashes and snow. . . ."

Suddenly there was noise on the beach. Sinking in the sand, the testers headed for the water—eight guinea pigs, eight failed zero-pilots. Seven carried the eighth, a blind man with a bandaged face. The blind man, head thrown back, was singing and playing the banjo, and they all sang along:

> When like the dark waters,
> Calamity, terrible and bad,
> Came upon you
> You didn't bend your head,
> You looked into the sky
> And went on . . .

Without looking around they walked into the sea, waist deep, then chest deep, and then they swam after the setting sun, bearing their blind comrade on their backs. To their right was a black wall reaching almost as high as they could see, and to their left was a black wall reaching almost as high as they could see, and there was only a narrow, dark-blue slice of sky, and the red sun, and a path of molten gold, down which they swam, and soon they were lost in the shimmering water, and there was only the banjo and the song:

> And you didn't bow your head
> You looked into the sky
> > And went on ...

The Second
Invasion from Mars

June 1 (3 A.M.)

*O this accursed
conformist world!*

L ORD, on top of everything else—Artemis!
Looks like she's gotten mixed up with that Nicostratus after
all. That's what you call a daughter. . . . Well, so be it.

About one o'clock this morning I was awakened by a terrific but distant rumbling and was startled by an ominous
play of red lights over the walls of my bedroom. The rumbling went on roaring and reverberating like the sound of an
earthquake, so that the whole house shook, the window-
panes rattled and the vials danced on the nightstand. I
rushed in a fright to the window. In the north the sky was
aflame: it seemed as if the earth was gaping out there beyond
the horizon and spewing fountains of multicolored fire up to
the very stars. But on the bench right under my window,
those two, seeing and hearing nothing, all lit up by the in-
fernal commotion and rocking with the subterranean
tremors, were embracing each other and kissing full on the
mouth. I immediately recognized Artemis and assumed that
Charon had returned, that she was so glad to see him she
was kissing him like a bride instead of leading him straight
to the bedroom. A second later, in the light of the red sky, I

recognized the illustrious foreign-made jacket of Mr. Nicostratus, and my heart sank. Such moments as these ruin a man's constitution. And yet you couldn't say that this hit me like a bolt from the blue. There had been rumors, hints, all sorts of little jokes. And still I was knocked dead.

Clutching my heart, completely at a loss what to do, I made my way in my bare feet to the living room and began to phone the police. But just try to get through to the police when you need them. The line at the station was busy for a long time, and when someone did answer, who should be on duty but Pandareus. I asked him what phenomenon was that observable on the horizon. He didn't know what a phenomenon was. I asked him, "Can you tell me what's happening on the northern horizon?" He tried to figure out where that might be. I was at my wit's end to explain it to him, when finally he caught on.

"Ah-h-h," he says, "you mean the big fire?" And he reported that some sort of burning had indeed been observed, but what kind of burning it was and what was being burned had not been determined as yet. The house was quaking, everything was creaking, people were on the street pitifully screaming about war, and this old horse's ass starts telling me that they'd just brought Minotaur into the station: he was dead drunk, he'd defiled the corner of Mr. Laomedon's estate, and he couldn't stand up or even fight.

"Are you going to do anything about it or not?" I interrupted him.

"That's what I'm trying to tell you, Mr. Apollo," says this ass, taking offense, "I have to make a report, and you're tying me up on the telephone. If you're all so upset about the fire——"

"What if it's a war?" I asked him.

"No, it's not a war," he declared. "I would've known."

"What if it's an eruption?" I asked. He didn't know what an eruption was. I couldn't stand it anymore and hung up. Sweaty all over from this conversation, I went back to the bedroom and put on my robe and slippers.

The rumbling seemed to have quieted down, but the flashing continued. Those two were no longer kissing or even sitting on the bench in each other's arms but were standing hand-in-hand where anyone could see them, since the fire lit up the horizon as bold as day. Only the light wasn't white, but reddish orange, with clouds the color of watery coffee drifting across it. The neighbors were running around in the street in whatever, Mrs. Eurydice was grabbing people by their pajamas and demanding to be saved, and only Myrtilus took a businesslike approach, rolled his truck out of the garage and along with his wife and sons set about loading his household possessions. It was a real panic, just as in the good old days—I hadn't seen one like it for a long time. But as for me, I understood that if an atomic war had broken out, you couldn't find a better place in the region than our town for hiding, waiting, sitting it out. And if it was an eruption, then it was occurring somewhere far away, so once again our town wasn't threatened. Besides, it was doubtful that it was an eruption. What kind of eruption could we have?

I went upstairs and tried to wake Hermione. It was the same old story: "Leave me alone, you sot. You shouldn't drink at night—I don't want to now. . . ." And so on. Then I started telling her in a loud and convincing voice about the atomic war and the eruption, laying on the colors rather thick, since otherwise I would never get anywhere. This got through to her, she leaped out of bed, shoved me out of the way and dashed straight for the kitchen, grumbling: "I'm going to take a look, and then you'd better watch out. . . ." Unlocking the cupboard, she examined the bottle of cognac. I kept cool. "Where'd you get yourself in this state?" she asked, sniffing at me suspiciously. "What den of iniquity did you go to tonight?"

But when she looked out the window and saw our neighbors half-dressed in the street, when she saw Myrtilus in his underdrawers propped up on his roof and peering through his field glasses to the north, she forgot about me. As it happened, the northern horizon had again sunk into silence and darkness, though you could still make out a cloud of smoke completely obscuring the stars. What can you say? My Hermione is no Mrs. Eurydice for you. A different age and a different upbringing. I'd barely managed to down a glass of cognac when she dragged out the suitcases and called to Artemis at the top of her voice. Go on and call her, call her, I thought bitterly, maybe she'll hear you.

At that moment Artemis appeared at the door to her room. Lord! Pale as death, shaking all over, but with her pajamas already on and curlers in her hair. She asks, "What is it? What are you all shouting about?"

You've got to admit it, she's got guts. If this phenomenon hadn't occurred, I'd never have found out anything, and Charon even less. Our eyes met, she smiled at me affectionately but with trembling lips, and I decided not to utter the words on the tip of my tongue. To calm myself down, I went to my room and began to pack my stamps. You tremble, I said to her mentally, you shake. You're lonely, scared and unprotected. But he didn't support you or protect you. He picked a flower of pleasure and ran off on his own business. No, my dear, when a man's without honor, he's without honor to the very end.

Meanwhile, as I expected, the panic was quickly subsiding. It became an ordinary night again, the earth no longer shook, the houses didn't creak. Someone had taken Mrs. Eurydice home. No one was shouting about war anymore, particularly since there wasn't anything more to shout about. Glancing out the window, I saw that the street was deserted, only one or two houses had their lights on and Myrtilus was still on his roof, standing out among the stars in his underpants. I called over to him and asked what he could see.

"Sure, sure," he said irritably. "Go to bed, snore. You snore, and they'll give it to you. . . ."

I asked who "they" were.

"Sure, sure," responded Myrtilus. "You wise guys know

it all. Along with your Pandareus. He's a fool, your Pandareus, and nothing else but."

Hearing about Pandareus, I decided to phone the police again. It took a long time to get through, but when at long last I did, Pandareus informed me that there was no special news, but as for the rest everything was in order, drunk Minotaur had been shot with a sedative, had his stomach cleaned out and dropped off to sleep. About the big fire, the burning had stopped a long time ago, especially since it turned out not to be burning at all, but a big holiday fireworks display. While I was trying to recall what holiday it was, Pandareus hung up. He really is stupid and revoltingly uneducated, and he always has been. It's strange to see people like that in our police force. Our policemen should be intellectuals, models for the youth, heroes to be emulated, people you can safely entrust not only with weapons and authority, but also with educational work. But Charon considers such a police force a "company of eggheads." He says no state would want my kind of police force because it would start arresting and reeducating the very people the state finds most useful, beginning with the Prime Minister and the Chief of Police. I don't know, I don't know, could be. But for the senior officer not to know what a phenomenon is and to act like a clod while performing his duties—who needs it?

Tripping over the suitcases, I made my way back to the cupboard and poured myself a glass of cognac just as Hermione came back in the kitchen. She said this was a madhouse, you couldn't depend on anybody here, the men were not men and the women not women. I'm a complete alcoholic, Charon lives here like a tourist and Artemis is a lily-white unfit for real life. And so on. Maybe someone would explain to her why she was awakened in the middle of the night and forced to get out the suitcases? I answered Hermione as best I could and sought refuge in my bedroom. I ached all over, and now I know for sure that my eczema will be worse tomorrow. I already feel like scratching, but so far I've been able to hold back.

About three o'clock the earth shook again. I could hear the noise of many engines and the grinding of metal. It turned out to be a column of military trucks and armored carriers full of troops moving past the house. They drove slowly, with dimmed headlights, and Myrtilus had latched onto some kind of armored vehicle and was trotting alongside, holding onto the lug of the hatchway and shouting something. I don't know what they answered him, but when the column had passed and he stood alone in the street, I called over to him and asked for the news.

"Sure, sure," said Myrtilus. "We know what kind of maneuvers these are. A bunch of wise guys riding around on my money." And finally I understood it all. Big military exercises are taking place—perhaps even with the use of atomic weapons. Big deal.

Lord, now if only I can get some sleep!

June 2

I ITCH all over. And above all I can't bring myself to have a talk with Artemis. I can't stand those excessively personal conversations, that intimate tone. Besides,
how do I know what she'll answer?

The devil knows what to do with daughters like this. If
only I had an inkling of what she needs! She's got a husband,
not some kind of puny egghead, but a real hunk of a man;
he's no slob, no cripple, and no lecher either. Though he
could be: the comptroller's niece looks at him suggestively
and Thyone makes eyes at him. Everyone knows about it,
not to mention the schoolgirls, the summer-cottage girls, or
Madam Persephone, the cattiest she-cat of them all—no cat
can stand up to her. But actually I do know what Artemis
would answer.

"Daddikins," she'd say, "it's boring, it's all so deadly boring around here."

And you can't argue with that! A young, beautiful woman,
no children, a model disposition: she ought to be whisked
away in a whirlwind of amusements, dances, flirtations, and
the like. But Charon, unfortunately, is one of those, what

shall we call them, philosophizers. A thinker. Totalitarianism, fascism, managerialism, communism. Dancing is a sexual stimulant, guests are blabbermouths, one's worse than the other. Don't breathe a word about a game of four kings. Yet, when it comes to drinking, he's nobody's fool! Get five of his know-it-all friends around a table and put five bottles of cognac in front of them, and they'll go on deciding the world's affairs till dawn. The lass yawns and yawns, she slams the door and goes to bed. You call that life? I understand, a man needs something manly, but, on the other hand, a woman needs something womanly! No, I love my son-in-law, he's my son-in-law, so I love him. But how long can you go on deciding the world's affairs? And what difference do those discussions make? It's obvious: you can talk about fascism till you're blue in the face and you won't make a dint in it. Before you can take a breath, it'll slap an iron helmet on you and—forward, long live the leader! But stop paying attention to your young wife, and she'll pay you back in spades. No philosophizing will help you then. I understand, a cultured man must discuss abstruse subjects now and then, but you must keep things in proportion, gentlemen.

A wonderful morning today. (Temperature: +19° C, cloud cover: 1, wind from the south at .5 meters per second. I ought to run down to the meteorological bureau and fix my wind gauge, since I dropped it again.) After breakfast I decided that a sleeping dog gets no pension, so I went to the mayor's office to look into it. As I walked along, pleased by the peace and quiet, I suddenly saw a crowd on the corner of Freedom and Juniper streets. It turned out that Minotaur had driven his cistern through a jeweler's front window, and the people had gathered around to watch him, all dirty, puffy and drunk again since early morning, try to explain it to the traffic cop. He made such an unwholesome contrast to the bright and shining morning that I immediately fell in the dumps. Obviously the police shouldn't have let him out so early, they must've known he'd drink himself into a stupor once he got going. But, on the other hand, how could they not let him out, since he's the only honey-dipper in town? Here you have only two options: either you take up the re-education of Minotaur and drown in filth, or you make a compromise in the name of hygiene.

Because of Minotaur I was held up, and when I got to The Five Spot all the boys had already assembled. I paid my fine, and then one-legged Polyphemus treated me to an excellent cigar in an aluminum case, which his oldest son Polycarpus, a lieutenant in the merchant marines, had sent to him for me. This Polycarpus once studied under me for several years, until he ran away to sea as a cabin boy. He was a lively lad, a playful scamp. When the scamp flew the city, Polyphemus almost took me to court, as if, so to say, the teacher had corrupted the child with his lectures on the vast multiplicity of worlds. Polyphemus is still certain that the sky is firm and satellites run around on it like cyclists in a circus. My demonstrations of the value of astronomy are beyond him: they were beyond him then, and they are just as far beyond him now.

The boys were talking about how the city comptroller had again misused funds allocated for the construction of the stadium. That makes it the seventh time already. We talked of ways to put a stop to it. Silenus shrugged his shoulders and asserted that nothing would do but a trial.

"Enough half-measures," he said. "An open trial. Gather the whole town at the foundation of the stadium and tie the embezzler to a pillory at the scene of his crime. Thank God," he repeated, "that our law is sufficiently flexible that the means of suppression can equal the seriousness of the crime."

"I would even say," remarked grouchy Paralus, "that our law is too flexible. The comptroller has been taken to court twice already, and both times our flexible law bent clean around him. But maybe you think it happened that way because he wasn't tried at the foundation, but in the town hall."

Morpheus, thinking it over carefully, said that from this day forward he'd never give the comptroller another shave and haircut. Let 'im go hairy.

"You're all stupid backsides," said Polyphemus. "You'll never get anywhere. He can just spit on the whole lot of you. He has his own cronies."

"That's exactly it," grouchy Paralus caught on, and he reminded us that in addition to the city comptroller there lived and flourished the city architect who had designed the stadium to the best of his abilities and now had a natural interest in seeing that the stadium, God forbid, not be built.

Calais the stutterer began to sputter and stammer, and having thus gained everyone's attention he recalled that he himself, Calais, had almost come to blows with the architect at the Flower Festival. This statement gave the discussion a decidedly new turn.

One-legged Polyphemus, as a veteran and a man not squeamish about blood, proposed that we jump both of them at the entrance to Madam Persephone's house and take them down a notch. In critical moments like these Polyphemus completely loses a hold on his tongue—the barracks language flows right out of him.

"Take the smelly bastards down a notch," he thundered. "Shovel away all that crap, crush their bones, polish 'em off!"

It's simply amazing how such speeches affect the boys. They all got furious and started waving their hands, and Calais sputtered and stammered more violently than ever, since he couldn't pronounce a word in his great agitation. But here grouchy Paralus, the only one of us to keep cool, noted that besides the comptroller and the architect, there still happened to be living in the city, in his summer residence, the best friend of these two—a certain Mr. Laomedon. At this everyone fell silent and began to puff on the cigars and cigarettes, which had gone out during the discussion, because you couldn't take Mr. Laomedon down a notch or polish him off so easily. And when in the settling silence Calais inadvertently burst out, finally, with his favorite curse —"S-s-sock 'em in the snoot!"—everyone looked at him with displeasure.

I remembered that I should have gone to the mayor's office a long time before, so I inserted the remainder of my cigar into the aluminum case and went up to the second floor, to the reception room of Mr. Mayor. I was struck by the unusual bustle of the office. All the employees were excited somehow. Even Mr. Secretary, instead of examining his fingernails as usual, was busy imprinting wax seals on large envelopes, although, to be sure, with an expression of distaste and obligation. Feeling very out of place, I approached this fashionably slicked-down beauty. Lord, I'd give anything on earth to have nothing to do with him, neither to see him nor to hear him. Even before this I hadn't liked Mr. Nicostratus, just as I didn't like any of our town dandies. To tell the truth, I didn't like him even when he studied under me, because he was lazy, crude and insolent. But after yesterday it makes me sick just to look at him. I had no idea what tone to take with him. But there was no getting out of it, and finally I decided to say "Mr. Nicostratus, have you heard anything concerning my case?"

He didn't even glance at me, didn't even, so to say, favor me with a glance. "Sorry, Mr. Apollo, but the answer hasn't come in yet from the ministry," he said, continuing to press the seals. I hung around a moment and then headed for the exit, feeling rotten, as I always do in official places. However, quite unexpectedly, he stopped me with a surprising piece of news. He said there had been no communication with Marathon since yesterday.

"What are you saying!" said I. "Haven't the maneuvers ended yet?"

"What maneuvers?" he asked in surprise.

Here I lost my composure. I still don't know if I should have done it, but I stared straight at him and said, "What do you mean—'what maneuvers?' The same ones you happened to see last night."

"So they were maneuvers, were they?" he declared with enviable indifference, again bending over his envelopes. "They were fireworks. Read the morning papers."

I should have, I really should have said a couple of words to him, especially since at that moment we were alone in the room. But can I be like that?

When I returned to The Five Spot, an argument was underway about the nature of last night's phenomenon. Our number had grown: Myrtilus and Pandareus had joined us. Pandareus had the jacket of his uniform unbuttoned; he was unshaven and tired after his night duty. Myrtilus didn't look any better, because he had spent the entire night patrolling the grounds around his house, expecting the worst. Everyone had the morning paper in hand, and they were discussing the column of "our observer," which bore the following heading: HOLIDAY IN THE OFFING.

"Our observer" reported that Marathon was preparing to commemorate its 153rd anniversary. From his usually well-informed sources he had learned that last night there had been a fireworks practice which residents of the surrounding towns and villages within a radius of up to two hundred kilometers had been able to enjoy.

That's all that was needed! Charon goes away on assignment, and our newspaper falls into catastrophic stupidity. They should at least have tried to figure out what a fireworks display would look like from two hundred kilometers away. And they should at least have asked themselves when fireworks displays began to be accompanied by subterranean tremors. I immediately explained this to the boys, but they answered that they knew perfectly well the time of day and advised me to read *The Milesian Herald*. In the *Herald* it was printed black on white that last night "the Milesians could admire the impressive spectacle of military exercises employing the latest devices of war technology."

"What did I tell you!" I burst out, but Myrtilus interrupted me. He related that early this morning an unknown driver from the Long-Distance Transport Company had driven up to his pump, had gotten 150 liters of gas, two cans of motor oil, and a crate of marmalade and had told him, in secret, that last night, for reasons unknown, the underground rocket-fuel factories had exploded. Supposedly the 23 guards and the entire night shift had perished, and 179 more men had vanished without a trace. This news threw us all into a panic, but then grouchy Paralus put forward the question "What then, I'd like to know, did he need the marmalade for?"

This question stumped Myrtilus. "Sure, sure," he said, "you heard it. That's all you're getting out of me."

We also had nothing to say. Really, what has marmalade got to do with it? Calais sputtered, sprayed, but didn't say anything. And then that old horse's ass, Pandareus, took the floor.

"Listen, old boys," says he, "those weren't any rocket factories. They were marmalade factories, obviously. Now, behave yourselves."

We sat down.

"Underground marmalade factories?" says Paralus. "Well, old-timer, you're in superb form today."

We began to slap Pandareus on the back, adding, "Yes, Pan, one can see right away that you slept poorly today, old-timer. Minotaur has run you ragged, Pan, it's a hard life. Time you took your pension, Pan, good old boy!"

"A policeman, and he plants the seeds of panic himself," said Myrtilus, highly offended. He was the only one who had taken Pandareus's words seriously.

"That's why he's Pan—to plant seeds everywhere," quipped Dymus. And Polyphemus also made a successful quip, although a completely indecent one. We went on amusing ourselves in this fashion, while Pandareus stood stock-still, then puffed himself up before our very eyes and tossed his head from side to side like a bull taunted by matadors.

Finally he buttoned his jacket up to the very last button, set his eyes above our heads and bawled: "You've had your say—enough! Dis-s-sperse! In the name of the law." Myrtilus went back to his gas pump, and the rest of us headed for the tavern.

In the tavern we all immediately ordered beer. This is a satisfaction I was denied until I went on my pension! In such a small town as ours, everyone knows the teacher. The parents of your pupils imagine for some reason that you are a wonder-worker and are able by your personal example to keep the children from following in their parents' footsteps. From morning to night the tavern literally swarms with these parents, but if you permit yourself an innocent mug of beer, then the next day without fail you will have a humiliating conversation with the principal. And yet I love the tavern! I love to sit in the company of good men, having leisurely and serious conversations on subjects of your choice, half catching the drone of voices and the clinking of glasses behind your back. I love to tell and to hear a salty little story, to play four kings—for a small amount, but with honor, and when I win I like to order a mug for everyone. Well, enough.

Iapetus served us our beer, and we began talking about the war. One-legged Polyphemus declared that if this were a war, they would already be mobilizing the troops, but grouchy Paralus objected that if it were a war, we wouldn't know anything about it. I don't like conversations about war and would gladly have turned the conversation to pensions, but who am I to do this?

Polyphemus laid his crutch across the table and asked what, in fact, did Paralus know about wars. "Do you know, for example, what a bazooka is?" he asked threateningly.

"Do you know what it means to sit in a trench when the tanks are coming at you and you haven't yet noticed that you've dumped in your drawers?"

Paralus objected that he didn't know anything about tanks and dumping in your drawers and he didn't want to know anything about them, but as for nuclear war we all knew the same thing about it. "You lie down with your feet in the blast and crawl to the nearest graveyard," he said.

"You were born a civvy and you'll die a civvy," said one-legged Polyphemus. "Nuclear war—that's a war of nerves, understand? They do us, we do them, and the first one to dump in his drawers loses." Paralus only shrugged his shoulders, and Polyphemus lost his temper completely. "Bazookas!" he yelled. "Tarzons! Ready, aim—dump in your drawers! Right, Apollo?"

Having shouted to his heart's content, he launched into recollections about how he and our troops had repelled a tank attack in the snow. I can't stand these recollections. Nothing but dump in your drawers. I don't know, maybe it all happened, I don't recall. But still I don't like to return to it. Polyphemus was gung-ho then, and he's gung-ho now. I simply don't know what you must take out of a man to make him stop being a noncommissioned officer. Maybe the problem is that he never happened to get caught in a pocket, as I did. Or is it a matter of character?

We had sat a long time, so I decided to go ahead and have lunch. Usually the fare at Iapetus's place is pretty good, but this time the chef's soup with dumplings gave off a heavy odor of cheap olive oil, and I told him about it. It turned out that Iapetus's teeth had been aching for three days, so unbearably that he couldn't prepare anything properly.

"Don't you remember, Phoebus, how I once knocked your tooth in?" he asked mournfully.

How could I not remember! It was in the seventh grade. We were both courting Iphigenia and we fought every day. My God, how distant are the times when I could have a good scrap! Iphigenia, it happens, is now married to some engineer in the south; she already has grandchildren and angina pectoris.

While on my way to Achilles' place, I passed Mr. Laomedon's house with that terrible red car of his with bulletproof windows standing outside. At the wheel that insolent punk who always makes fun of me was smoking himself silly. And this time he lit into me so viciously that I was obliged to cross the street in a dignified manner and pay not the slightest attention to him. Achilles was presiding over the cash register and looking through his *Cosmos*. Ever since he obtained that blue triangle with the little silver postage mark, he has made it a rule to take out his album just as I enter, as if by coincidence. I can see right through him, but I don't let on. Although, to tell the truth, every time he does it my heart contracts. My only consolation is that part of his triangle is glued on. I mentioned it to him.

"Yes," said I, "there's no denying it, Achilles, it's a nice item. Too bad, though, that it's glued together."

He squinted all over and mumbled that the grapes, it seemed, were sour.

"What can you do?" I answered him calmly. "Glued together is glued together, you can't get around it. I personally wouldn't have taken the stamp at that price. But some people, of course," said I, "are so broad-minded that they'll take stamps that are canceled and glued together. That's not for me, no kidding. I'd take them only for trading. You can always find some simpleton who doesn't care if they're glued together or not."

That'll teach you to stick your silver postmark under my nose!

But otherwise we had a good time together. He tried to persuade me that yesterday's fireworks were a rare type of northern lights which accidentally coincided with a special type of earthquake, and I informed him of the maneuvers and the explosion at the marmalade factory. It's impossible to argue with Achilles. Because you can see that the man

doesn't believe in his own words, but still persists in arguing. He sits there like some Mongolian stone image, looks
out the window and repeats the same thing over and over
again, that I'm not the only one in town who can interpret
the phenomena of nature. You'd think that in their pharma-
ceutical school they would actually train people in the serious sciences. But no, it's impossible to bring an argument
with any one of the boys to a reasonable conclusion. Take
Polyphemus, for example. He never argues to the heart of
the matter. Truth doesn't interest him, for him only one
thing is important: disgracing his opponent. Say that we're
arguing about the shape of our planet. Employing the precise arguments known to every educated person, I prove to
him that the Earth is, to put it crudely, a ball. He savagely
and unsuccessfully attacks every argument in turn, and
when we come to the shape of the Earth's shadow during a
lunar eclipse, he comes out with something like this: "A
shadow, a shadow! You bring in a shadow in the broad day-
light. First show the beard under your nose and grow the
hair on your bald spot before you start arguing about the
world." Or take Paralus. I once argued with him about ways
to cure alcoholism. I hadn't had time to bat my eyes before
we had turned to the foreign policy of our president, and
from there—to the problem of panspermia. And the most
surprising thing is that I had and still have nothing to do
with either panspermia or foreign policy, it's simply that
Hermione's cousin's son suffered from alcoholism and tor-
mented everyone around him. Now he's a medic in the army,
but at that time my life was an absolute nightmare. Yes,
alcoholism is the scourge of the people.

Our argument ended with Achilles taking out his trusty
bottle and our drinking a shot of gin. Achilles' business isn't
going very well. I have the impression that he wouldn't even
have enough for gin if it weren't for Madam Persephone.
Someone came from her place again today.

"I can recommend an antihistamine," said Achilles in a
discreet whisper.

"No," answers the messenger girl, "something more reliable was requested, please."

Something more reliable, you see, for her. The little cook from Iapetus's place ran in too, for tooth drops, but no one else came, and we talked our fill. I traded a pink "Monument" for his "Red Cross" series. Actually, I don't need "Red Cross," but the day before yesterday Charon told me that he'd received a personal announcement at the editorial offices, which read:

Will take "Red Cross." Offer any inverted postmark from the standard set.

I must confess that, strange as it seems, Charon is the only person in our house who doesn't giggle at me. In general, if you think about it, he's not such a bad fellow. Artemis is acting not only immorally, but also ignobly. And with the likes of Nicostratus!

Returning home at nine in the evening, I saw them again sitting in my garden, in the shadows. True, they weren't kissing this time, but still they ought to have a sense of decency. I went in the garden, took Artemis by the hand and said to that dandy, "Goodbye, Mr. Nicostratus, pleasant dreams." Artemis yanked her hand away from me and walked away without a word. And that rake, very ineptly trying to smooth over the awkward situation, struck up a conversation with me about the municipal recommendations which need to be attached to the request for a pension. And so I stand there and listen to him. I ought to drive him from the garden with a stick, but I listen to him. That damned delicacy of mine. And lack of confidence. I really have an inferiority complex.

And then he gave me a nasty smirk and said, "And how is charming Mrs. Hermione getting along? You didn't miss your mark there, Mr. Apollo. I wouldn't have refused such a housekeeper myself."

My heart sank and I lost the power of speech. But without

waiting for an answer (what did he need my answer for?), he went off, laughing all the way down the street. I remained alone in the dark garden.

No, there's nothing you can do about it. Still, relations between me and Hermione ought to be put in order. I know I won't get anywhere, but peace of mind requires sacrifices.

SOMETIMES I am seized with utter horror when I think that the matter of my pension is not progressing. Everything tightens up inside me, and I can't apply myself to anything.

But if you think it out logically, the matter should come to the most beneficial conclusion. First of all, I worked as a teacher for thirty years, not counting the break for the war. To be more precise, thirty years and two months. Second, I did not change my place of work even once, I never interrupted my term of service with transfers and other distracting circumstances, and only once, seven years ago, did I take a short leave of absence at my own expense. And participation in military activities cannot be considered a break in service, that's clear. By my best calculation, more than four thousand students passed through my classes, almost all of the present townspeople. Third, in recent years I have been constantly before the public and three times have substituted for the gymnasium director during his leave. Fourth, my work has been flawless; I have sixteen statements of gratitude from the ministry, a personal letter from the late minister on my fiftieth birthday, and likewise a bronze medal "For diligent work in the fallow field of public education." A whole compartment of my desk is specially set aside for letters of thanks from parents. Fifth, my speciality: today everything has turned topsy-turvy in this Cosmos; thus astronomy has become a timely subject. In my opinion, this is also a point in my favor. So, if you only glance at the matter, it would seem there could hardly be any doubt. In the minister's place I would certainly put me in the first-class category, without a moment's hesitation. Lord, then I could finally rest easy. After all, when you get right down to it, I don't need a lot in life. Three to four cigarettes, a glass of cognac, a pittance for cards, that's all. Along with stamps, of course. First class—that means 150 a month. One hundred I'll give to Hermione for household expenses; twenty goes into savings for a rainy day, and what's left is mine. That's enough for stamps and the rest. Really, haven't I earned it?

It's too bad that no one needs an old man. Squeeze him out like a lemon and then—kick off. Letters of gratitude? Who cares about them now? Medals? Who doesn't have them? And someone is bound to latch onto the fact that I was a prisoner. Were you a prisoner? I was. Three years? Three years. That's all! Your service was interrupted for three years, take your third-class pension and don't drag out our correspondence.

If only I had connections! Actually there is one student of mine, General Alcimus by name, who now sits in the Lower Congress. What if I write him? He ought to remember me, he and I had many of those little conflicts which students love to recall when they have grown up. By God, I will write him. I'll start right off: "Hi, boy. I'm an old man now. . . ." No, I'll wait a bit and then write.

All day today I sat at home. Yesterday Hermione visited an aunt and brought back a big package of old stamps. I derived great pleasure from rummaging through them.

There's nothing like it. It's like an endless honeymoon. Several fine specimens turned up, true, all of them glued to something. I'll have to restore them. Myrtilus has pitched a tent in his yard and is living there with his whole family. He was boasting that he could get up and go within ten minutes. He went on that there was still no communication with Marathon. He's probably lying. Drunken Minotaur drove his filthy cistern into Mr. Laomedon's red car and got into a fight with the chauffeur. Both of them were taken to the station. Minotaur was thrown in jail to sober up, and the chauffeur, so they say, was sent to the hospital. So there is justice in the world after all. Artemis is sitting as quiet as a mouse: Charon should be returning any time now. I haven't told Hermione anything about it. Maybe it will all blow over. But boy, I'd like to get first class!

June 4

JUST finished reading the evening papers, but just as before I don't understand anything. No doubt about it, some sort of changes have taken place. But what kind exactly? People around here like to tell whoppers, that's all.

This morning, after my coffee, I set off for The Five Spot. It was a good morning, warm. (Temperature: +18° C, cloud cover: 0, wind from the south at 1 meter per second by my wind gauge.) Coming through the gate, I saw Myrtilus fussing over his tent, which lay crumbled up on the ground. I asked him what he was doing.

"Sure, sure," he answered in extreme irritation. "You wise guys know it all. Just sit still and wait until they cut us all up." I don't believe Myrtilus any farther than I can throw him, but he always gives me the creeps when he talks like this.

"And what else is new?" I ask.

"Martians," he replied curtly and continued to smooth out the tent with his knee. I didn't understand him at first and maybe that's why I got such a funny feeling from that word, as if something terrible and unstoppable were on the way.

My legs went weak and I slumped back on the bumper of the truck. Myrtilus said nothing, only huffed and puffed.

"What'd you say?" I asked.

He packed up the tent, tossed it in the back of the truck and lit up a smoke. "The Martians have attacked," he said in a whisper. "It's the end of us all. They burned Marathon down to the ground, I hear. Ten million killed in one night, can you believe it? Today they paid a visit to our mayor's office. The power's theirs now, and that's that. They've already prohibited any planting, and now, I hear, they're going to slit open everybody's stomach. They need stomachs for some reason, can you believe it? I'm not going to wait for that, I need my stomach myself. As soon as I heard about it, I decided right away: these new rulings are not for me, they can all take a flying leap, 'cause I'm heading to my brother's farm. I've already sent the old lady and the kids on the bus. We'll sit it out, keep our eyes open, and see how things are going from there."

"Hold on," I said, keenly remembering how he always lies, but feeling myself getting weaker. "Hold on, Myrtilus, what are you talking about? Who attacked? Who burned? My son-in-law's in Marathon right now."

"Your son-in-law's had it," Myrtilus said sympathetically and flicked away his butt. "Consider your daughter a widow. The secretary has a clear road ahead. Well; I'm off. So long, Apollo. We were always on good terms. I've got no hard feelings toward you, so don't think badly of me."

"Lord!" I burst out in desperation, completely weakened. "Who was it that attacked?"

"Martians, Martians!" he said, again switching to a whisper. "From there!" He raised his finger to the sky. "They jumped in on us from a comet."

"You mean men from Mars?" I asked with a glimmer of hope.

"Sure, sure," he said, climbing into the cabin. "You're a teacher, you know better. But it's all the same to me who pokes out my guts."

"Lord, Myrtilus," I said, finally catching on that this was all a bunch of lies. "You can't go on like this. You're an elderly man, you have grandchildren. How can there be any men from Mars, when Mars is a lifeless planet? There's no life there, that's a scientific fact."

"Sure, sure," Myrtilus went on lying, but it was obvious that he was beginning to have doubts. "And what other facts are there about it?"

"Well, it's not 'sure, sure'; it's the way it actually is," I said. "Ask any scientist. But who needs a scientist, this is something every schoolboy knows!"

Myrtilus grunted and climbed out of the cabin. "It can all take a flying leap!" he said, laying his fingers on the back of his head. "Who am I to listen to? Am I to listen to you? Or to Pandareus? I don't understand a thing." He spat and went into his house.

I also decided to go back in, in order to phone the police. Pandareus, as it happened, was very busy, because Minotaur had broken out of his cell and Pandareus had to form a search party. It was true that someone, some kind of leaders, had driven to the mayor's office about an hour and a half before, and they might have been Martians, there were rumors that they were Martians, but as far as cutting open stomachs was concerned, no word had been given, and anyway he had no time for Martians, because Minotaur alone, in his opinion, was worse than all the Martians put together.

I hurried to The Five Spot.

Almost all the boys were crowding at the entrance to the mayor's office and arguing furiously about some kind of tracks in the dirt. The tracks had been made by the Martian who had come, they knew this for a fact. Morpheus asserted that he, as an old hairdresser and masseur, had never seen such marvels before. "Spiders," he was saying, "huge hairy spiders. That is, the males are hairy, but the females are naked. They walk on their back feet and grab you with their front. Did you see the prints? Horrifying! Like holes in the ground. That's where he walked by."

"He didn't just walk by," said Silenus thoughtfully. "The force of gravity is greater on Earth, as Apollo here will confirm, so that they can't simply walk with their legs. They need special stilts with springs, and that's what made the holes in the ground."

"Right, stilts," seconded Iapetus indistinctly with his bandaged-up jaw. "Only they're not stilts. They have a certain kind of car, I saw it in the movies. It doesn't run on wheels, but on levers, on stilts."

"Our comptroller has gone off the deep end again," said grouchy Paralus. "The last time it was a hail storm of unusual force, and the time before that he announced locusts, but now he's whipped up Martians—in keeping with the times, the conquest of space."

"I can't look at these tracks without getting excited," repeated Morpheus. "Horrifying. What d'ya say, buddies, let's go have a drink."

Calais stammered, sputtered and shook. Finally he pronounced: "G-g-good weather we're having, old boys! How d-d-did you sleep?" Due to his speech defect he always lags behind events. And yet he's a veterinarian; he could have said something worthwhile about the tracks.

"Myrtilus has already packed off," said Dymus, giggling stupidly. " 'Goodbye, Dymus,' he says, 'we were always on good terms. Look after my gas pump,' he says, 'and if you have to, burn it,' he says, 'so we leave nothing to the enemy.' "

Here I cautiously inquired what had been heard about Marathon.

"They say Marathon was burned down," Dymus answered readily. "They say people phoned from there with the terms for peace."

This absolutely convinced me that all of this was a bunch of senseless rumors, and I was getting ready to refute them when the wailing of a police siren cut through the air and we all turned around.

Minotaur came running across the square, staggering and

zigzagging like a bunny, splattered with mud and swollen, and hot on his heels came Pandareus in his police buggy, standing up and holding onto the windshield, shouting something and waving a pair of handcuffs.

"The jig's up, he'll catch him now," said Morpheus.

"That's what you think," objected Dymus. "See what he's doing?"

Minotaur ran up to a telephone pole, threw his arms and legs around it and began to scramble up. However, Pandareus had already jumped out of the vehicle and fastened onto his pants. With the help of a subordinate, he tore the honey-dipper away from the pole, packed him into the buggy, and put on the handcuffs. After this the subordinate drove away, and Pandareus, wiping his face with a handkerchief and buttoning himself up on the way, headed toward us.

"Got 'im," reported Morpheus, addressing Dymus. "You argue over everything."

Pandareus drew near and asked what was new with us. He was told of the Martian tracks. He immediately squatted down and became engrossed in an investigation of the matter. I even felt an involuntary twinge of respect for him, because right away you could see his true professional knack: he looked at the tracks sort of from the side and didn't touch anything with his fingers. I began to expect that everything would soon be cleared up. Pandareus moved alongside the tracks like a duck wagging its extruding backside and kept repeating: "Aha.... That's clear.... Aha.... Clear...." We waited impatiently, preserving silence, and only Calais strained to say something and sputtered. Finally Pandareus straightened up with a groan and, looking over the square as if to spy someone, pronounced in short bursts: "Two of them. Took the money in a bag. One has a cane with a spike. The other smokes Astras."

"I also smoke Astras," said grouchy Paralus, and Pandareus glared at him.

"Two of whom?" asked Dymus. "Martians?"

"Right from the start I thought they were not our sort," said Pandareus slowly, not taking his eyes off of Paralus. "Right from the start I thought these fellows were from Milesia. I know them."

Here Calais burst out: "N-n-no, he won't catch him in that buggy."

"But what about the Martians?" said Dymus. "I don't understand. . . ."

Pandareus, ignoring direct questions as before, looked Paralus up and down. "Hand me your cigarette, old man," he said.

"What d'ya need it for?" asked Paralus.

"I'd like to take a look at your bite," explained Pandareus, "and also, where were you today between six and seven in the morning?"

We looked at Paralus, and he said that in his opinion Pandareus was the biggest fool in the world, not counting the cretin who allowed him into the police force. We had to agree with him and started slapping Pandareus on the back, saying, "Yeah, Pandareus, you missed by a mile. You didn't know, Pan, old boy, that these were Martian tracks. But, of course, how could you know, old buddy, about Martians? They're not your usual honey-dippers, Pan!"

Pandareus began to puff up a bit, but here one-legged Polyphemus came out of the mayor's office and cut right into our enjoyment.

"It's a dirty business, boys!" he said in a troubled voice. "The Martians are attacking, they took Milesia! Our forces are retreating, burning the crops, blowing up the bridges behind them!"

My legs felt weak again and I didn't have the strength to push my way through to a bench and sit down.

"They've put down a landing party in the south: two divisions," croaked Polyphemus. "They'll be here soon!"

"They've already been here," said Silenus. "On special stilts. There are their tracks over there. . . ."

Polyphemus merely took a glance and said in disgust that those were his tracks, and everyone realized at once that, in fact, they were. Not even his, but his crutch's. For me it was a big relief. But Pandareus, as soon as it got around to him, buttoned his jacket up to the last button, cast his eyes over our heads and bawled: "You've had your say—that's all! Dis-s-sperse! In the name of the law."

I went into the mayor's office. The place was packed with some kind of flat bags set along the walls in the corridors, the stair landings and even the reception room. The bags gave off an unfamiliar smell and the windows were wide open everywhere, but other than that everything was normal. Mr. Nicostratus was sitting at his desk and polishing his nails. Grinning in a vague way and speaking with a very dubious intonation, he gave me to understand that the duties of his position did not give him the right to enlarge on Martians, however he could definitely state that all this hardly had any connection with the question of my pension. Only one thing was certain: it would no longer be profitable to plant wheat in these parts, but it would be profitable to plant a certain new kind of nutritive grain which had, as he put it, universal properties. The seeds were stored in those bags, and from today on they would begin to distribute them to all the neighboring farms.

"Where did the bags come from?" I asked.

"Supplied," he answered weightily.

I overcame my diffidence and inquired who supplied them.

"Official persons," he said. He raised himself from behind his desk, excused himself and took himself with his loose amble into the mayor's office.

I went into the general offices and chatted awhile with the typists and the watchman. Strange as it may seem, they confirmed almost all the rumors about the Martians, but did not leave me with the impression that they were truly informed. Oh, I've had it with these rumors! No one believes in them, but everyone repeats them. It goes so far that even the simplest facts are distorted. Like the blown-up bridges of Polyphemus. What actually happened? Polyphemus had been the first to arrive at The Five Spot. They saw him from the window and asked him into the general offices to repair a typewriter. While he was laboring, regaling the girls with stories of how his leg had been ripped off, Mr. Mayor came in, stood a moment, listened with a thoughtful expression and then uttered an enigmatic phrase: "Yes, ladies and gentlemen, it's evident that the bridges are burned out." And then he returned to his office, where he immediately ordered sardine sandwiches and a bottle of Phargossa beer. Polyphemus went on to tell the girls that in a retreat you usually blow up the bridges behind you in order to thwart the enemy. The rest is obvious. What stupidity! I considered it my duty to inform the employees of the mayor's office that Mr. Mayor's mysterious phrase signified only that a decision had been taken which could not be changed. Naturally, all their faces immediately expressed relief, mixed with a touch of disappointment.

No one was at The Five Spot, as Pandareus had driven them all away. Almost completely calmed down, I went over to Achilles to tell him about my new acquisitions and to test the water in regard to the architecture series: perhaps he would take a canceled one, since he couldn't get a clean one in any event. After all, he even takes them glued together. However, Achilles was also feeling the pressure of the spreading rumors. In answer to my proposal, he said absent-mindedly that he'd think about it, and at that moment, without even noticing it, he gave me a brilliant idea.

"The Martians," he said, "are a new regime. And as you know, Phoebus, a new regime means new stamps."

I was amazed that this simple thought had not entered my own head. That's right, if the rumors are only partly true, the first reasoned act of these mythical Martians would be to issue their own new stamps, or at least to print over our old ones. I said goodbye to Achilles hastily and headed straight for the post office.

Well, of course, there had been no correspondence with new stamps and nothing new at all at the post office. When will we ever learn to stop believing in rumors? For it is well known that Mars has an extremely thin atmosphere, its climate is excessively severe and almost lacks water, the basis of all life. The myths about the canals were thrown overboard a long time ago, since the canals turned out to be nothing more than an optical illusion. In brief, all this recalls the panic of the year before last, when one-legged Polyphemus ran around town with a fowling piece shouting that a gigantic man-eating triton has escaped from the zoo. That time Myrtilus cleverly managed to get his whole household out of the city, and he didn't decide to come back for two weeks.

The twilight reason of my uneducated compatriots, spoiled by a monotonous life, gives birth to truly fantastic spectres at the slightest disturbance. Our world is like a chicken coop sunk in nocturnal slumber, where you need only accidentally brush against the feather of some colorful old bird snoozing on his perch for the whole place to be thrown into indescribable confusion, with fluttering, clucking and slinging of muck in every direction. Life is already disturbing enough, in my opinion, without all that. We should all keep a check on our nerves. I've read that rumors are much more dangerous to health than even smoking. The author proved it with facts and figures. It was also written there that the force of a panic-rumor is directly proportional to the ignorance of the mass, and this is true, although it must be admitted that even the very best educated among us submit with surprising ease to the general mood and are ready to run with the stupefied crowd wherever their noses lead them.

I had intended to explain this to the boys, but on the way to the tavern I noticed that a crowd had again formed at The

Five Spot. I stopped off and discovered that the rumors had already exerted their pernicious influence. No one was willing to listen to my considerations on the matter. Everyone was aroused beyond all bounds, and the veterans shook firearms fresh from the grease pack and still not properly cleaned. I learned that the soldiers of the Eighty-eighth infantry had been discharged and expelled from their barracks. These soldiers told an incomprehensible story.

The night before last the regiment had been summoned by alarm and put on full military alert; they spent some time, until morning in fact, sitting in armored carriers and trucks on the parade grounds. In the morning the alert was called off, and yesterday passed in the normal fashion. But last night the same thing happened again, with this difference: this morning a colonel came from headquarters by helicopter, ordered the regiment to line up for punishment and without getting out of his helicopter delivered a long and completely incomprehensible speech, after which he flew away and almost the entire regiment was relieved of duty. It must be said that the soldiers, having slaked their thirst royally at Iapetus's place, spoke most inarticulately and now and then struck up the famous bawdy song:

> Nioba-Niobe-ya, always willing to obey-ya . . .

However, it was clear that the colonel from headquarters had not said a word about Martians. He had spoken, in fact, about only two things: the soldier's patriotic duty and his stomach juice. Somehow he had managed to combine these two concepts in a manner which couldn't be grasped. The soldiers themselves couldn't make head or tail of these subtleties, but they did understand that after this morning anyone the sergeant caught with Narco chewing gum or Opi cigarettes would be tossed in the brig for ten days and rot there. Immediately after the colonel's departure, the regimental commander, not countermanding the punishment, ordered the junior officers and sergeants to conduct a metic-

ulous search through the barracks to remove all cigarettes
and chewing gum containing stimulants. The soldiers knew
no more than this, and indeed they didn't want to know
more. Grabbing each other by the shoulders, they stormed
with such threatening looks,

> Nioba-Niobe-ya, how I want ya, baby . . .

that we hastily withdrew and left them.

Here Polyphemus with his crutch and fowling piece lum-
bered up on a bench and began to shout that the generals
had betrayed us, spies were all around us and true patriots
should rally round the flag, because patriotism and so on.
<u>Polyphemus can't live without patriotism.</u> He can live with-
out legs, but without patriotism he can't make it. When he
had shouted himself hoarse and shut up in order to have a
smoke, I tried in any event to elucidate some things for the
boys. I began by saying that there was no life on Mars and
could not possibly be—it was all imaginary. But again they
would not let me speak. First Morpheus stuck the morning
paper from the capital under my nose. It had a big article,
"Is There Life on Mars?" In this article all previous scientific
data were subjected to ironical doubt. But when I was not set
back and attempted to debate the matter, Polyphemus el-
bowed his way up to me, grabbed me by the collar and
hoarsely threatened: "Blunting our vigilance, you plague?
Martian spy, bald-headed turd! To the wall with you!"

I can't bear it when people address me that way. My heart
began to pound, and I yelled for the police. What a hooligan!
I won't forgive Polyphemus for the rest of my life. Who does
he think he is! I tore away, called him a one-legged swine
and went to the tavern.

It was nice to find that not only I considered Polyphemus's
patriotic yelps repellent. Two or three of our boys were already in the tavern. They were sitting around Cronidus the
archivist, pouring him rounds of beer and inquiring about
the morning visit of the Martians.

"What's so big about Martians?" said Cronidus, rolling the whites of his eyes with difficulty. "They're Martians like any other Martians. One's called Calchas, the other Eleius, both of them southerners, with such noses on them. . . ."

"Well, what about their car?" they asked him.

"It's a car like any other car, it's black and flies. . . . Nope, not a helicopter. It flies, that's all. What do you think I am, a pilot? How am I supposed to know how it flies?"

I had lunch, waited for them to leave him alone, took two shots of gin and sat down next to him.

"Heard anything new about pensions?" I asked.

However, Cronidus had already lost control of his faculties. His eyes watered, he simply downed one shot after another like an automatic machine and mumbled: "Martians are Martians, one's Calchas, the other's Eleius. . . . Black, they fly. . . . Nope, not blimps. . . . Eleius, I say. . . . Not me, a pilot. . . ." Then he fell asleep.

When Polyphemus roared into the tavern with his gang, I made a show of leaving for home. Myrtilus hadn't gone. He'd pitched his tent again and was sitting and cooking supper on a gas stove. Artemis wasn't home, she'd gone off somewhere without saying where, and Hermione was cleaning the rugs. To calm myself, I worked on restoring my stamps. It's nice anyway to think what mastery I have achieved. I don't know if anyone would be able to distinguish the glue I applied from the original stuff. In any event, Achilles can't.

Now about today's newspapers. Remarkable papers nowadays. Almost all the columns are filled with the reflections of various medical men about the most reasonable diets. Medical preparations containing opium, morphine and caffeine are spoken of with an extreme and somehow unnatural indignation. What is this, am I supposed to suffer if my liver begins to ache? Not one paper has a philately section, there's not a word about soccer, but all the papers reprint a gigantic and completely vapid article about the significance of gastric juice. Without them, I guess, I wouldn't understand the significance of gastric juice. Not one telegram from abroad, not a word about the consequences of the embargo; instead, they draw out a dumb discussion about wheat. Supposedly there are not enough vitamins in wheat; wheat supposedly is too easily infected by harmful agents. A certain Marsyas, an M.A. in agriculture, has come to the conclusion that the millennium-old history of cultivating wheat and other useful grains (oats, corn, maize) has been a universal mistake of mankind, one which, however, it is not too late to correct. I don't know anything about wheat, the specialists are more qualified, but the article is written in an insufferably critical, I would even say prejudiced, tone. It's obvious at a glance that this Marsyas is a typical southerner, a nihilist and fault-finder.

It's twelve o'clock already, and Artemis still isn't home. She hasn't come back, she can't be seen in the garden, and meanwhile the streets are filled with drunken soldiers. She might at least have phoned where she was. I keep waiting for Hermione to come in and ask what has happened to Artemis. I have no idea what I'll answer. I don't like such conversations, I can't stand them. You might ask who my daughter takes after. Her late mother was a very modest woman; only one time was she attracted to the city architect, but it was just an attraction—two or three notes, one letter. I myself was never a gay dog, as Polyphemus would put it. I still remember my visit to Madam Persephone's house with horror. No, such a pastime is not meant for a civilized man. Whatever you may say, love, even the physical kind, is a mystery, and to practice love in the company of people you even know well and who wish you well is not so amusing as certain books make it out to be. God forbid, I'm not thinking, of course, that my Artemis is reveling in bacchanalian dances amid bottles of booze at this moment, but she might at least have called. You can only be amazed at the stupidity of my son-in-law. In his place I would have returned a long time ago.

I was just about to close my diary and go to sleep when

the following thought popped into my head. Charon obviously didn't stay over in Marathon by chance. It's terrible to think of, but it seems I have guessed what the matter is. Did they really decide on such a step? I remember now all that rabble under my roof, those strange friends of his with their vulgar habits and uncouth manners. Some kind of mechanics with rough voices, drinking whiskey without seltzer and smoking revolting cheap cigarettes. Short-haired loudmouths with sickly complexions, parading about in jeans and colored shirts, never wiping their feet in the hallway; and all those conversations about world government, about some kind of technocracy, about those unthinkable "isms"; and their organic hostility to everything that brings peace and security to a quiet man. I remember it all now, and I understand what has happened. Yes, my son-in-law and his confederates are radicals, and so they acted. All those conversations about Martians—they're merely distorted echoes of the true facts. Conspirators have always loved bold and mysterious-sounding names, so it's not impossible that they now call themselves "The Martians," or something like "Society for the Preservation of the Planet Mars," or let's say "The Martian Renaissance." The fact that the M.A. of agriculture bears the name of Marsyas strikes me as most significant: he's most likely the ringleader of the coup. What I still can't understand is why the putschists dislike wheat and have such a ridiculous interest in stomach juice. Probably this is a diversionary tactic to confound public opinion.

Of course, I'm no good at interpreting putsches and revolutions, I find it difficult to explain everything that is going on, but I know one thing. When they drove us like sheep to freeze in the trenches, when the blackshirts pawed our women on our own beds, where were you then, Messrs. Radicals? You also put on the colors and shouted: "Long live the leader!" If you like revolutions so much, why do you always make them at the wrong time? Who needs you and your overthrows now? Me? Or Myrtilus? Or maybe

Achilles? Why don't you leave us alone? All of you, gentlemen, are noncommissioned officers, and no better than that fool patriot Polyphemus.

This eczema, blast it, is driving me crazy. I'm scratching like a monkey at a fair, no drops will help it, no salves. All the druggists are liars. I don't need any medicines. I need peace and quiet, that's what!

If Charon has enough brains not to remain in the back lines, I've got the first class made.

S LEPT poorly last night. First Artemis woke me up when she came in at 1 A.M. I firmly decided to make a clean breast of it with her, but nothing came of it: she kissed me and locked herself in her bedroom. I had to take a soporific to calm down. Began to snooze, dreamed some sort of nonsense. At 4 A.M. I was again awakened, this time by Charon. Everyone is sleeping, but he goes on talking loudly throughout the house, as if no one else were here. I threw on my robe and went out into the living room. Lord, he was a terrible sight. I understood at once that the overthrow had not succeeded.

He sat at the table greedily eating everything that drowsy Artemis was serving him, and on the table, right on the tablecloth, were lying the greasy dismantled parts of some kind of firearm. He was unshaven, his eyes were red and inflamed, his hair was disheveled and stuck out in matted clumps. He munched his food like a honey-dipper. He had no jacket on, so it must be assumed he came home in precisely that appearance. Nothing of the chief editor of a small but respectable newspaper remained in him. His shirt was

torn and smeared with dirt; his hands were filthy with broken fingernails, and horrible swollen scratches could be seen
on his chest.

He didn't bother to greet me, simply glanced at me with
crazy eyes and grumbled as he choked on the food: "You
asked for it, you bastards!" I let this savage remark pass by
my ears, because I saw the man was not in his right mind,
but my heart sank and my legs felt so weak that I had to sit
down on the couch. Artemis, too, was awfully scared,
though she tried every which way to hide it. But Charon
paid no attention to her and just barked for all the neighbor-
hood to hear: "Bread!" Or: "Brandy, damn it!" Or: "Where's
the mustard, Arta? I've asked for it twenty times already."

We had no conversation in the usual sense of the word.
Trying in vain to overcome my palpitations, I asked him
how he had ridden here. In answer he roared completely
unintelligibly that he had ridden on somebody's back, but
not the person he should have ridden. I tried to change the
subject, to direct the conversation along more peaceful channels, and inquired about the weather in Marathon. He looked
at me as if I had mortally insulted him and simply roared in
his plate: "Brainless idiots . . ." It was quite impossible to
talk with him. Every other word was a curse, both while he
was eating and afterwards, when he pushed the plates away
with his elbow and began to assemble his weapon with renewed vigor. It's a good thing Hermione sleeps so soundly,
so she wasn't present for this scene: she can't stand vulgarity. Everyone was a bastard to him; I just couldn't understand what had happened.

Here's the way it went: "All those bastards have become
such worthless bastards that now any miserable bastard can
do what he likes with the bastards, and not a single bastard
will raise a finger to stop the bastards from handing us any
old crap."

Poor Artemis stood behind his back wringing her fingers,
and the tears ran down her cheeks. From time to time she

glanced at me imploringly, but what could I do? I needed help myself; the nervous tension had practically blindfolded me. Without leaving off cursing for a moment, he assembled his weapon (it turned out to be a modern machine gun), inserted the cartridge and rose heavily to his feet, knocking two plates on the floor. Artemis, my poor daughter, her pale face drained of the last drop of blood, leaned over to him, and then, it seemed, he softened up a bit.

"There, there, kid," he said, dropping the cursing and hugging her awkwardly around the shoulders. "I could have taken you with me, but it wouldn't have been much fun for you. I know you like the back of my hand."

Even I felt the painful necessity for Artemis to find the right words at this moment. And, as if catching my tele-pathic thought, the girl gushed with tears and asked him, in my opinion, the main question: "What will happen to us now?"

I understood at once that, from Charon's point of view, these were not really the right words. He tucked his machine gun under his arm, slapped Artemis on the fanny, and said with a mean grin: "Don't worry, kiddie, nothing new will happen to you." After this he headed straight out. But I couldn't permit him to leave like that, without giving us any explanations.

"Just a minute, Charon," I said, overcoming my weakness. "What will happen now? What will they do to us?"

This question of mine drove him into an indescribable fury. He stopped on the threshold, turned half around and, knocking his knee painfully, hissed through his teeth these strange words: "If only one bastard would ask what he should do. But no, every bastard asks only what they will do to him. Rest easy, yours shall be the heavenly kingdom on Earth."

After this he went out, loudly slamming the door, and a minute later his car was heard roaring down the street.

The next hour was pure hell. Artemis had an attack of

something like hysterics, though it more resembled uncontrollable rage. She broke all the dishes left on the table, yanked off the tablecloth and hurled it at the television set, banged on the door with her fists and shouted something in a choked voice that sounded like this: "So to you I'm a fool? ... I'm a fool to you, huh? ... And what are you? ... What are you? ... I spit on the whole deal. ... You do what you want, and I'll do what I want! ... Got it? ... Got it? ... Got it? ... You'll come running, you'll come begging on your knees! ..."

Probably I should have given her some water, slapped her cheeks and the rest, but I myself was laid out on the couch, and there was no one to bring me a validus pill. It ended with Artemis dashing off to her room without paying any attention to me and with me, after resting a bit, crawling off to bed and falling into some sort of half-faint.

Morning came, overcast and rainy. (Temperature: +17° C, cloud cover: 10, no wind.) Fortunately I had slept through Artemis's explanation to Hermione of the mess in the living room. I only know that there had been a scene and both were now puffed up with anger. While she served the coffee, Hermione looked at me with the obvious intention of drawing me into the conversation, but she kept quiet. Most likely I looked pretty bad, and she's a kind woman, which is why I value her. After coffee, I was gathering strength to go to The Five Spot when a messenger boy arrived with a supposed piece of news signed by Polyphemus. It turns out I am a rank-and-file member of the city's "Voluntary Anti-Martian Patrol" and am already instructed to "appear at 10 A.M. on Harmony Square with firearms or sidearms and a three-day food supply." What does he think I am, a babe in the woods? Of course, I didn't go anywhere, purely on principle. From Myrtilus, who is still living in his tent, I found out that the farmers have been coming to the mayor's office since dawn; they are receiving sacks of the new grain-seeds and taking them back to their fields. Supposedly the wheat harvest, consigned to destruction, is being bought up before cutting by the government at a good price, and advances on the harvest of new grain are being offered. In all of this the farmers suspect the usual agrarian rigamarole, but since no money has been demanded of them, nor written contracts, they don't know what to think. Myrtilus assures me (!) that there are no Martians, because life is impossible on Mars. There is simply a new agrarian policy. Nevertheless, he is ready at any moment to leave the city, and, just in case, he also took a bag of seeds. In the papers, the same as yesterday, there is nothing but wheat and gastric juice. If it keeps on like this, I'm going to cancel my subscription. On the radio—also wheat and gastric juice. I don't even turn it on anymore, I just watch television, where everything is as it was before the putsch. Mr. Nicostratus drove up in his car, Artemis skipped out to him and they drove away. I don't want to think about it. Maybe, in the final analysis, it's fate.

Since all this babbling about wheat and gastric juice hasn't stopped, the putsch has apparently succeeded after all. Charon, due to his usual unsociability, didn't get what he'd counted on, argued with everyone there and found himself in the opposition. I'm afraid that because of him things will be unpleasant for us. When madmen like Charon take up a machine gun, they fire it. My God, will the time ever come when things are not unpleasant for me?

June 6

TEMPERATURE: +16° C, cloud cover: 10, wind from the southwest at 6 meters per second. Fixed my wind gauge.

The eczema is driving me crazy. I'll have to bandage up my hands. Besides that, my frozen ears are aching—probably from the change in the weather.

Martians are Martians. I'm sick of arguing about it.

June 7

M Y eye still hurts. It's all swollen up and I can't see anything out of it. Good thing it's the left eye. Achilles' eyewash only helps a little bit. Achilles says the shiner will be noticeable for no more than a week. Right now it's reddish blue, later it will turn green, then get yellow and disappear completely. Still, what a cruel and uncouth thing to do! To strike an elderly man who was only trying to ask an innocent question. If this is the way the Martians will start, I hate to think how they will end. And there's no one to complain to, I can only wait until the matter is cleared up. My eye hurts so much that it's terrible to remember how pleased I was with the peaceful morning today. (Temperature: +20° C, cloud cover: 0, wind from the south at 1 meter per second.)

When I went up to the attic after breakfast to make some meteorological observations, I noticed with some surprise that the fields beyond the city had acquired a definite bluish tinge. Farther off, the fields blended in so completely with the color of the sky that the line of the horizon was completely effaced, even though visibility was excellent and there was no smoke whatsoever. These new Martian seeds have sprouted up remarkably fast. It's to be expected that in a day or so they will wipe out the wheat altogether.

Arriving at the square, I found that almost all the boys, as *retirees?* well as a huge number of other townspeople, who should have been at work, not to mention farmers and schoolchildren who should have been playing games, were crowding around three large vans painted over with colorful posters and advertisements. I thought at first that this was a traveling circus, especially since the advertisements proclaimed incomparable tight-wire walkers and the other usual heroes of the arena, but Morpheus, who had been standing there a long time, explained to me that this was no circus, but a mobile donor station. Inside were installed special suction pumps with hoses, and next to every pump there sat a big husky guy in a doctor's uniform who offered to draw off the excesses of everybody who entered and to give a remarkable price: five bills per glass.

"What kind of excesses?" I asked. It turned out to be excesses of stomach juice. The whole world is founded on stomach juice. "Are they really Martians?" I asked.

"What do you mean, Martians?" asked Morpheus. "They're big husky hairy guys. That fellow has one eye."

"So what if he does?" I naturally objected. "A member of any race, be he on Earth or on Mars, has one eye, if the other one is injured."

I didn't realize then that these words of mine would prove prophetic. I was simply irritated by Morpheus's presumptuous attitude.

"I've never heard of one-eyed Martians in my life," he declared.

The people around us were listening to our conversation, and so he, in an attack of vanity, deemed it necessary to maintain his dubious reputation as a debater. But he still doesn't know what he's talking about.

"These are no Martians," he states. "Just ordinary guys

from the suburbs. You can find a dozen like them in every tavern."

"Our information about Mars is so scanty," I say calmly, "that to propose that Martians are like ordinary guys in suburban taverns at least doesn't contradict any scientific truth."

"You said it," puts in an unknown farmer standing by. "You said that very convincingly, Mr. What's-Your-Name. The one-eyed guy has his arms tattooed up to his elbows, full of naked women. The way he rolled up his sleeves and the way he came over to me with that hose—no, I thought, we don't need any of this."

"So what does science have to say about tattooing on the Martians?" Morpheus asked spitefully. He wanted to stick me with that one. A cheap trick, it smells of the barber in him. You can't beat me with stunts like that.

"Professor Zephyrus," said I, looking him straight in the eye, "the chief astronomer of the Marathonian observatory, has never denied in any one of his numerous articles such a practice among the Martians."

"That's right," confirmed the farmer. "Professors wear glasses, they see more."

And Morpheus had to swallow all that. He piped down and made his way out of the crowd, saying, "Time for a beer." I stayed to see what would happen next.

For a while nothing happened. Everyone just stood around, staring and talking quietly to one another. Farmers and merchants—they're an indecisive folk. Then a movement occurred in the first rows. Some villager suddenly whipped off his straw hat, stomped on it with all his might and cried out loudly: "Heh! Five bills—that's money too, isn't it?" Uttering these words, he walked decisively up the wooden steps and thrust himself in the door of the van, so that all we could see was the back of his body, all dusty and covered with burrs. What he was saying and what he was asking could not be heard because of the distance. I saw only that at first his stance was stiff, then he sort of went soft, began to shift his weight, stuck his hands in his pockets and backed out, shaking his head. Then, without looking at anyone, he gingerly stepped down to the ground, picked up his hat and, thoroughly knocking the dust off of it, rejoined the crowd.

In the door of the van there appeared a man who was indeed very tall and indeed blind in one eye. If it hadn't been for his white uniform, he would certainly have passed for an inhabitant of some thieves' den, what with the black string of his eye patch across his face, his unshaven stubble and his hairy tattooed arms. Looking us over darkly, he rolled down his sleeves, pulled out a cigarette and, after lighting up, said in a rough voice: "Well, come on! It's worth five bills. Five bills for every little glass. That's real money! On the spot. How much drudging do you have to do for five smackers? But here all you have to do is swallow a hose, and it's over in no time. Well?"

I looked at him and couldn't help but wonder at the short-sightedness of the administration. How could they expect a townsman, or even a farmer, to entrust his organism to such a loud-mouthed thug? I made my way out of the crowd and went over to The Five Spot.

All of the boys were already there, every one of them with his fowling piece, and some of them with white bands around their sleeves. Polyphemus had pulled on his old army cap, and, drenched with sweat, he delivered a speech. According to him, the evil deeds of the Martians had already become unbearable and all patriots were moaning and sweating blood under their yoke and the time had finally come to give them a decisive rebuff. And the ones responsible for it all, Polyphemus asserted, were the deserters and traitors such as those fat-assed, gobbling generals, the druggist Achilles, the coward Myrtilus and that backslider Apollo.

My eyes clouded over when I heard these last words. I

completely lost the gift of speech and recovered myself only when I noticed that no one but myself was listening to Polyphemus. All of them, it turned out, were listening not to the one-legged stooge, but to Silenus, who had just returned from the mayor's office and was relating that from now on all the taxes would be levied exclusively in stomach juice and that an order had come from Marathon converting stomach juice into the usual units of money. Supposedly stomach juice would now be transferable, and all banks and savings trusts were ready to change it into cash.

"How can that be?" said Dymus. "I don't understand. What are we going to do, carry some sort of container instead of wallets? And what if I bring them water instead of juice?"

"Listen, Silenus," said Morpheus, "I owe you a tenner. Will you take juice?" He got very excited, since he always lacks money for drinks and has always drunk at another's expense. "Good times are here, buddies!" he exclaimed. "For example, if I feel like a drink, I just go to the bank, discharge my excesses for them and get cash in exchange. Then—off to the tavern!"

Here Polyphemus began to shout again. "They've bought you out!" he shouted. "You've sold yourself to the Martians for stomach juice! Here you've sold yourselves out, and they drive around like they were on their own Mars!"

And at that moment there came across the square, slowly and noiselessly, a very strange black car, which seemed to have no wheels, no windows and no doors. Children were running behind it yelling and whistling; some of them tried to catch hold of it from the back, but it was completely smooth, like a piano, and there was nothing for them to hold onto. A very unusual car.

"Could it really belong to the Martians?" I asked.

"Who else?" said Polyphemus irritably. "Is it yours?"

"No one's saying it's mine," I objected. "There are all sorts of cars in the world. Do they all have to belong to the Martians?"

"I'm not saying they all belong to the Martians, you old hunk of dung!" Polyphemus roared. "I'm saying the Martians are riding around town as if they were at home, the bastards! And all of you here have sold yourselves out."

I only shrugged my shoulders, not wanting to get involved, but Silenus answered him very thoughtfully: "Excuse me, Polyphemus, but your shouting is beginning to wear on me. And not only me. In my opinion, we have all fulfilled our duty. We enlisted in the volunteer squad and we cleaned our weapons—what more do you want, if you don't mind me asking?"

"Patrols! Patrols are needed!" said Polyphemus, choking with emotion. "To cut off the roads! To keep the Martians out of the city!"

"But how are you going to keep them out?"

"Blast you, Silenus! How can you keep them out? Very simple! Halt, who goes? Halt or I'll fire! You asked for it, bang!"

I couldn't stand this. He's not a man, he's a gung-ho.

"Well, maybe we could form patrols," said Dymus. "It's not too hard for us, is it?"

"It's not our job," I said decisively. "Silenus here will tell you that it's against the law. That's the army's job. Let the army worry about patrols and whatever shooting has to be done."

I can't stand these military games, especially when Polyphemus is in command. Some kind of sadism. I remember once when we had civil-defense training in the city in the event of a nuclear attack, and he went around throwing smoke bombs to create a realistic effect, so no one would go without his gas mask. How many people were asphyxiated —well, it's simply a nightmare. He's a noncommissioned officer, you can't trust him with anything. Or the time he barged into the gym class at school, chewed out the instructor in the most vulgar language and took it upon himself to show the kiddies how to march in step. If they put him on patrol, he'd fire his shotgun at everyone until they stopped bringing goods into the city. He'd lash out at the Martians, and they, most likely, would burn the whole city down in retaliation. But our old-timers are like children, honest to God. Patrol they want, patrol they'll get. I spat for all to see and went off to the mayor's office.

Mr. Nicostratus was polishing his nails. He answered my hesitant questions more or less as follows. The government's financial policies will change somewhat under the new conditions. A large role in monetary matters will now be played by the so-called stomach juice. It may be expected that in the near future the aforementioned juice will begin to have the same currency as money. So far there have been no special instructions about pensions, but there are substantial grounds for assuming that once taxes are levied in the so-called stomach juice, pensions will be paid out in the same so-called stomach juice. My heart sank, but I collected myself and asked Mr. Nicostratus directly if it wasn't possible to understand his words to mean that the so-called stomach juice was not actually stomach juice, but some sort of symbol of the new financial policy. Mr. Nicostratus shrugged his shoulders indefinitely and, continuing to examine his fingernails, stated, "Stomach juice, Mr. Apollo, is stomach juice."

"What good is stomach juice to me?" I asked in complete desperation.

He shrugged his shoulders a second time and remarked, "You know perfectly well that every person needs stomach juice."

It was absolutely clear to me that Mr. Nicostratus was either lying or holding something back. I was so desperate that I requested an audience with Mr. Mayor. But I was refused. Then I left the mayor's office and signed up for the patrol.

If a man who has worked flawlessly for thirty years in the fallow field of public education is offered a vial of stomach juice, this man has the right to demonstrate any degree of indignation he so desires. Whether Martians or non-Martians are responsible is beside the point. I cannot abide any anarchic activity, but I am willing to fight for my rights with a rifle in my hands. And even though everyone will know that my protest has a purely symbolic value, let them think about this, let them know that they are not dealing with some dumb animal. Of course, if the donor stations should become our system and the banks and savings trusts should accept stomach juice in exchange for cash, I would take a different stand on the matter. However, so far only Silenus has spoken about banks and savings trusts, so it's only an unconfirmed rumor. As regards the donor stations, Morpheus, after signing up for the patrol, decided to anoint the deal right away and gave himself into the hands of the one-eyed thug. He returned with teary red eyes, showed us a crisp new fiver and reported that the vans were presently leaving. That means there can be no talk about any new system: they came and they left. If you managed to donate your excesses—good for you. If you didn't—blame yourself. In my view, this is outrageous.

Polyphemus appointed me along with Calais the stutterer to patrol Harmony Square and the adjoining streets from 12 to 2 A.M. After giving us our certification made out in Silenus's hand, he slapped me on the back with great emotion and said, "The old guard! What would these crappy civvies do without us, Phoebus? I knew when we got down to brass tacks you'd be with us." We embraced and both shed tears. Actually, Polyphemus is not such a bad guy, he simply likes people to follow his orders without question. A completely understandable desire. I requested his permission for free time and headed for Achilles' place. A patrol's a patrol, but you ought to play it safe.

What sort of a thing is stomach juice? I asked Achilles. Who can benefit from it? What can it be used for? Achilles said it was necessary for the proper digestion of food and most likely nothing else. I'd known that before I'd asked him.

"Soon I will be able to offer you a large batch of the so-called stomach juice," I said. "Will you take it?"

He answered that he would think about it, and right here offered to trade his unserrated air-mail stamp of '28 for my incomplete "zoo park" series. You have to admit, the unser-rated beauty is unique, but the one Achilles showed me has two strips glued together and some kind of greasy spot. I don't know, I just don't know.

Coming out of the drugstore, I saw the Martian car again. It might have been the same one, but perhaps another. Breaking all the traffic laws, it floated down the middle of the street, but with the speed of a pedestrian, so I was able to get a good look at it. I was walking to the tavern and it was going the same way. My first impression proved to be correct: the car most resembled a streamlined piano covered with dust. From time to time something underneath it flashed and the car shuddered a bit, but this was apparently not a malfunction because it continued to move steadily forward without stopping for a moment. I couldn't make out any windows or doors even from a close distance, but the absence of wheels struck me most of all. True, my build did not permit me to bend down low enough to look at the bottom. Perhaps there were wheels there after all—it couldn't be that there wasn't even a single wheel.

Suddenly the car stopped. And wouldn't you know it, it stopped right in front of Mr. Laomedon's estate. I recall that I thought bitterly: it seems there are people in the world to whom it makes no difference whether it's a new president, an old president, Martians or anybody else. Every power always pays them respect and attention, I thought, which they don't deserve; in fact they deserve the opposite. But something completely unexpected happened. Assuming with good reason that someone was going to get out of the car and that I would finally see a real live Martian, I stood to the side and watched along with the other townspeople, whose line of thinking apparently coincided with mine. To our amazement and disappointment, there emerged from the car not Martians, but some kind of proper young men in tight coats and identical berets. Three of them went to the grand front entrance, while two of them stayed with the car, sticking their hands deep in their pockets and leaning casually on the car with various parts of their bodies. The front door opened, the three entered and immediately strange but not very loud noises were heard, as if someone were trying to move the furniture around by himself and others were beating a carpet with regular blows. The two standing by the car paid no attention to these sounds. They kept their same positions, one looking carelessly down the street, the other yawning and glancing at the top floor of the estate. They also didn't change their positions when a minute later the front door opened slowly and my insulter, Mr. Laomedon's chauffeur, came out cautiously, like a blind man. His face was pale, his mouth hanging open, his eyes bulging and glassy, and both his hands were pressed to his stomach. Coming out onto the sidewalk, he walked a few paces, dropped with a groan, sat for a while bending over farther and farther, and then toppled over on his side, curled up, kicked his legs and froze stock still. I must confess that at first I understood nothing. Everything proceeded so leisurely, in such a calm businesslike manner, against the background of the usual city noise, that the feeling arose and stuck with me that this was the way it should be. I did not experience any anxiety and did not seek any explanations. I felt such trust in those young men—so proper, so restrained. . . . Now one of them distractedly glanced at the chauffeur lying there, lit up a cigarette and again began to examine the top floor. It even seemed to me that he was smiling. Then a stamping of feet was heard, and one after another there came out of the entrance the young man in the tight coat, wiping his lips with a handkerchief; Mr. Laomedon in a splendid eastern robe, without a hat and in handcuffs; another young man in a tight coat, taking his gloves off on the way; and finally a third young man in a tight coat, loaded with weapons. With his right hand he held three or four machine guns to his chest, and in the left he carried several pistols, dangling the trigger loops on his fingers, and besides these a tommy gun hung from each shoulder. I glanced at Mr. Laomedon only once, but this was enough for me: I can still see something red, wet and sticky. The whole cavalcade crossed the street leisurely and disappeared into the inner recesses of the car. The two young men remaining outside lazily pushed off from the polished side, walked over to the prostrate chauffeur, carefully took him by the hands and feet and, swaying him slightly, tossed him into the house. One of them then drew a piece of paper out of his pocket and neatly stuck it next to the doorbell, after which the car, without turning around, moved with its former speed in the opposite direction, and the two young men with the most unassuming faces walked through the parting crowd and disappeared around the corner.

When I came out of the stupor into which the unexpectedness and unusualness of this occurrence had thrown me and again recovered the ability to think, I felt something like a psychic shock, as if a turning point in history had been reached right before my eyes. I am sure that the other witnesses experienced and felt something similar. We all crowded in front of the entrance, but no one resolved to go inside. I put on my glasses and over the heads of the crowd read the proclamation stuck below the doorbell.

It read:

Narcotics are a poison and the disgrace of the nation! The time has come to make an end of narcotics. And we shall make an end of them, and you will help us. We shall punish unmercifully those who spread narcotics.

If it had been anyone else, there would have been enough to talk about for two hours or more, but this time everyone only exchanged interjections, not having the strength to fight against their initial timidity: "Aiee-aiee-aiee.... Better do it! ... Ehe-he-he.... Egads! Oh, no!"

Someone had called the police and a doctor. The doctor went into the house and attended to the chauffeur. Then Pandareus arrived in the police buggy. He stomped around on the porch, read the proclamation several times, scratched the back of his head and even peeked in the door, but was afraid to go inside, even though the doctor was calling him irritably in the most disrespectful language. He stood in the doorway, spreading his legs, sticking his palms under his strap and puffing up like a turkey.

With the appearance of the police the crowd grew somewhat bolder and began to speak out more definitely:

"So that's the way they do it, huh?"

"Yeah, that's the way, it seems...."

"Interesting, interesting, isn't it, gentlemen?"

"I never would have believed it."

I sensed with alarm that the tongues were becoming untied and decided to leave, although I was eaten up with curiosity, but here Silenus turned to Pandareus with a direct question: "So, Pan, did the law triumph after all? Is this what you finally decided?"

Pandareus pursed his lips significantly and, hesitating a bit, stated, "I assume this was not our decision."

"What do you mean, not yours? Whose, then?"

"I suppose, the gendarmerie in the capital," declared Polyphemus in a thunderous whisper, glancing around on all sides.

"What kind of gendarmerie is that?" people in the crowd objected. "Suddenly the gendarmerie is riding around in a Martian car! No, that's no gendarmerie."

"So what's your opinion, huh? Were they really Martians?"

Polyphemus puffed up even more and bawled: "Hey, who's that talking about Martians? Watch out!"

But they paid no more attention to him. The tongues came completely unhinged: "The car might be Martian, but they themselves are not Martians, that's for sure. Their ways are the same as ours, human."

"Right! What do Martians care about narcotics, I'd like to know."

"Hey, you old-timers, a new broom sweeps clean. But what business of theirs is our stomach juice?"

"No, gentlemen, those were no people. Too calm, you see, too quiet. I think they were Martians. They work like machines."

"Right, machines! Robots! Why should the Martians dirty their hands? They have robots."

Pandareus, unable to hold back, also joined in the guessing game. "No, old fellows," he declared, "they're not robots. That's just the system now. They take only deaf-and-dumb men into the gendarmerie. For reasons of state security."

This hypothesis at first caused confusion, but then brought poisonous retorts, very witty for the most part. I recall only the remark of grouchy Paralus. He delivered himself of the opinion that it wouldn't be a bad thing if the police took only deaf-and-dumb men, only not for reasons of state security, but to protect innocent people from all the rubbish dumped on them by official spokesmen. Polyphemus, who earlier had unbuttoned his jacket, now puffed up, buttoned up again and hollered: "You've had your say— that's all!"

And so we unfortunately had to disperse, although at just that moment the ambulance pulled up. The old horse's ass flew into such a fury that we could only observe from afar how they carried the injured chauffeur out of the entrance-way and afterwards, to our surprise, the bodies of two others. We still don't know who these two were.

All of the boys headed for the tavern, and me too. Those same two young men were standing casually at the bar. As before, they were calm and quiet, they drank gin and looked distractedly over the heads. I ordered myself a complete meal and, eating my fill, watched how the most curious of our group gradually moved closer to the young men. It was fun to watch how ineptly Morpheus tried to start a conversation with them about the weather in Marathon, and Paralus, intending to take the bull by the horns, offered them a drink. The young men, as if seeing no one around them, briskly gulped down the drinks pushed toward them, but maintained an impartial silence. Jokes didn't amuse them, they didn't catch hints and seemed to miss direct questions altogether. I didn't know what to think. I was so taken with their exceptional restraint, their complete indifference to the amusing attempts to draw them into conversation, that I began to incline to the thought that they were indeed Martian robots, that the repulsive appearance of the Martians prevented them from openly showing their true faces. Then I suspected that they were the Martians themselves, about whom we still know nothing, when you get right down to it. The boys, giving themselves away completely, clustered about the young men and made remarks about them without any restraint; some even dared to try touching their coats. All were now convinced that these were robots before them.

Iapetus even began to worry. Serving me brandy, he said nervously, "How can they be robots? They've each had two gins, two brandies, two packs of cigarettes, and who's going to pay?"

I explained to him that the robot's program would have accounted for drinks and cigarettes and therefore would certainly account for some means of payment. Iapetus calmed down, but at this moment a fight started at the bar.

As we learned later, grouchy Paralus had made a bet with that fool Dymus that Dymus could touch a burning cigarette to the robot's hand and nothing would happen. Here is what

I saw with my own eyes. From the crowd of people enjoying themselves Dymus suddenly burst like a cork from a bottle. He flew backwards all the way across the room, pumping his feet in tiny circles and knocking down tables and people in his path until he dropped in a corner. Not a second passed before Paralus, in exactly the same manner, found himself in another corner. The boys flung themselves in all directions, and I, without understanding a thing, saw the young men sitting quietly at the bar as before, thoughtfully raising the glasses of alcohol to their lips with identical movements.

Paralus and Dymus were picked up and dragged behind the curtains to be revived. I took my glass and also went behind the curtains. I wanted to find out what had happened. I arrived just as Dymus came around and sat there with the most idiotic expression on his face, feeling his chest. Paralus had not yet recovered consciousness, but was already gulping gin and washing it down with soda. The waitress was standing beside him with a towel ready to bandage up his chin when he came to. Here I learned the version of the incident just described and agreed with the rest that Paralus was a provocateur and Dymus was simply a fool no better than Pandareus.

However, having expressed these reasoned considerations, the boys were by no means satisfied, but took it into their heads to do something about it. Polyphemus, who had kept in the shade up to this point, announced that this would be the first military action of our voluntary patrol. We'd jump the hoodlums when they came out of the tavern, he said, and he began to order who should stand where and when we would attack. I immediately disassociated myself from this venture. First of all, I am an opponent of violence, there's nothing of the noncommissioned officer in me. Second, I didn't see that the young men had been in the wrong. And finally, I planned not to fight with them, but rather to have a talk with them about my own affairs. I quietly came out from behind the curtains, returned to my table and by these very movements initiated another occurrence, one very bitter for me.

But even now, when I look over the events of the day with completely different eyes, I must state that the logic of my actions was and remains faultless. The young men were not from our area, I reasoned. The fact that they had arrived in the Martian car indicated that they most likely came from the capital. Moreover, their participation in the arrest of Mr. Laomedon proved without a doubt that they belonged to the new regime: they would hardly have sent some minor agents against Mr. Laomedon. Therefore, it followed from the logic of things that these young men must certainly be well informed about the new conditions; they would be able to tell me things of interest. Being in the position of a little man who was ridiculed by Mr. Laomedon's chauffeur and refused information by Mr. Mayor's secretary, I couldn't pass up this opportunity to get some true facts. On the other hand, the young men did not raise any fears in me. The fact that they had handled Mr. Laomedon and his bodyguards rather brutally did not alarm me at all. It was their duty and Mr. Laomedon had deserved a good hiding for a long time. As regards the incident with Paralus and Dymus, well, my friends, Dymus is an idiot, it's impossible to deal with him, and Paralus is able to bring out anyone's worst side with his grouchy wisecracks. I won't even mention the fact that I myself would not allow anyone to call me a robot, let alone stick a cigarette on my hand.

Consequently, when I had finished my brandy, I went over to the young men, completely confident of the success of my undertaking. I had thought out the plan of the impending conversation in all its details, having taken into consideration the nature of their occupation, their mood immediately after the incident and their evidently innate taciturnity and restraint. I had intended at first to ask their forgiveness for the thoughtless behavior of my compatriots. Further, I would introduce myself, express the hope that I was not bothering them with my conversation, complain about the quality of the brandy, which Iapetus frequently dilutes with cheaper sorts, and offer to treat them from my personal bottle. And only after this and after we had discussed the weather in Marathon and in our town, did I intend very lightly and delicately to pass to the main question. Approaching them, I noticed that one of them was busy smoking his cigarette, while the other, turning away from the bar, observed my approach intently and with some interest, as it seemed to me. I decided therefore to address him directly.

Coming up, I doffed my hat and said, "Good evening." And then this hoodlum made a sort of lazy movement with his shoulder and it suddenly seemed as if a hand grenade had exploded inside of my head. I don't remember anything. I recall only that I was lying for a long time next to Paralus behind the curtains, glugging gin, washing it down with soda, and someone was applying a cold wet napkin to my wounded eye.

And now I ask myself: What more can you expect? No one interceded for me, no one raised a voice of protest. Everything repeats itself. Hoodlums are again spreading terror, beating up citizens in the streets. And when Polyphemus drove me home in his miniature car, my daughter, as unconcerned as everyone else, was kissing Mr. Secretary in the garden. No, even if I had known how it would all turn out, I still had a duty, an obligation to try to engage them in conversation. I would have been more careful, I wouldn't have approached them, but from whom else can I find out anything? I don't want to worry over every copper, I can't force myself to teach anymore, I don't want to sell the house in which I have lived for so many years. This is what I fear, and I want peace and quiet.

June 8

TEMPERATURE: +17° C, cloud cover: 8, wind from the south at 3 meters per second. I'm sitting at home, not going out, not seeing anybody. The swelling has gone down and the injured spot almost doesn't hurt, but it still looks terrible. All day I examined my stamps and watched television. Everything is the same in town. Last night our golden youth besieged Madam Persephone's house, which was loaded with soldiers. They say it was a real free-for-all. The field of battle was held by the army. (They're no Martians, you can be sure of that.) Nothing special in the newspapers. Not a word about the embargo; you get the impression it's been called off entirely. There's a strange address by the war minister, set in brevier type, which says that our membership in the Military Commonwealth represents a burden for the country and is not so well founded as might appear at first sight. Thank God, they've finally figured it out after eleven years! But most of all they are writing about a farmer named Periphas who is remarkable in that he can give up to four litres of stomach juice a day without any harm to his organism. His hard life is reported with many intimate details. Interviews with him are recorded and scenes from his biography are acted out on television. A sturdy, rather crude man of forty-five years, without a grain of intellect. You look at him and never suspect that you are looking at such an amazing phenomenon. He kept insisting it was his habit of sucking a piece of sugar every morning. I'll have to try it.

Yes! In our papers there is an article by Calais the veterinarian about the danger of narcotics. There Calais writes that the regular use of narcotics by large-horned cattle is exceptionally harmful to the production of stomach juice. A diagram is even attached. An interesting observation: everything is printed black on white in Calais's article, yet it's unbearably difficult to read. It seems as if he were writing and still stuttering. However, it turns out that Mr. Laomedon was exterminated because he prevented the citizens from freely drawing off their stomach juice. One gets the impression that stomach juice is the foundation stone of the new governmental policy. Such a thing has never occurred before. But then, when you think about it, why not?

Hermione returned from a visit to friends and related that in the former estate of Mr. Laomedon a permanent donor station for the collection of stomach juice was being set up. If this is true, then I approve and support it. I always stand for permanence and stability.

Ah, my stamps, my little stampies! You alone never upset me!

June 9

TEMPERATURE: +16° C, cloud cover: 5, a slight rain. The swelling has completely vanished; however, as Achilles predicted, the whole area around the eye has taken on a hideous greenish tinge. I can't show myself on the street: you wouldn't hear anything but stupid jokes. This morning I phoned the mayor's office, but Mr. Nicostratus was pleased to be in a humorous mood and did not communicate anything new to me regarding my pension. Of course, I became very upset, tried to calm myself with my stamps, but even the stamps did not console me. Then I sent Hermione to the drugstore for tranquilizers, but she returned with empty hands. It turned out that Achilles had received a special notice instructing him to distribute tranquilizers only by prescription of the city physician. I flew into a fury and phoned Achilles, started up an argument, but to tell the truth—what could I expect from him? All medicines containing narcotics are under the strict supervision of the police and specially appointed people from the mayor's office. What can you do: if you cut down a forest, the chips will fly. I got my cognac and took a drink, right in front of Hermione.

It helped. I even feel better. And Hermione didn't let out a peep.

This morning Myrtilus's family returned, even though he is still living in his tent. To be honest, I was glad. This was the first sign that the situation in the country was becoming stable. But then suddenly after lunch I saw Myrtilus putting them all on the bus again. What was the matter?

"Sure, sure," Myrtilus answered me in his usual manner. "You're all such wise guys, and I'm a fool. . . ."

It seems he had gone to The Five Spot and learned that the Martians intended to call the comptroller and architect to account for their machinations and squandering of funds; supposedly they had already summoned them somewhere. I tried to explain to Myrtilus that this was a good thing, it was fair. But where would it lead!

"Sure, sure," he answered. "It's fair. . . . Today the comptroller and architect, tomorrow the mayor, and the day after tomorrow I don't know who, maybe me. Nothing doing. Look at you—they hung a black eye on you, was that fair?"

I can't talk with him, he can go . . .

A Mr. Corybantus phoned. It turns out he is replacing Charon at the newspaper. A pitiful, trembling voice; the paper must be having difficulties with the authorities. He begged me to tell him if Charon would be returning soon. I spoke very sympathetically with him, of course, but I didn't say a word about Charon having already returned once. Intuitively I feel it isn't worth spreading around. God knows where Charon is now and what he's doing. That's all I need: unpleasantries over politics. I don't talk to anyone about him, and I've forbidden Artemis and Hermione as well. Hermione understood me at once, but Artemis had to make a scene.

June 10

ONLY now have I recovered somewhat, though I am as sick and distraught as before. The eczema has spread as never before. I'm covered all over with blisters and keep scratching, though I know I shouldn't. And terrifying phantoms pursue me without a letup; I try to get away from them, but can't. I understand: take up arms and kill, kill or be killed. It's vile and disgusting, but in the final analysis it's natural. Still, no one is forcing them. Partisans! I certainly know what it's all about. But how could I know that in my declining years I would live to see it all over again?

It began yesterday morning.* Contrary to all expectations, I received a very friendly response from General Alcimus. He wrote that he remembers me well, regards me highly and wishes me all sorts of successes. This letter greatly excited me. I simply didn't know what to do with myself. I talked it over with Hermione, and she was forced to agree that I

---

* From what follows, it appears that Mr. Apollo is writing on the morning of the eleventh about the events of the tenth. (Editor's note.)

shouldn't let such a chance slip by. Only one thing worried us—the troubled times. At this point we saw Myrtilus breaking his temporary camp and beginning to carry his things back into the house. That was the last straw. Hermione made me a very elegant black patch for my wounded eye, I took my portfolio with documents, got in my automobile and set off for Marathon.

The weather favored me. I drove peacefully along the deserted highway between fields which were turning blue and thought over the various courses of action available to me. However, as always, something unforeseen soon happened. About 40 kilometers from town the motor began to sneeze, the car started to shudder and then it stopped altogether. It happened at the top of a rise, and when I got out on the road the peaceful country landscape spread out before me, looking rather unusual, to be sure, what with the blueness of the ripening grains. I recall that I was completely calm in spite of the delay and did not restrain myself from admiring the neat white farms scattered in the distance. The blue grains stood very high, attaining the height of a man in some places. Never before had such abundant crops grown up in our parts. The highway, straight as an arrow, could be seen to the very horizon.

I lifted the hood and looked at the motor for a while, hoping to find the malfunction. But I am such a poor mechanic that in a short while I had to give up, straighten out my aching back and look around for help. However, the nearest farm was still rather far off, and on the road only one car could be seen approaching from the direction of Marathon at a rather great speed. At first I rejoiced, but soon, to my great chagrin, I became certain that it was one of the black Martian cars. Still, I did not completely lose hope, since I remembered that ordinary people might also be inside Martian cars. The prospect of hailing that grim black car did not appeal to me too much; I was still afraid there might be Martians inside, for whom I felt an instinctive aversion. But what else was there for me to do? I held my hand out across the highway and took a few steps toward the car, which was already approaching the foot of the rise. And then something horrible happened.

The car was 50 meters from me when suddenly a yellow light flashed; the car jumped and reared up like a horse. A thunderous blast reverberated, and the highway was wrapped in a cloud of smoke. Then I saw the car apparently trying to fly; it just about cleared the cloud, listing badly on its side, when one after the other two more lights flashed right beside it. The double blow tossed it over, and it crashed with its full weight on the asphalt, so hard that I could feel the tremor of the earth in my legs, now weak from this unexpected development. A terrible accident, I thought in the first moment. The car caught fire, and some kind of black figures surrounded by flames came climbing out of it. At the same moment, shooting broke out. I couldn't tell who was shooting from where, but I clearly saw who was being shot at. The black figures dashed about in the smoke and flames and fell one after the other. Through the barrage of bullets I heard heartrending inhuman cries, and then they were all stretched out next to the overturned car, which continued to burn. And even then the shooting did not stop. Then the car exploded with a horrifying boom, an unearthly white light struck me in my good eye and a thick hot gust of air whipped me about the face. I squinched involuntarily, and when I opened my eye again I saw to my horror a twisted black creature running down the highway straight toward me. It was wrapped in flames, with a tail of black soot, and looked just like a huge ape. At that moment, to the left of me, a man in a military uniform, with a machine gun at the ready, jumped out of the blue wheat, stopped in the middle of the road with his back toward me, squatted down quickly and started blasting the flaming black figure almost point blank. I was so horrified that the initial shock left me and I found sufficient strength to turn around and run at full speed to my car. Like a madman I turned the ignition, unable to see anything in front of me, forgetting that the motor wouldn't work; and then my strength again deserted me, and I remained sitting in the car, senselessly staring ahead, a passive and dumbfounded witness of a horrible tragedy. Indifference overcame me. As if in a dream, I saw armed men come out one after the other onto the highway, surround the scene of the catastrophe, bend over the burning bodies, turn them over and shout brief exchanges, barely audible for the blood pounding in my temples. Four of them gathered at the foot of the rise, and the man in the military uniform—an officer, judging by his epaulets—stood in his former place, several steps from the last victim and reloaded his gun. Then I saw him approach the prostrate figure without haste, tilt the muzzle of the gun and give a short burst. The figure shuddered repulsively and I threw up on the steering wheel and my pants. But after this the worst thing of all happened.

The officer quickly surveyed the sky, then turned toward me, looked—I will never forget that cold merciless glance —and, holding his machine gun by the strap, headed toward my car. I heard the men below shout something at him, but he didn't turn around. He headed toward me. Probably I fell unconscious for a few seconds, because I don't remember anything more until I found myself standing beside my automobile in front of the officer and two more insurgents. God, what a lot! All three were crusty and long unshaven; their clothes were ragged and splattered, and the officer's overcoat was in a disgraceful condition. The officer wore a helmet; one of the civilians, a black beret; the other one with glasses, nothing at all on his head.

"What's wrong with you, gone deaf?" said the officer sharply, shaking me by the shoulder, and the man in the beret frowned and bit out the words: "Why don't you leave him alone, what do you need to do that for?"

I gathered up the last vestiges of strength and forced myself to speak calmly, for I knew it was a matter of my life.

"What do you want?" I asked.

"An ordinary townsman," said the man in the beret. "He doesn't know anything and doesn't want to know anything!"

"Wait a minute, engineer," said the officer irritably. "Who are you?" he asked me. "What are you doing here?"

I answered all his questions without hiding anything, and while I was speaking he kept glancing around and looking at the sky from time to time, as if expecting rain. The man in the beret interrupted me once, shouting: "I don't want to risk it! I'm leaving—you do what you want!"—after which he turned and ran downhill. But the other two remained and heard me out to the end, while I kept trying to guess my fate from their faces, without seeing anything good for myself. And then a saving thought came into my head, and forgetting everything I had just said, I burst out: "Keep in mind, gentlemen, that I am Mr. Charon's father-in-law."

"Who's Mr. Charon?" asked the insurgent with glasses.

"The chief editor of the newspaper in this area."

"So what?" asked the insurgent with glasses, and the officer kept surveying the sky.

I really got scared: they obviously didn't know Charon. But anyway I said, "My son-in-law took his gun and left home on the very first day."

"Is that so?" said the insurgent with glasses. "That's to his credit."

"That's a load of bull," said the officer. "What's going on in the city? Where are the troops?"

"I don't know," I said. "Everything's quiet with us in the city."

"Is there free access to the city?" asked the officer.

"I believe there is," I said and considered it my duty to add: "But you may be stopped by the men of the city's Voluntary Anti-Martian Patrol."

"What?" said the officer, and for the first time something like surprise registered on his hardened face. He even stopped looking at the sky and looked at me. "What patrol?"

"The Anti-Martian," I said. "Commanded by Noncommissioned Officer Polyphemus. Perhaps you know him? He's an invalid."

"The devil knows what to make of it," said the officer. "Can you lead us into the city?"

My heart sank. "Certainly," I said, "but my automobile . . ."

"Yes," said the officer. "What's wrong with it?"

I plucked up courage and lied: "It seems the motor froze."

The officer whistled and without another word turned and disappeared in the wheat. The insurgent with glasses continued to eye me closely and then suddenly asked, "Do you have any grandchildren?"

"Yes!" I lied in complete desperation. "Two! One's still at the breast. . . ."

He nodded sympathetically. "That's terrible," he said. "That torments me most of all. They know nothing, and now they will never know anything. . . ."

I didn't understand a word he was saying, and I didn't want to understand, I only prayed that he would soon leave and not do anything to me. For some reason I suddenly imagined that this quiet fellow with glasses was the most terrible of the lot. For several seconds he awaited my answer, and then tossed his machine gun over his shoulder and said, "I advise you to get the hell out of here. Goodbye."

I didn't even wait for him to go in the wheat. I turned and walked as fast as I could down the hill toward town. As if some storm carried me on its wings. I wasn't aware of my legs, I didn't notice my short-windedness, I seemed to hear some mechanical rumbling and buzzing behind my back, but I didn't even turn around and simply tried to run. But I hadn't gotten very far when a small truck full of farmers turned out toward me from the crossroad. I was nearly unconscious, but found the strength to stand across their way. I waved my arms and shouted: "Stop! Not that way! Partisans ahead!"

The truck stopped and I was surrounded by rough simple people, for some reason armed with rifles. They grabbed me by the chest, shook me and cursed me with filthy language; I understood nothing, I was horrified and only after a while figured out that they had taken me for an accomplice of the partisans. My legs gave way under me, but here the driver got out of the cabin, and luckily he turned out to be a former student of mine.

"Hey, what are you guys doing!" he yelled, grabbing their upraised threatening hands. "That's Mr. Apollo, the town teacher! I know him."

Not immediately, but eventually they all calmed down, and I told them what I had seen.

"Aha," said the driver. "We knew it. Now we'll catch them. Let's go, you guys."

I wanted to continue on my way to the city, but he convinced me that it would be safer to stay with them, and he would fix my car in good time, after they had caught the bandits. They sat me in the cabin, and the truck rolled to the scene of the tragedy. There was the top of the rise, there was my automobile, but the road ahead was completely empty. There were no bodies, no fragments, only burned spots on the asphalt and a little dent in the place where the explosion had occurred.

"Pretty obvious," said the driver, stopping the truck. "They've already cleaned up. There they go flying . . ."

Everyone started yelling and pointing at the horizon in the direction of Marathon, but no matter how I stared into the untroubled sky with my one good eye, I couldn't see anything.

Then the farmers, with an alacrity demonstrating a certain amount of training, without any unnecessary fuss or argumentation, split up into two groups of ten men each. These groups spread out into two chains and began the comb through the wheat—one to the right and one to the left.

"They have machine guns," I warned them, "grenades too, it seems."

"We are well aware of that," I was answered, and after a

while shouts announced that the search party had hit on a trail.

Meanwhile the driver was fixing my car, while I, sitting in the back seat, let myself fall into a blessed half-sleep, having finally managed to calm my nerves. The driver not only got rid of the problem (it turned out to be an air lock in the fuel line) but also cleaned up the front seat, the splattered steering wheel and dashboard. Tears of gratitude burst from my eyes, I shook his hand and paid him as much as I could. He was satisfied. This simple, good man (I can't recall his name) turned out to be quite talkative, unlike most farmers, who are also simple and good, but stern and tight-lipped. He explained what had been going on.

It turned out that the insurgents, whom the peasant folk simply call bandits, had shown up in the area the very day after the arrival of the Martians. At first they were friendly toward the farmers, and it was learned that most of them were residents of Marathon, people well educated as a rule and harmless at first glance, if you don't count the military men. Their intentions remained moot to the farmers. In the beginning they encouraged the villagers to rise up against the new regime, but their reasons for the necessity of this were vague—they all kept repeating that it meant the ruination of culture, degeneration and other bookish things of little interest to the man in the village. Nevertheless, the farmers fed them and gave them shelter, because the situation was still unclear and no one knew as yet what to expect from the new regime. When it came out that nothing bad and only good was to be seen from the new powers, when the powers bought up the crop (not only the standing crop, but also the shoots) at a good price, when they made a generous advance on the new blue wheat, when money seemed to pour from heaven for the previously useless stomach juice and when, on the other hand, it was learned that the bandits were laying ambushes for the representatives of the administration as they were transporting money to the village, when a deputy from Marathon let them know that this outrage must be brought to a swift end for the good of everyone, then the farmers' attitude toward the insurgents changed completely.

Several times we interrupted our conversation and listened. Occasional shots could be heard from the fields, and every time we nodded at each other and winked with satisfaction. By now I had completely recovered and sat down at the wheel with the intention of turning around and driving home. (I had no thought, of course, of continuing my trip to Marathon. God be with him, that Alcimus, if this is what happens on the road.) At this moment, the search party returned to the highway. At first four farmers dragged two unmoving bodies to the truck. One of the dead men I recognized—it was the man in the beret whom the officer had called an engineer. The other, a young man, was unknown to me. With some relief I saw that fortunately he was not dead, but only seriously wounded. Then the rest of the search party returned in a mass, talking merrily to one another. They led forward a prisoner with tied hands whom I also recognized, although he was now without glasses. It was a complete rout, not one of the farmers had suffered. I felt a great moral satisfaction seeing how these simple people, still apparently fired up by the battle, nevertheless showed unquestionable spiritual nobility by addressing the defeated enemy in almost chivalrous terms. They bandaged the wounded man and laid him fairly gently in the back of the truck. And although they didn't untie the prisoner's hands, they gave him something to drink and stuck a cigarette in his mouth.

"Well, they've done a good job," said my friend the driver. "Now it'll be a bit quieter around here."

I considered it my duty to inform him that there were at least five insurgents.

"No matter," he answered. "That means two got away. They won't get far. Either in our district or the next, it's the same thing. They'll get kilt or caught."

"And what are you going to do with these three?" I asked.

"Drive 'em away. About forty kilometers from here there's a Martian post. They take all kinds there: dead or alive, however you bring 'em."

I thanked him and again shook his hand, and he headed for his truck, saying to the others, "What d'ya say, let's get a move-on."

And here they led the prisoner past me: he stopped for a moment and peered at my face with his myopic eyes. Perhaps it only seemed that way to me. Now I hope that it only seemed that way to me. Because in his eyes there was something that made my heart sink. Miserable world! No, I'm not justifying that man. He's a radical, he's a partisan, he has committed murder and should be punished, but still I'm not blind. I saw clearly that this was a noble man. Not a blackshirt, not a goon, but a man with convictions. However, I hope now that I made a mistake. All my life I have suffered because I think too well of people.

The truck rolled away in one direction, I in the other, and an hour later I was already home, completely bushed, aggravated and sick. I will note, by the way, that Mr. Nicostratus was sitting in the living room and Artemis was treating him to tea. But I was in no mood for them. Hermione started to fuss over me, turned back the bedspread, put an ice pack over my heart, and soon I fell asleep, and when I woke up during the night I knew that my eczema was getting worse again. It was a horrible, tormenting night.

Temperature: +17° C, cloud cover: 10, pouring rain.

Yes, they are rebels, people who destroy the peace and quiet. Yet I can't help but feel sorry for them, soaked to the bone, dirty, chased like wild beasts. And in the name of what? What is this—anarchism? A protest against injustice? What injustice? I simply don't understand them. Strange, now I remember that during the search there were no bursts of machine-gun fire nor grenade explosions. They must have run out of ammunition.

June 11 (MIDNIGHT)

HERMIONE wanted me to spend today in bed, but I didn't obey her, and rightly so. By midday I felt quite well, and right after lunch I decided to go to town. Man is weak. I won't conceal the fact that I couldn't wait to tell the boys about the terrible and tragic events I had had the misfortune to witness yesterday. True, by lunchtime these events appeared to me in more a romantic light than a tragic one. My story had a huge success at The Five Spot, questions were hurled at me, and my petty vanity was fully satisfied. It was amusing to look at Polyphemus. (He, by the way, is the only member of the Anti-Martian Patrol to still drag a shotgun around with him.) When I reported my conversation with the officer-rebel to the boys, Polyphemus began to act important, assuming himself to be a part of the desperate and dangerous activity of the insurgents. He even went so far as to call the insurgents brave lads, even though they were acting outside of the law. What he meant by this, I don't know—in fact, no one knew. He also declared that in the insurgents' shoes he would have shown "that peasant rabble" what a pound of smoke was worth, and then a fight almost broke out, because Myrtilus's brother is a farmer and Myrtilus himself comes from peasant stock. I don't like arguments, can't stand them, so while the disputants were wrangling I went off to the mayor's office.

Mr. Nicostratus was a model of politeness with me. He inquired considerately about my health and listened to my tale of yesterday's adventure with great sympathy. And he wasn't the only one—all the other employees left their current business and gathered around me, so I enjoyed a complete success here as well. Everyone agreed that I had acted courageously and that my behavior spoke to my credit. I had to shake a lot of hands, and pretty Thyone even asked my permission to kiss me, which permission I granted, of course, with pleasure. (Blast it, I haven't been kissed by young girls for such a long time! I must admit I'd even forgotten how delightful it is.) Regarding my pension, Mr. Nicostratus assured me that everything would probably be all right, and he informed me in the greatest confidence that the matter of taxes had now definitely been decided: beginning in July taxes would be collected in stomach juice.

This engaging conversation was unfortunately interrupted by an outright scandal. The door of the mayor's office suddenly burst open and Mr. Corybantus appeared on the threshold with his back to us, shouting at Mr. Mayor that he would not let this pass, this was a violation of the freedom of speech, this was corruption, Mr. Mayor should remember the lamentable fate of Mr. Laomedon, and so on. Mr. Mayor also talked in a raised voice, but his timbre was a bit softer than Mr. Corybantus's, and I couldn't understand what he was saying. Mr. Corybantus at long last went away, slamming the door forcefully, and then Mr. Nicostratus explained to me what it was all about.

It happens that Mr. Mayor fined our newspaper and closed it for a week because the issue the day before yesterday had published some verses sent in by a certain XYZ, which contained these lines:

And where the sky meets with the Earth,
The planet Mars burns bright and fierce.

Mr. Corybantus refused to submit to Mr. Mayor's decision, and for the second day now he has been cursing him over the telephone and in person. Discussing the affair, Mr. Nicostratus and I came to the same conclusion, namely that both sides in this dispute are right in their own way and wrong in their own way. On the one hand, the penalty Mr. Mayor leveled at the newspaper is excessively severe, especially since the poem in its entirety is absolutely harmless, as it speaks only of the author's unrequited love for the night fairy. But on the other hand, the situation is such that you shouldn't tease the geese: Mr. Mayor has enough troubles without this, if only the same old Minotaur, who got plastered again the day before yesterday and ran his stinking cistern into a Martian car.

Returning to The Five Spot, I joined the boys again. The argument between Polyphemus and Myrtilus had already been cleared up, and conversation was proceeding in the usual friendly atmosphere. Not without satisfaction, I noticed that my story had apparently led the collected minds down the same path. They were talking about insurgents, the military methods at the Martians' disposal and similar topics.

Morpheus related that not far from Miletus a Martian flying machine had made a forced landing because the pilot was not accustomed to the increased force of gravity; it was then attacked by a group of malefactors, but it shot down every last one of them with a special electric gun, after which it blew up, leaving a huge hole with glass sides. All of Miletus was supposedly taking trips to look at the hole.

Myrtilus, repeating what his farmer brother had told him, said that there was a ferocious band of Amazons attacking the Martians and abducting them for the purpose of procreation. One-legged Polyphemus, for his part, said the following. Last night, as he was patrolling Park Street, four Martian cars slipped noiselessly up on him. An unfamiliar voice, in broken speech and with an unpleasant lisp, asked him how to get to the tavern, and although the tavern does not represent any governmental significance, Polyphemus refused to answer out of pride and contempt for the conquerors, so the Martians had to move on with long faces. Polyphemus assured us that his life had been hanging by a thread all the while, he had even supposedly spied long black barrels aimed right at him, but he had never flinched and never budged.

"What's wrong with you, would it put you out to tell them?" asked Myrtilus, who hadn't forgotten the insult to his family. "I know bastards like that. You drive into an unfamiliar place, you feel like having a drink, and for no reason at all they won't tell you where the tavern is."

It almost came to a fight again, but here Pandareus came up and, smiling joyfully, reported that finally Minotaur had been deported from our city. The Martians had deported him. They suspected him of connections of terrorists and of sabotage. We all objected: to leave the city without a honey-dipper in the hottest time of the year—why, it's a crime!

"Enough!" roared one-legged Polyphemus. "We've suffered this damned yoke long enough! Patriots, follow my command! Fa-a-all in!"

We had already begun to form lines when Pandareus calmed everyone by saying that the Martians intended to begin work next week laying in a sewer system, and meanwhile a young policeman would be put in place of Minotaur. Everyone said that his was another matter, and again they turned to conversation about the terrorists. And about how dirty it was to lay ambushes.

Dymus, rolling his eyes, told us a frightening story. For three days now some kind of people have been roaming the town and treating everyone they meet with candy. "You eat a piece of that candy—and boink!—you've had it." They hope to poison all the Martians this way. We, of course, didn't believe his story, but it was scary anyway.

Here Calais, who had been twitching and sputtering for some time, suddenly babbled: "B-b-but Apollo here has a son-in-law who's a terrorist."

Everyone sort of moved away from me, and Pandareus, thrusting out his lower jaw, announced weightily: "That's right. We have information to that effect."

I became highly indignant and told them all that, first, a father-in-law is not responsible for his son-in-law; second, Pandareus himself has a nephew who spent five years inside for licentious behavior; third, I have always been at logger-heads with Charon, as anyone could confirm; and fourth, I know nothing of the sort about Charon—the man left on assignment and neither hide nor hair of him has been seen since. These were unpleasant moments, but the flimsiness of the accusation was so obvious that everything ended hap-pily and the conversation turned to stomach juice.

It turns out that the boys have been giving stomach juice for two days already and receiving cash for it on the spot. Only I am left out. In some incomprehensible way I am al-ways left out of something profitable to me. There are such hapless people in the world: in the barracks they are always cleaning the urinals, at the front they fall into the "buckets," they are the first to get the worst, the last to get the best. That's the sort of man I am. Well, so be it. All the boys were boasting about how pleased they were now. How could they not be!

Here a Martian car drove across the square, and one-legged Polyphemus pronounced thoughtfully: "What do you think, old buddies, if we let her have it with the shot-gun, would it go through or not?"

"Well, if it's a bullet," said Silenus, "then it ought to go through."

"That depends on where you hit it," objected Myrtilus. "If it's fore or aft, then no way will it go through."

"And if it's broadside?" asked Polyphemus.

"Broadside it'll probably go through," answered Myrtilus.

I was about to say that a grenade wouldn't even go through it, but Pandareus beat me to the punch by saying profoundly, "No, old boys, you're arguing over nothing. They're invulnerable."

"Broadside they're invulnerable?" asked Myrtilus venomously.

"All over," said Pandareus.

"What, even by a bullet?" asked Myrtilus.

"Even to cannonfire," said Pandareus with great gravity.

Here everyone began to shake his head and slap Pandareus on the back. "Yeah, Pan," they said. "You're the one. You slipped up that time, Pander, old fellow. You didn't think, old-timer, you just babbled." And grouchy Paralus rubbed it in right away, saying that if you fired a cannon at Pandareus broadside, you might make a dent, but if you hit him aft, in the head, it would just bounce off.

Well, Pandareus puffed up, buttoned his jacket all the way up to the top button, rolled his crayfish eyes and bawled: "You've had your say—that's it! Dis-s-perse! In the name of the law."

Losing no time, I headed for the donor station. Of course, failure awaited me once again. They didn't take any juice from me, so I didn't get any money. It turns out they have a rule that they must draw off the juice on an empty stomach, and I had had lunch only two hours before. They gave me a donor card and invited me to come tomorrow morning. By the way, I ought to say that the donor station produced a most favorable impression on me. The most recent equipment. The probe is smeared with the very best brands of Vaseline. The stomach juice is obtained automatically, but under the supervision of an experienced physician, not some kind of ruffian. The personnel are without exception polite and well mannered; it's immediately apparent that they are well paid. Everything is spanking clean, the furniture is new. While waiting your turn in line you can watch television or read fresh newspapers. And what kind of line is there? Far shorter than in the tavern. And the money is paid out immediately, straight from the machine. Yes, a high level of culture, humaneness and concern for the donor are felt throughout. And to think that only three days ago this house was the den of such a man as Mr. Laomedon!

However, thoughts of my son-in-law did not leave me, and I felt it necessary to discuss this vexing new problem with Achilles. I found him, as always, behind the cash register looking through his issue of *Cosmos*. The tale of my adventures made a big impression on him, and I felt that he was looking at me now with completely different eyes. But when we came to Charon, he simply shrugged his shoulders and said that my course of action and the dangers I had faced would not only fully rehabilitate me, but possibly Charon as well. Besides, he pretty much doubted that Charon was capable of becoming involved in anything illicit. Charon, he claimed, was most likely in Marathon helping to re-establish order, thereby trying to do something useful for his hometown, as behooves every cultured citizen, and all those envious townsmen, those Pandareuses and Calaises, who can only spout irresponsible gibberish, were simply slandering him.

I had my doubts on that score, but naturally I kept silent and simply marveled that we, the residents of really only a small town, knew each other so poorly. I realized it had been pointless to talk about this matter with Achilles, and so, pretending that his considerations had calmed me, I turned the conversation to stamps. But here is where the surprising event occurred.

I recall that at first I was speaking with some constraint, because my main purpose was somehow to distract Achilles from our conversation about Charon. But it happened that we began to talk about that blessed inverted lithographic overprint. Some time ago I had expounded completely irrefutable proof to Achilles that this was a forgery, and it seemed the question had been settled. However, the day before, Achilles had read some miserable pamphlet and deemed himself qualified to put forward his own considerations. This was something unprecedented in our relationship. Naturally, I lost my temper, flew into a rage and said straight out that Achilles didn't know anything about philately, a mere year ago he didn't know the difference between a Klemmtasche and a Klassier and it was no wonder that his collection was chock full of defective specimens. Achilles also flared up, and we began a real knock-down drag-out fight, of which I am capable only with Achilles and only over stamps.

I seemed to become vaguely aware, while we were arguing, that someone had come into the drugstore and extended a paper to Achilles over my shoulder, and Achilles had fallen silent for a moment, which silence I immediately used to drive a wedge into his incompetent observations. After that I recall an irritating difficulty, something extraneous persistently pressing into my consciousness, preventing me from thinking systematically and logically. However, this eventually passed, and the next stage of this occurrence, which is most interesting from the psychological point of view, was the moment when our argument ended and we fell silent, tired and somewhat offended at each other.

I recall that at that precise moment I suddenly felt an overwhelming need to look over the premises, and I experienced a dull surprise when I discovered no particular change. At the same time I distinctly knew that some kind of change should have occurred during our argument. Here I noticed that Achilles was also experiencing some emotional discomfort. He also looked around and then walked along the counter, glancing under it. Finally he said, "Tell me, would you, Phoebus—didn't someone come in here?" He was disturbed by exactly the same thing as I. His question dotted all the i's, and I understood what all my confusion was about.

"A blue hand!" I exclaimed, enlightened by a suddenly bright recollection. As if before my very eyes, I could see blue fingers holding the piece of paper.

"No, not a hand!" said Achilles excitedly. "A tentacle! Like an octopus!"

"But I distinctly remember fingers. . . ."

"A tentacle, like a polyp!" Achilles repeated, looking around feverishly. Then he grabbed the book of prescriptions from the counter and hurriedly flipped the pages. I went numb all over from a dark foreboding. Holding the piece of paper in his hand, he slowly raised his wide-open eyes to me, and I knew what he would now say.

"Phoebus," he uttered in a hushed voice. "It was a Martian."

We were both shaken, and Achilles, as a man close to medicine, considered it necessary to fortify me and himself with cognac, a bottle of which he took from a big cardboard box labeled "Norsulphazolum." Yes, while we were arguing over that inauspicious overprint, a Martian had stopped in the drugstore, handed Achilles a written order to turn over to the bearer all medicinal compounds containing narcotics, and Achilles, without understanding or remembering anything, had handed him a package of such medicines prepared in advance, after which the Martian had gone away without leaving anything in our memory besides snatches of recollections and a dim image caught out of the corner of the eye.

I distinctly recalled a blue hand with short sparse hairs and meaty fingers without nails, and I was amazed that a sight like that did not instantly knock out of my head any ability to carry on an abstract argument.

Achilles did not recall any hand, but he did remember a long tentacle, incessantly pulsating, extended toward him as if out of nowhere. Besides this, he recalled that the sight of this tentacle had caused him extreme irritation, for he considered it a joke that was quite out-of-place. He recalled also how he had angrily tossed the package of medicines on the counter without looking, but on the other hand he absolutely did not recall whether he had read the prescription and entered it in the book, although it was obvious that he had read it (since he had released the medicines) and had entered it (since it was there).

We drank another glass of cognac, and Achilles called to mind that the Martian had stood to the left of me and had worn a fashionable sweater with a V neck, and I recalled that on one of the blue fingers there had been a sparkling ring of white metal with a precious stone. Besides this, I recalled the sound of an automobile. Achilles wiped his brow and announced that the sight of the prescription reminded him of the sensation of dissatisfaction at someone's attempts, insistent to the point of impoliteness, to break into our argument with some completely ridiculous point of view about philately in general and inverted overprints in particular.

Then I remembered that, yes, the Martian had actually spoken and his voice had been piercing and unpleasant.

"Rather, it was low and condescending," objected Achilles.

However, I held my own view, and Achilles, getting hot again, called his assistant out of the laboratory and asked him what sounds he had heard during the last hour. The assistant, an uncommonly dim-witted young man, blinked his stupid eyes and mumbled that all the time he heard only our voices, but once it seemed that someone had turned on the radio, but he hadn't paid any special attention to it. We sent the young pharmacist away and downed another drop of cognac. Our memories cleared up completely, and although we differed in our opinion of the Martian's appearance as before, we fully agreed on the sequence of events. The Martian, without a doubt, had come to the drugstore in a car; he did not turn off the motor, he entered the premises, he stopped to the left of me, almost beside me, and he stood for a while without moving, examining us and listening to our conversation. (My flesh crawled when I realized my complete helplessness at that terrible moment.) Then he made several remarks to us, apparently concerning philately and apparently completely incompetent, then he extended the instructions to Achilles. Achilles took it, looked at it hastily and stuck it in the book. Further, Achilles, put out by this intrusion, handed over the package of medicines, and the Martian left, having understood that we did not wish to admit him into the conversation. Thus, leaving aside the details, there arose the image of this creature who, although poorly versed in matters of philately, was by no means devoid of a proper education and a certain humanity, if you take into consideration that he could have done with us whatever he'd wanted. We drank another glass of cognac and felt that we could no longer remain here and keep the boys in ignorance of this occurrence. Achilles hid the bottle, left the assistant pharmacist in charge and we beat it to the tavern on the double.

The boys reacted to our story about the Martian's visit in various ways. One-legged Polyphemus openly called it a lie. "Just take a sniff, they're reeking of it. They've guzzled so much, they're seeing blue devils."

Rational Silenus proposed that it had not actually been a Martian, but some kind of Negro—sometimes Negroes have a bluish tint to their skin.

Paralus—well, he was the same old Paralus. "A good druggist we've got," he said grouchily. "Someone unknown comes from somewhere unknown, slips him some unknown piece of paper, and he gives it to him without a peep. No, we won't build a reasonable society with druggists like that. What kind of druggist is it who doesn't know what's going on because of his lousy stamps?"

But all the others were on our side, the whole tavern gathered around us. Even the golden youth with Mr. Nicostratus in the lead poured over from the bar to listen. They made us repeat again and again where I had stood and where the

Martian had stood when he'd extended his extremity, and so on. Very soon I noticed that Achilles was beginning to embellish the story with new details, shocking for the most part. (Such as that the Martian blinked only two eyes like us when he was silent, but when he opened his mouth some additional eyes opened, one red, the other white.) I commented on this, but he objected that cognac and brandy had a remarkable effect on human memory, this was, so to say, a medical fact. I decided not to argue with him, asked Iapetus to serve me supper and, laughing to myself, began to observe how Achilles was surely becoming his own worst enemy. In ten minutes or so they all knew he was talking through his hat, and they stopped paying any attention to him. The golden youth returned to the bar, and soon the same old complaint was heard from there: "I'm tired of it. . . . It's so dull around here. Martians? Bull, senility. . . . What should we knock off tonight, sports?"

At our table the old argument about stomach juice was renewed. What in the world is it, what good is it, what do the Martians need it for, and what do we ourselves need it for? Achilles explained that man needs stomach juice for the digestion of food, it would be impossible to digest food without it. But his authority had already been undermined, and no one believed him.

"You ought to shut your trap, you old enema bag," Polyphemus told him. "What do you mean, impossible. This is the third day I've given the juice, and nothing's wrong, I'm digesting. You should digest so good. . . ."

In despair they turned to Calais for consultation, but this naturally led to nothing. After prolonged spasms, which kept the entire tavern on tenterhooks, he only burst out: "A g-g-gendarme's already an old man at thirty, if you really want to know." These words referred to some half-forgotten conversation which had taken place at The Five Spot sometime before lunch, and in fact was meant not for us, but for Pandareus, who had gone to work a long time before. We left

Calais to work up an answer to our question, while we fell to speculation.

Silenus proposed that the civilization of Mars had come to a physiological dead end; they no longer could produce their own juice, and so they had to locate other sources.

Iapetus put in his two bits from behind the bar, stating that the Martians use the stomach juice as a ferment for the production of a special kind of energy. "Like atomic energy," he added as an afterthought.

But that fool Dymus, who had never distinguished himself for bold flights of fancy, stated that human stomach juice for a Martian was the same as cognac or beer for us, or say, juniper vodka, and with this statement spoiled the appetite of everyone who was just beginning to eat.

Someone proposed that the Martians obtained gold or rare metals from stomach juice, and this obviously illiterate proposal prompted Morpheus to a very true thought. "However you look at it, old buddies," he said, "whether they get gold or energy out of it, you must realize that our stomach juice is a very important thing for the Martians. Have they pulled a fast one on us, huh?"

At first no one understood, but finally we caught on that no one really knew the true price of stomach juice or what kind of price the Martians had set. It was quite possible that the Martians, being practical people, as we must suppose, were making a disproportionately large profit out of this enterprise, taking advantage of our ignorance.

"They're cutting us down to dirt cheap," one-legged Polyphemus flared up in a white heat, "and then those rotten bastards will drive it up to the true price on some comet!"

I ventured to correct him, that it's not on any comet, but on a planet, to which he responded with his usual vulgarity that I should have my eye treated and then get into arguments. But that's not the point.

Morpheus's idea got us all excited, and a very pithy and valuable discussion might have developed, but at this point

Myrtilus barged into the tavern with his farmer brother, both stewed to the gills. It turned out that Myrtilus's brother had been experimenting with the distillation of malt from the blue wheat and today, at long last, his experiments had been crowned with success. Two hefty jugs of the first lot of blue brew were set up on the table. Everyone took an immediate interest and began to sample it, and I must say that "blue-beer" made a big impression on us. As luck would have it, Myrtilus invited Iapetus to the table to give it a try. Iapetus drank two short glasses, stood a moment screwing up his left eye, as if cogitating, and then suddenly said, "Pack off, I never want to see you here again." This was said in such a tone of voice that Myrtilus, without saying a word, grabbed the empty jugs and his groggy brother and cleared out. Iapetus surveyed us with a heavy eye and with the words, "That's a new one—coming into my establishment with their own swill," he returned to the bar. To smooth things over, we all ordered a round, but the previous free and easy atmosphere had vanished. After sitting for another half hour, I headed home.

In the living room Mr. Nicostratus, occupying Charon's armchair, was sitting across from Artemis and drinking tea with preserves. I didn't interfere in their affair. First of all, Charon, it seems, has been cut off entirely, and no one can say if he will ever return at all. Second, Hermione was somewhere in the immediate vicinity, and I stank so much of alcohol that I could smell it myself. Therefore I preferred to slip quietly to my room, without attracting anyone's attention. I changed clothes and looked at the paper. It's simply amazing! Sixteen pages of type, and nothing of substance. Like chewing a wad of cotton. The press conference of the president was published. I read it twice and didn't understand anything—nothing but stomach juice.

I'm going to go see how Hermoine feels.

June 12

TEMPERATURE: +12° C, cloud cover: 0, no wind. Terrible belching from that bluebeer. My migraine has flared up. Sat home all day. A new gastronomical novelty has appeared: blue bread. Hermione praised it, Artemis liked it too, but I just ate it without any appetite. It's bread like any other bread, only blue.

June 13

FINALLY, it seems, summer weather has arrived. Temperature: +22° C, cloudy . . .

What things are going on! I don't even know how to begin. In regard to my pension nothing is known, but in the final analysis it's not a matter of my pension anymore. Just now, when I began today's entry, I suddenly heard a car approaching. I thought it was only Myrtilus bringing the quart of bluebeer he promised from the farm, and I looked out to see. As it happened, I looked out at just the right time. At first I saw an unfamiliar car under the streetlight, very deluxe, and then I noticed that coming across the garden with a decisive step, straight toward the bench where Artemis and Mr. Nicostratus had settled down since evening, was Charon. Before I could blink my eye, Mr. Nicostratus had flown higgledy-piggledy over the fence. With superhuman strength Charon hurled his walking stick and hat after him, but Mr. Nicostratus did not stop to pick them up and only ran faster. Then Charon turned to Artemis. It was hard for me to see what happened between them, but I have the impression that at first Artemis tried to fall in a faint; however, when Charon pasted her one up against the side of the head, she changed her mind and decided instead to show her celebrated temperament. She let out a long, ear-splitting scream and slashed at Charon's physiognomy with her fingernails. I repeat, I did not see all of this. But when I looked into the living room a few minutes later, Charon was pacing from corner to corner like a caged tiger, holding his hands behind his back, and a fresh scratch was turning crimson on his nose. Artemis was setting the table matter-of-factly, but I noticed that her face looked a little bit asymmetrical. I can't stand family scenes, I get all weak inside and feel like going away somewhere where I will see and hear nothing. However, Charon noticed me before I could slip out and contrary to all expectations greeted me so cordially and warmly that I considered it impossible to go into the living room and strike up a conversation with him.

Above all, I was pleasantly surprised by the fact that Charon looked quite unlike what I had expected. This was no longer that shaggy and raggedy bum who had clanked his gun around and railed at me a week ago. In fact, I had expected him to be even more ragged and dirty. But before me sat the previous Charon of peaceful times, smoothly shaven, neatly combed, elegantly and tastefully dressed. Only the crimson scratch on his nose somewhat spoiled the overall impression, and also his complexion, which was unusually swarthy, testified to the fact that in recent days this office worker had spent a lot of time under the open sky.

Hermione came in wearing hairpins, excused herself for her appearance and also sat down at the table. And there we sat, the four of us, just as in the old days, one peaceful family. Until the women cleared the table and left, the conversation revolved around general subjects: the weather, health, how Charon looked. But once we were left alone, Charon lit up a cigar and said, looking at me strangely, "Well, what do you think, father, is our cause lost?"

In answer I simply shrugged my shoulders, although I

very much felt like saying that if anyone's cause was lost, it certainly wasn't ours. But then, in my view, Charon didn't expect an answer. Around the women he had kept calm, and only now did I notice that he was in a state of extreme agitation, almost to the point of sickness, that state in which a man is able to switch abruptly from nervous laughter to nervous weeping, when everything is bubbling inside him and he feels an overwhelming need to release this bubbling in words and therefore talks, talks, talks. And Charon talked.

There is no more future for people, he said. Man has ceased to be the pinnacle of nature. For now and evermore and throughout all eternity man would be an ordinary phenomenon of nature like a tree or horse, nothing more. Culture and progress together had lost all meaning. Mankind no longer required self-development, it would be developed from outside, and so schools would no longer be needed, institutes and laboratories would no longer be needed, social thought would no longer be needed—in a word, everything that distinguished man from beast and was called civilization would no longer be needed. As a factory of stomach juice, Albert Einstein was no better than Pandareus, most likely worse, since Pandareus was marked by rare gluttony. Not in the boom of a cosmic catastrophe, not in the flames of nuclear war and not even in the clutches of overpopulation would the history of mankind come to an end, but, don't you see, in calm, sated tranquility.

"Just think," he said with his voice breaking, holding his head in his hands, "civilization wasn't destroyed by ballistic missiles, but by nothing more than a handful of coppers for a glass of stomach juice. . . ."

He spoke, of course, much longer and much more effectively, but I understand abstract reasoning poorly and remembered only what I remembered. To be frank, he succeeded in depressing me. However, I rather quickly understood that all this was simply the hysterical verborrhea of a cultured man who had experienced the collapse of his personal ideals. And so I felt it necessary to raise an objection. Not, of course, because I hoped to convince him of the opposite, but because his judgments deeply wounded me, they struck me as grandiose and immodest, and besides I wanted to get away from that oppressive feeling produced by his lamentations.

"You've had too easy a life, my son," I said pointedly. "You're getting picky. You don't know anything about life. Right away one can see that you've never been bashed in the teeth, you've never frozen in the trenches and you've never hauled logs in prison. You've always had enough to eat and money to pay for it. You've gotten used to looking at the world through the eyes of a god in heaven, that superman of yours. What a pity—civilization has been sold for a handful of coppers! Just say thanks that you're given these coppers for it! For you, of course, they're not worth much. But for a widow who has to bring up three children, to feed them, educate them, raise them? And for Polyphemus, a cripple who receives a meager pension? And a farmer? What would you offer a farmer? Some dubious little social ideas? Booklets, brochures? Your esthetic philosophy? Well, a farmer would spit on the whole deal! He needs clothes, machines, he needs the certainty of tomorrow! He needs the constant possibility of raising a crop and receiving a good price for it! Could you give him that? You and your civilization! No one has been able to give him that for ten thousand years, but the Martians did it! Where's the wonder that the farmers now hound you like wild beasts? No one needs you and your discussions, your snobbery, your abstract prophecies which so easily change into machine-gun fire. The farmer doesn't need you, the city dweller doesn't need you, the Martians don't need you. I am even certain that most reasonable educated people don't need you. You imagine yourself the flower of civilization, but in fact you are the mold growing over its juices. You've elevated yourself in your own mind and now you imagine that your downfall is the downfall of all civilization."

It seemed to me that I had literally slain him with my

speech. He sat with his face in his hands, shaking all over. It was so pitiful that my heart flooded with blood.

"Charon," I said as gently as possible, "my child! Try for a moment to descend from the cloudy spheres to the sinful earth. Try to understand that what man needs most in the world is tranquility and the certainty of tomorrow. After all, nothing so terrible has happened. Here you say that man has been converted into a stomach-juice factory. Those are ringing words, Charon, but in fact the reverse has occurred. Man, coming upon new conditions of existence, has found an excellent way to utilize his physiological resources to simplify his position in the world. You call this slavery, but every reasonable man considers it an ordinary business deal which should be mutually profitable. What kind of slavery can it be if the reasonable man is already figuring out whether or not he is being cheated, and if he really is being cheated, I can assure you, he will have justice. You speak of the end of culture and civilization, but this is completely untrue! It's impossible even to say what you have in mind. The newspapers come out every day, new books are being published, new television shows are being created, industry is working. . . . Charon! What more do you need! You've been left everything that you had: freedom of speech, self-determination, the constitution. Not only that, you've been protected from Mr. Laomedon! And, finally, you have been given a constant and reliable source of income, which doesn't depend on any competition."

I ended on this, because I discovered that Charon was by no means slain and was not sobbing, as it had seemed to me, but was giggling in the most indecent way. I considered myself highly offended, but here Charon said:

"Forgive me, for God's sake, I didn't want to offend you. I simply remembered an amusing story."

It happened that two days ago Charon and his group of five insurgents had seized a Martian car. How amazed they were when out of the car clambered a completely sober Minotaur with a portable device for sucking out stomach juice. "What d'ya say, fellows, feel like a drink?" he asked. "C'mon, I'll set you up right away. Who's first?" The insurgents were dumbfounded. When they recovered their senses, they half-heartedly slapped Minotaur around for being a traitor and then let him go with his car. They had thought of seizing the car to learn to drive it, and then to penetrate a Martian post with it and stage a battle there, but this episode had such an effect on them that they began to spit on everything. That very evening two of them went home, and the next day the rest of them were taken by the armers.

I didn't quite get the connection between this story and the topic of our conversation, but I was struck by the thought that Charon had consequently been held captive by the Marians.

"Yes," he answered by question, "that's why I was laughing. The Martians told me the same thing as you, point for point. True, a bit more coherently. And they especially emphasized that I was the elite of society, they felt deep respect for me and failed to understand why I and others like me were carrying out terroristic activities instead of forming a reasonable opposition. They proposed that we fight them by legal means, guaranteeing us complete freedom of the press and the right of assembly. Great fellows, the Martians— right?"

What could I answer him? Especially when it became clear that they had treated him most civilly, bathed him, clothed him, treated his wounds, given him an automobile confiscated from the owner of some opium den and let him go with their blessing.

'Words fail me," I said, throwing up my hands.

"Me too," replied Charon, darkening again. "Words still fail me too, but we must find them. We're worth a pittance if we don't find them."

After this he completely unexpectedly wished me a good

night and went to his room, while I remained sitting there like a fool, seized by an unpleasant foreboding. Oh, we are going to have more trouble with Charon! Oh, we are for sure! And what a disgusting way to leave, without having finished the argument. It's already 1 A.M., and my eye is wide open.

Incidentally, today I gave stomach juice for the first time. No big deal, only it's unpleasant to swallow; but they say that soon you get used to it. If you give 200 grams every day, that makes 150 bills a month. Wow!

June 14

TEMPERATURE: +22° C, cloud cover: 0, no wind. The new stamps have finally come out. My God, how exquisite! I purchased the whole issue in quarter-sheet and then couldn't resist and bought the full sheets. Enough economizing. Now I can permit myself a few things. Went with Hermione to give stomach juice; from now on I'll go alone. There's a rumor that a notice arrived from the ministry of education confirming the previous status of pensions, however I failed to get any details. Mr. Nicostratus didn't come to work—he sent his younger brother to say he had caught the flu. People are saying, though, that he doesn't have the flu at all, but accidentally fell down somewhere and received internal injuries. Oh, you Charon! Artemis creeps as quiet as a mouse all through the house.

Yes, I completely forgot. I looked into the living room and saw Charon sitting there along with some pleasant gentleman with big glasses. I recognized him and literally turned to stone. It was the same insurgent whom the farmers had captured before my very eyes. He also recognized me and also turned to stone. We looked at each other for some time, then I recovered and bowed my way out. I don't know what he told Charon about me. But soon he left. I really mean it: this doesn't please me. If they plan to make a legal battle and organize all sorts of meetings, brochures and newspapers, as they were officially advised, then go right ahead. But if only once I see automatics and other such hardware in my home, then I beg your pardon, dear son-in-law. Here our paths must part. That's the most I can do.

To calm myself down, I just now re-read yesterday's entry of my conversation with Charon. In my opinion, my logic was flawless. He didn't even manage to make an objection. It's a shame, though, that I wrote it down more coherently and convincingly than I said it. I have absolutely no talent for speaking, that's my weak point.

The morning papers carried an interesting report on the general demobilization and demilitarization of the country. Thank God, they've finally thought of it! It must be that the Martians have taken the matter of defense entirely into their own hands, and now this defense won't cost us a penny, if you don't count stomach juice, of course. Nothing was said directly about this in the president's speech, but you could read it between the lines. The previous military expenditures, he said, will be used for raising the standard of living and developing shipbuilding. Certain difficulties now stand in the way of reducing the arms industry; however this will be a purely temporary phenomenon. And he also emphasized several times that no one will suffer from the reorganization. I take this to mean that the military industrialists and generals will get a lump sum. Rich people, these Martians! The demobilization has already begun. Paralus is spreading the rumor that the police will also be abolished. Pandareus wanted to haul him in, but we wouldn't let him. Rumors, of course, are only rumors, but if I were in Pandareus's shoes I would be more careful.

Actually, I don't feel like writing anything down today. I'm going to take the speech I made to Charon yesterday and make a clean copy. It's a good speech.

June 15

THE morning has turned out exceptionally clear and pure. (Temperature: +21° C, cloud cover: 0, no wind.) How pleasant it is to get up early in the morning, when the sun has already dispersed the morning haze, but the air is still fresh and cool and preserves the nocturnal aromas. The minutest drops of dew tremble in myriad rainbows and flicker iridescently like precious stones on every blade of grass, every leaf, every web stretched at night by the industrious spider from his little home to the quivering twig. No, I don't do too well with artistic prose. On the one hand, everything seems to be in its proper place, it's beautiful, but all the same somehow ... I don't know, something's not right. Well, so be it.

For the second day we are all enjoying an excellent appetite. They say it comes from the blue bread. Truly, it's a remarkable product. I never used to eat bread outside of sandwiches and generally ate little bread at all, but now I am literally stuffing myself with it. It melts in your mouth like a cookie, and it doesn't sit heavily on your stomach. Even Artemis, who always worried more about keeping her figure than keeping her family, can't control herself and eats like a young, healthy woman of her age should eat. Charon also eats it and praises it. In answer to my remarks, which are not entirely free of spite, he only answers, "One thing does not contradict the other, father. One thing does not contradict the other."

After breakfast I headed for the mayor's office and arrived just at the beginning of reception time. The boys had not yet come to The Five Spot. Mr. Nicostratus looked rather bad. With every movement he grimaced, grabbed his side and moaned quietly from time to time. He spoke in a pained whisper and paid no attention to his fingernails. During the course of our conversation he didn't once look at me, but he did speak politely, respectfully and without the slightest touch of his usual irony. A notice confirming the previous status of pension payments had indeed been received. My papers were probably at the minister's office. It seems likely that everything will turn out favorably and I will get the first category; however this will not prevent me from asking Mr. Mayor to send a special letter to the minister confirming my personal involvement in the armed struggle against the insurgents. This thought pleased me greatly, and Mr. Nicostratus and I agreed that I should compose a rough draft of such a communiqué, which he would edit and present to Mr. Mayor for consideration.

In the meantime the boys had gathered at The Five Spot. Morpheus was the last to arrive, and we fined him. Enough liberalism—we've neglected our club business in recent days. Everyone was terribly interested in one question: had the matter between Charon and Mr. Nicostratus been settled? They forced me to describe everything I had seen in great detail, and for a while one-legged Polyphemus argued with Silenus what part of Mr. Nicostratus exactly had been injured. As an experienced man and a noncommissioned officer, Polyphemus asserted that in such a scuffle Mr. Secretary's coccyx should have been injured, for only a well-placed kick with the point of the boot in the appropriate place could have caused Mr. Nicostratus to abandon the field of battle in the manner I had described. Silenus, as a man no less experienced and a former lawyer, objected that precisely the same effect was produced by a well-aimed blow to the body, and if you took into account the postures which Mr. Nicostratus now assumed, you had inevitably to conclude that a rib on his left side had been injured: either a crack, or perhaps a fracture. Both, however, agreed that the matter was far from settled and that Mr. Nicostratus, being young, hot-blooded and athletic, would not fail to meet Charon in some dark corner along with his buddies.

They also dunned me whether Artemis continued to be favorably inclined toward Mr. Nicostratus, and when I decisively refused to answer this tactless question, they concluded almost unanimously that yes, of course, she did.

"A woman is a woman," said grouchy Paralus. "One man is never enough for a woman, that's her biological nature."

I lost my temper and observed that when a woman is like that it lies more within the biological nature of certain men, such as Paralus, and everyone found my joke very witty, since they were fed up with Paralus and his grouchiness, and second, they recalled that in time past, before the war, his young wife had run off with a traveling salesman. A very propitious moment had arisen in which to put Paralus, with all his eternal quasi-philosophical sentiments, in his proper place.

Morpheus, who had already thought up a new wisecrack and was bursting with laughter in anticipation, grabbed everybody by the hands and shouted: "No, listen to what I'm going to say!" But here, as inopportunely as always, that old horse's ass Pandareus pushed his way in and without paying attention to the subject under discussion announced in his thunderous voice that a new fashion had come to us from abroad—two to four men living with one woman, just like cats. Well, what can you do! Just throw up your hands. Paralus immediately latched on to this pronouncement and at once changed the conversation to the subject of Pandareus.

"Yes, Pan," he said, "you're in good form today, old fellow. I haven't heard such things even from my younger son-in-law—the major."

Paralus's second son-in-law was known far beyond the city limits; it was impossible to restrain ourselves, and we all doubled over with laughter. But Paralus quickly topped that with a sorrowful look: "No, old boys, demilitarizing isn't enough. We ought to depolicetize or, if worse comes to worst, depandareusize."

Pandareus immediately puffed up like a blowfish, buttoned his jacket up to the top button and bawled: "You've had your say—that's all! . . ."

It was still too early to go to the donor station, so I headed for Achilles' place. I read him the fair copy of my speech to Charon. He listened to me with his mouth hanging open. It was a total success. Here are his precise words when I had finished reading: "That was written by a real orator, Phoebus! Where did you take it from?"

I posed a bit for better effect and then explained how it had come about. But he didn't believe me! He stated that a retired astronomy teacher simply wasn't capable of formulating the thoughts and aspirations of the simple people so accurately.

"Only great writers are capable of that," he said, "or great statesmen. But I see nothing of the sort in our country," he said, "neither great writers nor great statesmen.

"Phoebus, you stole it from the Martians," he said. "Admit it, you old duffer, I won't tell anybody."

I was nonplussed. His disbelief both flattered me and vexed me at the same time. And then he suddenly showed me a sealed envelope made of heavy black paper.

"What's that?" I asked with deliberate casualness, while my heart sensed disaster and sank with bad forebodings.

"Stamps," says the bold man. "Real ones. From there!"

I don't know how I managed to control myself. As if in a fog, I listened to his raptures, expressed with intentional sympathy. And he twirled the envelope under my nose and kept telling me what a rarity it was, how impossible it was to obtain them anywhere, what fabulous sums Chtonius had already offered him for them, and how adroitly he, Achilles, had acted by demanding stamps instead of money as compensation for the banned medicines. The sums which he casually named completely flabbergasted me. It turns out that the market price for Martian stamps is so high that no first-class pension and no stomach juice could ever alter my situation. But finally I recovered myself and had a brain wave. I asked Achilles to show me the stamps. And everything became clear. The conner began to hedge: he lost his composure and babbled something about the stamps' being sensitive to light, like photograph paper, since they were from Mars. They could be examined only under a special light, and here, in the drugstore, there was no proper equipment. I took heart and asked him if I could drop by in the evening, before he went home. Utterly without life, he invited me, saying that, honestly, he didn't have the special equipment at home yet either, but he would try to think up something by tomorrow night. Now that I can believe. He will surely think up something. Most likely it will turn out that these stamps dissolve in the air or you can't look at them at all, but only feel them with your fingers.

In the heat of our discussion I suddenly heard someone's breathing by my left ear, and out of the corner of my eye I caught a movement beside me. I remembered at once the mysterious visitor and turned around sharply, but it was only Madam Persephone's maid, who had come to ask for something more reliable. Achilles went to the laboratory to search for a preparation which would satisfy Madam Persephone, and apparently he intended not to return until I had left. I left without concealing my irony.

At the donor station a pleasant surprise awaited me: the

appropriate tests revealed that owing to my chronic internal irritations, my stomach juice must be put in the first category, so that for 100 grams of juice they are going to pay me 40 percent more than all the rest. Not only that, the medical attendant suggested that if I consume a moderate but sufficient quantity of bluebeer, I might get switched to the category of extra-fine and receive 70 to 80 percent more than 100 grams. I don't want to hex it, but finally it seems for the first time in my life I've lucked out a bit.

In the most sunny disposition I headed for the tavern and sat there till late at night. We had a great time. First, Iapetus is now doing a lively business in bluebeer, which the neighboring farmers supply him wholesale. Bluebeer makes you belch terribly, but it's cheap, goes down easy and gets you pleasantly tipsy. We were greatly amused by one of the young fellows in tight coats. I still haven't learned how to distinguish them from one another and up until tonight felt a natural aversion to both of them, as did most of the boys. Usually these fearful conquerors of Mr. Laomedon come alone or together to the tavern and stay from lunch until closing time; they sit at the bar, drink and keep stone silent, as if oblivious of everyone around them. However, today this young man suddenly tore himself away from the bar, came over to our table and, when everyone had shut up in expectation, broke the silence by ordering a round of drinks for the whole crowd. Then he sat down between Polyphemus and Silenus and stated quietly: "Ee-akk."

At first we all thought he had burped, and Polyphemus, as was his habit, said to him, "How do you do?" However, the young man, somewhat offended, explained that this was his name—Aeacus—and that he was so named in honor of the son of Zeus and Aegina, the father of Telamon and Peleus and grandfather of Greater Aias. Polyphemus immediately made his apologies and proposed a toast to Aeacus's health, so the incident was completely closed. We all introduced ourselves, and very soon Aeacus felt quite at home with us.

He turned out to be a superb raconteur; we simply split our sides listening to him.

We especially like the one about how they soap the floor in the living room, undress the young ladies and have a race for them. They call this "playing touch," and he spoke about it in the drollest manner. I must admit that we all nevertheless felt somewhat embarrassed for our dull backwater, where you would never hear the like of such a thing, and therefore the escapade of the young rowdies from Mr. Nicostratus's band proved to be very timely.

They appeared on the square leading a sizable reddish-orange rooster on a string. Lord, how funny it was! Singing "Nioba-Niobe-ya," they traversed the whole square and came into the tavern. Here they gathered around the bar and ordered brandy for themselves and bluebeer for the rooster. At the same time they announced to the congregation that they were celebrating the rooster's coming of sexual maturity and they invited everyone who wanted to join in. We nearly burst. Aeacus laughed along with us, so that our city, as center of witty entertainments, was somewhat rehabilitated in the eyes of this visitor from the capital.

Achilles arrived with interesting news. He reported that six semiupholstered chairs had been stolen from the courtroom in the town hall. Pandareus had already investigated the scene of the crime and announced that he had found the track. He said there were two burglars, one of them with a velure hat and the other with six toes on his right foot, but actually everyone was certain that the city comptroller had stolen them.

Grouchy Paralus stated straight out: "Looks like he's pulled another fast one. Now everyone will talk about these idiotic chairs and completely forget about his last embezzlement."

When I got home, Charon was still sitting up with his editorial work, and the two of us had supper together.

Just now I looked out the window. The marvelous summer

night has fanned over the city a bottomless sky, spangled with myriads of sparkling stars. A warm breeze strews magical aromas and caresses the branches of the slumbering trees. Hush! One can hear the slight buzzing of a lightning bug wandering through the grass, hastening to a rendezvous with his emerald beloved. A benevolent paradise of sleep has lowered onto the little town wearied of its daily labors. No, it still doesn't seem quite right. Well, so be it. I'll just say it was beautiful when high above the huge spaceships, shining with magical lights, passed over our city as symbols of peace and security—you could see at once they weren't ours.

I'm calling my speech "Peace and Certainty," and I'm giving it to Charon for the paper. Just let him try not to print it. That's how it is: the whole city for, and he alone, don't you know, against! It won't work, dear sonnie-in-law, it won't work!

I'm going to Hermione, to see how she feels.

8272